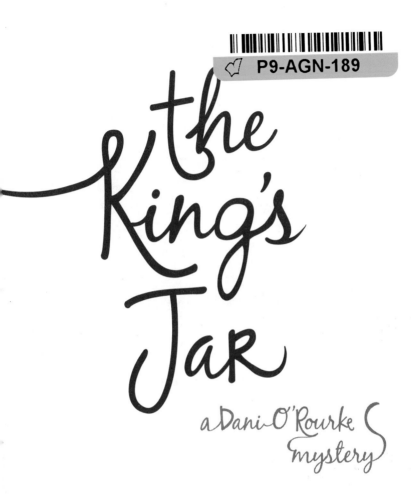

the King's Jar

a Dani O'Rourke mystery

Susan Cummins Miller

Top Five Books

2013

A TOP FIVE MYSTERY

Published by Top Five Books, LLC
521 Home Avenue, Oak Park, Illinois 60304
www.top-five-books.com

Library of Congress Cataloging-in-Publication Data

Shea, Susan C.
   The king's jar : a Dani O'Rourke mystery / Susan C. Shea.
      pages cm
   ISBN-13: 978-1-938938-04-7 (pbk.)
   ISBN-10: 1-938938-04-6 (pbk.)
   I. Title.
   PS3619.H39985K55 2013
   813'.6—dc23

                                        2012043947

Cover design & illustrations by Megan Moulden
Book design by Top Five Books

Printed and bound in the United States of America
10 9 8 7 6 5 4 3 2 1

*To Justin, Lana, Nicolas, and Decima,
and to Tim, forever*

chapter 1

"IT'S NOT GOING to happen, Dickie. I don't care how many times you ask, the answer is N-O."

I might as well have been talking to the other cars on the street for the good it did. In fact, I probably looked like I was talking to the Mini Cooper in front of me, although I was actually glaring at the speaker attached to the sun visor. The little device blinked cheerfully at regular intervals, which wasn't unlike my ex-husband's steady and persistent attempts to wriggle his way back into my life. A life that was, to be honest, not exactly swimming with competing offers.

Arguing with Dickie is difficult, in part because he doesn't hear what doesn't suit his purposes. Today, his purpose was to convince me that going with him to a mutual friend's wedding was not a date, and so didn't contradict my pledge to never go out with him again.

Our relationship, actually our non-relationship, is complicated. It started with fireworks, literally. We met at a Fourth of July party in San Francisco's fashionable Cow Hollow on one of those nights when the fog is low and dense and the fireworks being set off in a park nearby were only watercolor stains in the sky, fading quickly to the accompaniment of muted thuds. The party crowd was young, beautiful, and, judging by the clothes, rich.

I was there as a guest of a woman who had managed to make a shocking amount of money in the dot-com bubble before she turned thirty-five, and who had sold her company only months before the bottom in the market for untested Internet ideas dropped out. She had told me cheerfully, one night when I was pouring wine at a Devor Museum for the Arts and Antiquities event, that she was buying her way into society. I had dutifully reported it to my boss, who put her on a list to research further. It was sweet of her to invite me to her party, even though I was a lowly staffer at the museum.

I thought she had her eye on Dickie, but he was following me around as the fireworks boomed mysteriously, and he eventually cornered me at a bay window.

"Hey," he said and smiled. Great opening line. I knew who he was, of course. Everyone in San Francisco did. The gossip columns were always speculating about whom he'd marry, although the names changed every few months.

"We've met," he said when I didn't rise to the bait.

"I don't think so," I said, glancing at him and then out the window quickly. A bit of blond hair that had fallen into his blue eye was making my fingers twitch. It would not do to reach over and push it away.

"Yes. You poured me a glass of wine, remember? The night of the Matisse opening. I distinctly remember, a so-so cabernet from Sonoma."

"You remember that?" I said skeptically.

"Sure I do. First floor, in the atrium. Blue dress. Looked great with that red hair. Your boss told me you were new on the job."

"Chestnut," I said, "not red. You talked to my boss?" I really wanted to succeed at the Devor, to become a senior fundraiser in a great museum setting, for which this entry-level job was a stepping stone. If a rich donor was already complaining about me, I'd never make it. "It wasn't my fault the wine was crappy. Thanks a lot." I made a move to walk away, but Dickie reached over and touched my wrist.

"No, no, not complaining. I wanted to know who you were. In fact, I told him you'd said something that made me realize I should be thinking about joining the Curators Circle. He was impressed." He grinned at me.

Confused now, I said, "What did I say?"

"Nothing. But I'm hoping you get a little bonus as a result. How much should I give to the museum, by the way?"

And that was how I met Dickie, and a good example of why he was—and is—so difficult to deal with. Turned out he had asked the dot-com millionaire to invite me to her holiday party. He marches to his own drummer, thinks he is brilliant, and works hard to get what he wants. That he wanted me for such a long time was always something of a mystery to me—and to his Pacific Heights friends.

His pestering on the phone was a distraction I didn't need on this day. I was on my way to meet with an elder states-man in the academic world, someone whose help I needed on a major project for the Devor Museum. I'd been warned he was a hard man to work with. I needed to concentrate as I prepped for the meeting. Fending off Richard Argetter III was not the best way to accomplish that. I'm the museum's chief fundraiser now, a job I take seriously even if the director of the Devor probably rehired me because I had been married to a man with two Porsches, a Paris pied à terre, and four hundred and fifty million dollars.

I sighed. "I'm about to park the car, Dickie. I'm busy now. Do not RSVP for me and do not show up at my apartment on the great day. If I go, I'll go alone, and that's final." I hit the button on the cell phone quickly so I wouldn't hear another word, pushed some strands of unruly hair out of my face, and plucked my briefcase from the seat next to me. Five minutes later, I was sitting on a hard wooden chair in Rene Bouvier's office, focused on the business of the day— getting his cooperation for one of the most exciting coups in the Devor's history.

Dr. Bouvier had seemed anxious when I arrived, looking pointedly at his watch and telling me he had another appointment after me. He seemed restless, which probably meant he wanted to get rid of a visitor with no scientific standing as quickly as possible. Still, he was polite in an old-fashioned way. "Please call me Rene," he said as we settled into our meeting.

"Beautiful, isn't it?" Bouvier said as he leaned across his desk and handed me a photo. His eyes bored into mine. His tone was one of command, and it was clear that the only acceptable answer was yes. It was an awkward moment because, if I were being brutally honest, I'd have to say no.

I was looking at a large photograph of the so-called King's Jar taken in the lab, judging by the wooden shelf and hand-lettered sign in the background. It was about two feet tall, with a pale green, crackled glaze and a lid with a handle in the form of a rhinoceros. Handsome, maybe. Important, definitely. To many scholars of sub-Saharan Africa, almost a holy grail object. But beautiful? My idea of beautiful runs toward Impressionist paintings, vintage evening dresses, and fields of lavender in Sonoma County. But what do I know?

Fortunately, my employer doesn't pay me to be an expert in fine arts or history, or even to be candid. San Francisco's Devor Museum of Arts and Antiquities rehired me two years ago to persuade people with money and treasure to part with some of it in order to make the museum a more exciting place for visitors. The King's Jar, currently locked up somewhere in this lab waiting to be transported to the Devor, was a major prize.

"Absolutely," I said, injecting what I hoped was the right amount of awe into my voice. "It will look gorgeous sitting in its case at the center of the new exhibition."

Rene nodded at me, apparently satisfied with my reaction, and leaned back in his swivel chair. The distinguished professor didn't own the valuable artifact, but he had discovered it more than twenty years earlier in a small, landlocked African country, stunning the archaeological world. Ever since then, he'd had custody of the King's Jar in his large laboratory at Warefield University in San Francisco.

He fiddled with a shard of pottery on his desk as I explained that I needed his help. From the large workroom behind me, I could hear researchers talking over the high-pitched whine of a miniature electric sander they were using to remove hard-packed dirt from the surface of another object from the same site.

"We want to raise five million dollars this year. That's how much Tom Burns says it will take to maintain the exhibit he's creating, plus make the King's Jar available for research as you've stipulated."

"You're wasting your time with me," he said. "I'm not rich, you know. And, it's not my job to ask people for money. That's not part of the deal."

Noticing his mottled skin, almost bald head, and the deep lines that scoured his face, I reminded myself to count to ten. Most people don't like asking for money, although he had pulled in major government grants. Admittedly, people

5

look at me strangely when I admit I enjoy the challenge of asking wealthy people to part with money in a good cause. "I'd like to schedule a few lunches with you as the guest of honor. You won't have to talk money at all."

"Get Fritz to pay for it. This whole thing is his idea, anyway." His chin lifted with a jerk and his pale eyes examined me.

Was this his ego talking? After toiling in relative anonymity for years, Rene had found himself sitting on the hottest discovery to come out of Africa since "Lucy," evidence of a complex thirteenth-century African civilization in what was now modern Kenobia. It had changed forever the way archaeologists and historians understood sub-Saharan Africa and its precolonial civilizations. Rewarded with tenure at Warefield, the adulation of graduate students, major grants with which to continue his fieldwork, and the patronage of a billionaire philanthropist, Rene had made his reputation at a relatively late age with the King's Jar. Why wouldn't he be pleased about this move to ensure a permanent home for the artifact now that he was retiring from the university?

"Simon says—"

Rene Bouvier leaned forward suddenly, his expression morphing into a mask of dislike. The vertical lines in his cheeks dug deeper and, with spittle coming out of the corners of his mouth, he practically hissed his dislike. "Simon Anderson is a liar, a crook, and a fraud." He slammed his fist on the desktop, making me jump, and glared at me with those rheumy eyes. "That's for starters, young lady, and you can tell him I said so."

Bouvier's outburst shocked me. Simon was the popular writer and television host whom the Devor had hired to coauthor the exhibition catalog. "But, Rene, he knows so much about Kenobia. He's written about your discovery and even filmed a segment of his show at your site. I—we—thought you would be pleased," I said.

I remembered Simon's enthusiasm for the King's Jar and the starring role it would play at the Devor. "There's nothing like it," Simon had declared when a group of museum administrators met to talk about the catalog project. "Look at it," he said, grinning as he held up a color photo. "Nine hundred years old, delicate celadon finish intact."

I learned that day that the King's Jar was crafted by sophisticated, late Song Dynasty ceramists in China in a distinctive style reserved for royalty.

"The Chinese traded with African coastal groups, but this piece amazed everyone because it was found so far inland and north of trading centers," Simon said, passing around photographs. "The jar is too delicate to have been traded around like beads or shells. It must have been personally presented to an important individual as a gift from a Song Dynasty ruler."

Our PR director scribbled notes as Simon continued. "The most spectacular aspect of the jar is the sculpted figure of a rhinoceros on the lid. It's amazing that the lid is in such good shape, given the spiky horn that extends so far out of the body."

Someone said, "It's a Chinese vessel, but there are no rhinos in China, right?"

Simon paused dramatically, looking around the table. "There are, and were. But Asian rhinos have short, stubby horns. Black rhinos, found only in Africa, have two horns. The area where this civilization flourished and where our jar was found, south of the Rift Valley, was the only place white rhinos lived. And only white rhinos have a super-long, single horn." Simon's deep voice resonated with the excitement that hooked viewers of his *Explore!* show every season, "And that rhino, my friends, is what a Song Chinese ceramist tried to sculpt into this jar's lid, probably with the advice of the Song trader who had seen one on a previous trip to this spot in Africa."

Tom Burns, our Non-Western Arts curator had winked at me across the table and permitted himself a smile at Simon's theatrics, but nodded in agreement about the singularity of the King's Jar.

Now, in his office, Rene jabbed a finger at me. "Anderson doesn't respect Kenobians, the rules of our profession, or the science," he said. "He may have made Fritz McBeel happy by arranging a deal with the Kenobians to sell the Song jar to us. But I guarantee you someone was bribed, and Anderson probably got paid, too."

Peter and Tom had told me about the rumors that McBeel's agents bribed Ministry officials to get it approved for export and sale, rather than being retained as a prime piece of the little country's historical treasure. Simon's name had even come up, but vaguely. The circumstances of McBeel's purchase had kept the lawyers busy for months. The board's acquisition committee had demanded documentation that would protect the Devor should Kenobia ever protest our ownership. Ultimately, Fritz McBeel's foundation executive produced signed and stamped export papers, and Peter and the board decided to chance it.

"Did you know Simon in those days?" I asked.

"Oh, yes. We all knew each other, like it or not. There weren't many foreigners out there."

"Since you found it," I said, deciding it might be best to change the subject, "did you have some say in who would get the jar?"

"You obviously don't know much about field research," Rene said, a small smile taking the sting out of his words. He sketched the protocols that foreign academics went through over the next few minutes, relaxing into a professorial voice that was warmer than the forbidding manner in which he had begun our meeting. When he finished, he explained, "The vessel belonged to the Kenobians by rights. To tell the truth, I was shocked after I returned to the States and Fritz told me he had managed to purchase it and was delivering it to me for safekeeping."

"But you accepted custody, as it were?" I said.

"Sadly, I had no choice. Fritz insisted he wouldn't return it to the Kenobians. He told me that it was too precious to have it anywhere but under lock and key in a place where people understood its importance. If I could have stopped it right then, I would have." Rene paused and sighed. "That's been a bitter thing for me to accept for twenty years."

I struggled for a diplomatic response. Fritz McBeel was a billionaire donor to the Devor, which meant he could do no wrong in our eyes. Simon Anderson was going to collaborate with our curator on the exhibit catalog whether or not Rene liked it. Simon's name on the cover would add cachet and help sell the coffee-table book.

Some heavy-duty persuasion was called for and, as the Devor's vice president and chief fundraiser, I was pretty good at buttering people up. I took a deep breath. "Simon's story-telling skills will bring the meaning of your discoveries to a wider audience. And think how it will please African scholars and political leaders who have been so frustrated by persistent stereotypes of a primitive continent. It's such an opportunity."

I stopped. Rene pursed his lips. The amiable professor was gone again. I noticed a gray patch on his chin where he had failed to shave properly, and the purple veins on the backs of his hands, which lay curled on the arms of his chair.

Just then, there was a knock at the door, and a chunky young man in baggy shorts and a badly faded green T-shirt poked his head in. "Uh, Rene, can you take a look at this? I got some results on the soil testing that don't add up." We both turned to look at him. "I hate to bother you, but you always read these better than anyone else."

It wasn't warm in the office, but the guy was sweating noticeably. When he took his hand away from the frame to push his glasses up his nose, he left prints on the wall. "Oh, sorry," he mumbled, seeing me for the first time. He pushed a fringe of shaggy hair off his forehead. "Didn't know you were in a meeting."

"No problem, Oscar," Dr. Bouvier said, raising a hand to signal him to come in. "This is Miss…"

"O'Rourke," I said when he hesitated. "Danielle. From the Devor."

"Come to tell me I have to help raise rent money for our jar." His mouth twisted in a bitter smile.

Before I could protest, Oscar started nodding. "You'll be great. You know you always…" Abruptly he stopped, and a blush swept over his features. "Um," he said, backing out of the doorway. "Later's fine," his voice came from the hallway as he retreated. He probably feared I would snag him, too.

"Don't let him fool you," Bouvier said in a warmer voice than I'd heard before. "First-rate researcher and as loyal as they come. He'll succeed me here if the dean has half a brain. No social graces, but tops in the field, where it counts."

The deferential assistant's presence seemed to have softened him. "You'll do what you have to and I'm sure it will be a success. I apologize for snapping at you," he said as he pushed himself slowly out of his chair. "We get pretty possessive about our treasures in this field, young lady. The King's Jar has aroused strong feelings from the day I first brushed the dirt away from its surface, and Fritz McBeel and I have never agreed on its future. But that's not your problem."

He glanced surreptitiously at his watch for the third or fourth time since I arrived. Clearly, the meeting was over as far as Dr. Rene Bouvier was concerned. We left his office and, after showing me a few particularly important pottery shards he took from locked glass cases, he escorted me to the door. I turned to thank him once more, but he had already disappeared into the long rows of shelves that went up to the ceiling and far into the corners of the laboratory. Each shelf was lined with wooden boxes, which I now knew were lined with foam. Hundreds of fragments from the site he and his team had been excavating all these years were labeled and stored meticulously in each.

I stood there for a minute, frustrated. The buzzing sound of the sanding tool had stopped, and Oscar and a couple other equally unkempt guys in their twenties and even older were glancing sideways at me, undoubtedly curious as to why I was there. I stood up to my full five-foot-ten and tried to look as professional as my trendy cardigan sweater and ballet flats permitted. For an instant, I envied the shoulder pads and crispness of the 1980s power suits that would have signaled I was someone to be reckoned with in this all-male enclave. Going over to a long table they were clustered around, I asked Oscar if he could explain a little about what he was working on, as much to counter the impression that I had been summarily dismissed as because of any deep interest.

Ten minutes later, I realized I was way out of my depth. Oscar and his buddies might look like slackers in their sandals and shorts, but they lived and breathed African archaeology. They had all been trained by Bouvier, but Oscar was the closest to him, judging by the number of times he brought the older man's name into the conversation.

"Rene seems conflicted about this gift to the museum. Do you have reservations about the jar coming to the Devor?" I asked him at one point.

He looked unhappy. "I just want it to be safe and for everything to be settled."

"It will be safe for sure. And it's definitely settled."

He nodded and fiddled with a wire brush for a minute before looking up at the wall clock behind me. I got the message I was overstaying my welcome, such as it was. Oscar walked me to the door, wiped his hand on his pants, and pushed his wire-framed glasses up higher on his nose before shaking hands with me. I felt for him. The thick lenses made his eyes appear huge and beseeching somehow, like one of those paintings of big-eyed waifs. When I said good-bye, he merely nodded. The others had already gone back to their work.

As I unlocked my car door, I tallied the morning's work: 0 for me, 1 for Dr. Bouvier. He hadn't agreed to help raise money, and all I knew for sure was that Rene Bouvier was no fan of Simon Anderson's.

» » »

The rest of the day was hectic. The only good thing about being in my San Francisco office at seven o'clock when the phone rang was that it was ten P.M. in New York City, too late for the call to be from Louise Johnson, the chairwoman of the Devor's volunteer gala committee.

Louise was in over her head as the date for our black-tie dinner at the Pilgrim Club loomed. My job before joining her in Manhattan on Saturday was to make things work to her satisfaction. Unfortunately, the Pilgrim's chef was taking it as a personal insult that the committee had decided, against his recommendation, to use only organic beef tenderloins for four hundred entrees. The florist simply could not be held accountable for the fact that it had been raining in Central America for weeks now and roses were in short supply, especially the apricot color Louise's committee had chosen.

And, worst of all, dozens of late responses kept upping the head count. The Pilgrim Club steward was warning Louise that we would have to start saying no when the elegant, old dining room with its quartet of massive crystal chandeliers reached capacity. Saying no to the United Nations ambassadors who had finally, a week before the party, decided they would honor the Devor with their presence was anathema to Louise Johnson.

"We can't turn them away," Louise had phoned to tell me in a harried voice a couple of hours ago. "Dani, you have to talk to the steward. He didn't listen to me."

Because my role at the Devor is to keep everyone happy while artfully picking their pockets, and Louise's husband, Geoff, is chairman of the board and a man whose pockets I have picked more than once, I was willing to do battle with the steward and the florist on Louise's behalf.

In two days, I would take the red-eye to New York to do the final on-site preparation for what was to be one of the Devor's most impressive dinners. The following Thursday, we would celebrate the donation of the King's Jar to the museum by Fritz McBeel, a powerful San Francisco–based billionaire, and his wife. Tonight, I wanted to lock my door and head home to my perennially starving cat, a glass of pinot noir, and an hour in front of the boob tube with my feet up.

No such luck. The phone rang and I winced. "Dani O'Rourke here," I said warily.

"Dani, it's me and I have some bad news."

"Me" sounded like Thomas Burns, whose collection would get said artifact, by far its most significant acquisition.

"Hi, Tom. You're still here?" Tom was a workaholic, passionately dedicated to making his section of the Devor the most exciting antiquities wing west of the Hudson River. He was also a favorite of mine because he was endlessly patient with my dear old lady prospects when they wanted to tell him about their family histories over fundraising dinners at the museum.

"Yeah, I was working on my annual budget request. It was due yesterday."

"Is the bad news about the budget?"

"No, much worse. Rene Bouvier was found bashed in the head in his lab this afternoon."

I gasped, and my stomach lurched. "That can't be." My brain skittered in all directions, working to absorb the unthinkable. "I was there this morning. How is he?"

"He's dead."

I swallowed hard but couldn't speak for a minute.

"Dani, you there?"

"Are you sure?" I said. "How could anyone attack him? The lab was crawling with people when I left."

"Yeah, well, I heard everyone went out for a late lunch together, and when they came back, there he was. I'm as shocked as you are."

"Can you come upstairs?" I said weakly, my head spinning.

While I waited, I brooded. Simon Anderson had told me that Rene Bouvier had built a reputation in scientific circles for living on a diet of professional jealousies. Simon said Rene wasn't well liked outside his inner circle, the former students and researchers he had brought onto his team and who defended his scientific standing aggressively. I had seen that side of him this morning, aimed at Simon himself.

"Terrible news," I said to Tom when he walked into my office and dropped his two hundred and thirty pounds onto the sofa, releasing a small cloud of dust from the cushions. "He wasn't the most popular man in the world, but that hardly seems like a reason to kill him."

"It could have been a robbery gone wrong," Tom said. "What scares the hell out of me is the idea someone would do that to get the jar. I mean, it's priceless, but to kill for it?"

"Wait a minute. You're saying the jar is gone?"

"Yeah. The staff did a search right away, and it's definitely missing from the lab."

"Oh, hell, this complicates everything." I said, thinking of the New York dinner and hating myself for being so crass. "Could it be somewhere else on campus?"

Tom was silent for a minute. "Possibly, but I wouldn't count on it. We'll know tomorrow." When he looked up at me, I saw that his eyes glistened.

"I'm sorry for sounding so callous," I said, getting up and coming around to sit next to him on the sofa. I put my arm through his. Tom might be focused on his work, but I knew him well enough to realize he had a big heart, and his reaction chastened me. "Tunnel vision brought on by too many conversations about place cards and champagne prices. It's a tragedy. Did he have family?"

"No," Tom said, scratching the ginger goatee that complemented his thinning hair. "He was married to his work. In a way, grad students were his family. They worshiped the old man."

"Do you think the media will jump on this?" I said, my gut twisting at the idea that the Devor would be dragged into a murder investigation when the missing artifact was understood to be an intended gift to the museum.

"Yeah, the science reporters will," Tom said, frowning at the floor.

"I was there today, and he was agitated. I put it down to the fact that I mentioned Simon. He seems to hate Simon."

"I know. He isn't—wasn't—happy Simon's been hired to do the catalog. But that can't be helped. After all, Rene didn't own the jar. Giving it to us wasn't his decision."

"How did you hear about it?"

"A friend of mine called. Everyone in the archaeology building is shocked."

"I better give Peter a heads-up tonight," I said. Peter Lindsey was my boss and the museum's director.

Tom rose, grunting, from the couch. We hugged briefly, and as he lumbered out the door, he said, "McBeel won't be a happy man when he hears this."

That was an understatement. Fritz McBeel and his wife, Jamie, were the billionaire couple we were supposed to honor in New York in less than a week. Fritz was the man responsible for whisking the priceless archaeological find out of Kenobia twenty years ago when it looked like it might disappear into the dusty rooms of what was then a poorly run Ministry of Antiquities. He had entrusted it to Rene for research and care ever since. And, with Rene about to retire from Warefield's faculty, Fritz had had decided to give the vessel to the Devor Museum, which is why I was trying to raise funds. I didn't want to think about what Fritz McBeel would say if anything went wrong at this point.

chapter 2

PETER WAS LONG GONE from the office, so I left a message on his cell phone. As I pulled on my jacket and turned off the office lights, I told myself the McBeels probably knew about Bouvier's death already. They have their tentacles into everything in San Francisco. In an insular community like ours that worships money and power, too many people look for any excuse to suck up to people like the McBeels, who are the epitome of both. An I-thought-you-should-know item like this would be a golden opportunity for someone to lay the news at their feet, tail wagging, long before Peter or the morning paper could.

Not that Fritz McBeel would appreciate the gift of infor-mation. He would expect it. He had inherited the millions his father made in mining, which had become billions with-out his help as he played unsuccessfully at a variety of jobs. His only sibling had died in a boating accident when both boys were college-age, which left Fritz even richer.

Jamie McBeel had pounced on the money a decade ago, elbowing the former Mrs. McBeel out of the way with breathtaking energy and skill. Jamie played up to Fritz's image of himself as intellectually gifted. He accommodated her desire to be the queen of the city. My relationship with them was strictly on behalf of the Devor, the King's Jar, and their annual membership in the Curator's Circle of million-dollar donors, a group I massaged.

I pulled into the nighttime traffic and made the turns that aimed me north and west to my apartment in a condominiumized old mansion in Pacific Heights. My cell phone rang, and I fumbled with the hands-free device that made it legal to talk while driving.

"Thank god I found you. Have you heard about Rene? Where are you?"

"Hello, Peter," I said. "Yes. Headed home from the office. I left you a message. Poor guy. I hear he got hit over the head."

"Jesus," Peter said.

"Yeah, I know. I'm trying not to visualize the scene and am having a hard time even believing it happened. Why would anyone want to hurt him?"

"Has Tom checked to make sure the jar is safe in the vault at Warefield?"

"More bad news. Tom says it's missing."

There was an ominous silence. Then, Peter erupted with questions, none of which I could answer. "Look, you need to relax, Peter. The cops will do their thing, and after all, this is not a Rolex someone can peddle on Market Street. I'm sure they'll find it."

Suggesting to my boss that he should relax is a waste of breath. Peter Lindsey is brilliant; widely praised for his ability to attract donors, collectors, and artists; and vigilant at keeping the Devor in the forefront of West Coast museums. He charms benefactors, courts the media, and pushes his staff hard. He has the saving grace of making effusive apologies afterward. I actually like Peter.

When he finally calmed down a little, he said, "Let's focus on Fritz. He'll be upset. He may insist on staying in San

Francisco to monitor the investigation. What if he and Jamie skip the dinner? How will we explain that to the guests? We can't cancel it, can we?" The last was said wistfully. Translated, it meant: if they don't come, you have to get us out of the dinner that is costing us a mint.

"A, it won't happen, and B, I can't cancel it. Don't get ahead of yourself. Jamie's totally into being the center of attention at this year's dinner. She won't let her husband bail, no matter what. I heard from Louise that Jamie hired a New York PR firm to make sure her picture is in the *Times*, the *Post*, and *W* after the dinner."

Peter managed a rueful laugh. "Then I better get a haircut since I intend to be standing right next to her."

That wouldn't be hard. Peter sparkled at social events, was always current on cultural news and gossip, and was sought after by hostesses as a bachelor of no known persuasion. I had my hunches, but if he wasn't saying, neither was I.

"Something's bugging me," Peter said. "I tagged along when Fritz walked the fourth floor with Tom a few weeks ago to talk about how the piece would be displayed. Tom made some flattering comment about Rene, and Fritz said Rene had made mistakes in his day and that the future was with younger men. Tom had the good sense to shut up at that point."

"I've heard Jamie doesn't like Rene," I said. "He and the first Mrs. McBeel stayed friends after the McBeels divorced. Maybe Jamie's influenced her husband."

"Could be. I asked Tom later if he thought Fritz was trying to tell us something, but he shrugged it off. Said Fritz is right in a way. A few super smart geeks with big ambitions pretty much do the work these days."

"How about I ask Simon?" I said. "If there was a rift between Fritz and Rene, he'll know. He's known them both for ages."

"Ah, yes, the great Simon Anderson," Peter said.

"His contacts all over the world are amazing," I said too quickly. Just because I was single and Simon was, well, Simon, and we were having dinner in New York next week didn't mean I was looking for an excuse to call him.

Peter sighed. "I'll call Fritz right now. How about if I ask Geoff Johnson to call him, too? Geoff wants Fritz to join the Devor board, and a courtesy call might be a nice touch."

I've heard people say that fundraisers are by trade a manipulative and insincere bunch. The first is true, in a way. So are parents, lawyers, and people who write clever commercials. As for insincere, I object. I'm sincerely interested in making wealthy people feel good about the Devor Museum so they will give it money, appreciated stock, and valuable artwork. This is what we "development officers" do for a living and, in the end, everyone benefits.

» » »

An hour later, I had changed into the size twelve jeans that fit again thanks to a newfound love of fruits and vegetables. I had released my thick hair from the clips that held it in some kind of order and poured a glass of wine to counteract the shock. Fever, my chubby bundle of cat fur, was drowsing happily on his chair and didn't even stir when my phone rang. Peter again.

"Neither Geoff nor I got through to Fritz. The butler said they weren't taking calls."

"It was a little late to call," I said.

"Yeah, well…maybe. Anyway," he breezed past my observation, "he told me they had heard about Bouvier. I tried to get him to tell me more, but he clammed up. I forgot to ask you earlier, how is the catalog coming along?"

"Tom's happy. Simon's a terrific writer, knows everything that's been recovered in that region of Africa."

"Maybe a little arrogant because of that?" Peter said.

"Maybe a lot, but all of his books get rave reviews and this one will, too. I predict *The Test of Time: African Antiquities* will be a bestseller in the museum bookstore for years."

We signed off, promising to touch base in the morning. I let myself consider Simon Anderson's other winning qualities, starting with tall, dark, and handsome, a perfect description even if it is a cliché. The tall is about six feet, three inches, and the dark is deep brown hair a tad longer than other men dare to wear it. The handsome is all of that plus a dazzling smile set off by the kind of tan you get clambering around pyramids, Caribbean reefs, and the African savannah. He does the climbing around on television, where his wildly popular archaeology series has made him a celebrity.

One other upside: he's single and a regular on magazine Most Eligible Bachelor lists. Since he was taking me to dinner in New York during my trip to celebrate the book project, he was right at the top of my eligible bachelor list.

Actually, he was currently the only man on the list, although my friends insist that Dickie and SFPD Homicide Inspector Charlie Sugerman are on it, too. They exaggerate. I long ago deleted Dickie, and even though he makes noises about getting back into my good graces, I can't forget his public fling with the synthetically endowed underwear model. Forgive, yes. He can't help it that his background as the only child of older, doting parents makes self-restraint a foreign concept. Forget my humiliation at the hands—or heart—of my own real-life Ritchie Rich? Not likely.

Charlie "Green Eyes" Sugerman might be another matter if the demands of being half of the most successful San Francisco homicide team didn't preclude regular time off work. That, and if his reserve with women, well, with me, anyway, didn't result in the slowest dating process one could sustain. Example: a movie and pizza followed by two cancelled dates in two months, followed by another movie and pizza interrupted by a gang shootout. At this rate, I'd be dyeing my hair back to its chestnut self by the time we got to a white tablecloth meal.

I finished my wine and shook myself into action. I needed to pack since tomorrow would be even busier than today. Yvette, my downstairs neighbor, would take care of Fever as usual while I was away. Last time, I had brought her a flirty, fringed cowgirl skirt from Santa Fe, and this time she let me know a long, wooly scarf from Barney's would be appreciated. She's a real sweetheart, even if the men I know all have a tendency to swoon when they meet her.

I travel with one suitcase, a buttery leather Louis Vuitton number Dickie got me for our honeymoon. For my trip to New York, I planned to pack it with black everything— slacks, skirt, sweaters, camisoles, flat-heeled boots, and four-inch heels. My evening dress for this year's dinner was black, backless, and about as slinky as my size-twelve-on-a-good-day allowed. I would tame it with a black and gold Florentine shawl, another remnant from my married days. As I checked off the last item on my list, I wondered briefly why black is New Yorkers' virtual uniform. It's a pulsing, chic, upbeat city, and, for some reason, all that black looks quite cheerful when you're in Manhattan. In San Francisco's pastel skies, it sucks up all the light.

I was climbing into bed when the phone rang. The clock said midnight. Why was Peter calling so late?

"Yes?" I snapped, taking in a deep breath to start my protest.

"Hey, it's me," said a mellow baritone voice.

"Simon?"

"I didn't wake you up or anything, did I? I thought you might want to know—"

"—that Rene Bouvier is dead and the King's Jar is missing? I've already heard. Where are you calling from?"

"I'm still at my friend's house in Berkeley. I put off my flight to New York. My plan was to be downing large quantities of ancient cognac with a pal at a private club in the East Sixties tonight, telling each other lies about our Explorer Club expeditions. Rene's death changed that."

"How so?" I said, biting a yawn.

"The editor of the London Sunday *Times* reached me in the cab on the way to airport. A schoolmate of his is on the Warefield faculty and said the campus grapevine was buzzing. The editor wants me to do an obituary that includes interviews with a few people out here. Poor Rene, his murder is news, but it's the theft of the piece that will have the archaeology world reeling. You don't have any information, by any chance?"

"Hardly. I don't even know that it was stolen. Are you sure?"

"It wasn't in its regular, locked spot in the lab. Are the cops looking somewhere else?"

"I'm not the right person to ask, Simon. Maybe I'll get more information in the morning. Your getting the obit assignment is kind of strange. I mean, Rene told me this morning how much he hated your guts."

"Yeah? What did he say?"

"Only that you were a liar and a thief because of what you did to help get the King's Jar out of Kenobia."

"That's an old story. I'm sorry he still felt that way, but that's how it goes in this field. Once, we were great pals. Paranoia runs wide and deep in the discipline. Comes with the turf."

"So I'm learning. I'm guessing—hoping, actually—that's not why you called me. This has been an unsettling day, to say the least. I'm a working girl and get grumpy without at least six hours of sleep. Don't you ever go to bed?"

"Frequently," he said, and paused for me to get it.

"Ha, ha," I dutifully responded.

"Seriously, plenty of time for that when I'm old and gray." Ouch. I felt several gray hairs sprout on the spot and wondered if I had gone down a few notches in Simon's estimation for needing sleep.

"You're going somewhere with this, right?"

I heard myself sounding bitchy and reminded myself whom I was talking to. How many women could brag that Simon Anderson, safari-jacketed media darling and adventurer, called them late at night to chat? Maybe my experiences with my ex had soured me on men. It bore thinking about at some more reasonable hour.

"Okay, I know it's late," he said and laughed. "How about coffee tomorrow morning? I'd like to talk to you about something."

"Something about Rene's death? I'm really not involved—"

"No, about the McBeels. You're involved with them about this gift, right?"

"True. Okay, tomorrow it is."

After we signed off, I thought about turning off the phone but decided I'd better not. As it turned out, I got no more calls and slept pretty well, although I did dream that Dickie was trying to steal my suitcase from the baggage carousel while wearing roller skates and Bermuda shorts. Weird, because Dickie never ever wears Bermuda shorts, but I'm not in charge of my subconscious.

chapter 3

THURSDAY MORNING'S PAPER carried the story. Distinguished scholar killed at prestigious university, priceless artifact missing. A quote from the protégé, Oscar. Poor guy was almost incoherent with grief. He described his boss as "the most brilliant researcher ever, a giant in the field."

"Bad news," said a grim Tom, standing in my office doorway an hour later, his hands jammed into his pants pockets. "The scientists have confirmed the vessel is gone. The cops had the campus officials check the vault and everywhere else they could think of. Fritz McBeel's gone ballistic. His foundation guy called me twenty minutes ago to ask if we have it in storage. I assured him it wasn't at the Devor."

"Here? Why would they think that?"

"Reaching for straws. He told me university officials were reviewing the logs and other security systems. Nada. They're sweating bullets over there."

"Could it be at his house?" I said.

"If it is, they'll find it. But the word is Fritz is threatening to withdraw his gifts from the university."

"Fat chance he'll get any money back," I said. "Realistically, isn't the jar likely to show up soon? What could anyone do with it that wouldn't be noticed?"

"That's all I can hope. The vessel's way too important and much too fragile to be moved carelessly. If it's a common thief who doesn't know that, it will be another tragedy. Rene would know how to handle it, and it's possible he might have moved it. You know, if it's gone, our exhibit is kaput." Tom massaged his head, stirring up the red hair he had left.

"As is the rationale for my lovely dinner," I said, "which will especially disappoint our new best friend, the ambassador to the United Nations from Eritrea. He has apparently invited his entire village, all of whom miraculously landed visas and jobs in New York City two months after he was appointed."

My phone rang and, after agreeing we'd stay in close touch for the rest of the day, Tom left.

It was Simon, downstairs in the coffee bar. I put lipstick on more carefully than usual, hoped the new eye shadow made my brown eyes half as alluring as the ads promised, and headed to the elevators.

Five minutes later, my cappuccino and his double espresso in hand, we settled at a sunny table, followed by a score of sidelong glances.

"Rene despised me, as you mentioned last night," Simon said, tilting his head to one side and looking straight into my eyes, a trick that worked terrifically well on television. "I did a magazine story years ago that included comments from other archaeologists challenging his thesis on what scholars call 'cultural diffusion' in Africa. When he threatened me with a ridiculous libel suit, we stopped speaking to each other."

"Does this kind of thing happen a lot in your business?"

"Absolutely. Happens in any scientific field where physical evidence is rare. Discovering something important is one part skill and two parts luck. Those who do make an important find frequently have their legs chewed off by the envious pack."

"Ugh. And I thought fundraisers were a competitive lot."

"This will sound crazy, but Rene was a highly ethical guy, which I genuinely respected. He felt responsible for using these finds to increase scientific knowledge and public understanding. On that, we agreed."

I nodded.

"To the point," Simon said, "here's what you need to know. The drinking buddy I mentioned last night runs in the same circles as Fritz McBeel. When I called him to beg off our evening at the club, he told me Fritz had a burr up his ass about Rene. He suspects Fritz's wife Jamie stokes the fire."

"That's the impression I got," I said, "although I don't know why."

"A dusty old scientist hardly greases the skids in New York society."

"But is that enough to influence Fritz McBeel? I mean, he's been a supporter of the lab for twenty years at least."

"Maybe Rene wasn't as comfortable with the idea of handing his treasure over to the Devor as you thought, although I did hear he was determined not to leave it at the university once he retired. Thought it would molder away in a storage room since no other team in the archaeology department is focused on that era in Africa."

"It'll get plenty of attention here, especially because our collection of materials from that time is small. I wish the McBeels were considering leaving us the rest of their collection, although my spies say that's not likely."

"Why am I not surprised, given Jamie's death grip on the money?" Simon chuckled.

"Agreed. She's a lot younger than he is, and I expect she'll sell his collection when Fritz passes on. Not that we won't keep trying. How well do you know her?"

"I met her once, for a few minutes, at a book launch. The impression I got was that she was a calculating bitch, if you'll pardon the expression. Are you laying odds on how long the marriage will last?"

"I haven't seen any friction, although he's a pretty cold guy at best. But, hey, that's a rather strong reaction," I said.

"Mostly what I've heard from other people, I admit," Simon said, shrugging. "Probably not even fair. I expect a lot of people jump to that conclusion. You know, the gold-digger thing?"

I winced. My former mother-in-law's face swam into my head. I knew that's what she thought I was. Time to change the subject. "By the way, I'm still planning on dinner with you Tuesday in New York, right? I'm staying at the Algonquin. I guess I already told you that." For some reason, my face was getting warm.

"Yes, ma'am," he said, grinning so the white teeth sparkled. Damn, he was hot. "I won't be headed to New York until the weekend but I will see you Tuesday for a spectacular dinner at one of my favorite restaurants. In the meantime, if I pick up any juicy gossip about Fritz and Rene, I'll let you know," he said, raising his eyebrows and twinkling at me.

We did the European kiss-kiss thing, and I went back to the office, trying not to skip as I walked across the wood floor to the elevator. It does something for a girl to have the attention of someone like Simon, even if it is only business and only for thirty minutes.

I was still a little spaced out when my phone rang again. Perhaps Simon, saying we should have dinner in San Francisco tonight as long as he was in town?

My nerves jumped to attention at the sound of the overly modulated voice on the other end of the phone. "Danielle? This is Victoria Peerless." It would be fair to say Victoria Peerless, Perfect Peerless to those of us who got calls from her on a regular basis, was conscious of her proximity to power even if she had none of her own. As Jamie McBeel's social secretary, she radiated self-importance.

"Such dreadful news about Rene Bouvier, don't you agree? Mrs. McBeel wishes to speak with you. Please hold." All this with no pause for me to reply, to make up some excuse why I couldn't take the call, or to jump up and run from my office, screaming. And now, of course, I would be on hold for as long as Jamie McBeel thought necessary to remind me of my place.

When I moved in the same social circles by dint of my status as Dickie's wife, a.k.a. Mrs. Richard Argetter III, Jamie was still cementing her place. Dickie's mother, Mrs. Richard Argetter II, was among the blue-haired set that tried to shut Jamie out of the top echelons of San Francisco society, reasoning that she had, in essence, stabbed one of their number, the first Mrs. McBeel, in the back. They loved to gossip about the prenup that Fritz had insisted upon as a condition of elevating Jamie. I got uncomfortable when I heard any of that talk since my own prenup with Dickie had been a source of grim satisfaction to Mrs. A. when Dickie and I split. Dickie, motivated by embarrassment, I'm sure, did his best to modify it, scaring his mother to death. I had enough pride to turn down payoff money.

The loyal ladies hung on to their outrage about the second Mrs. McBeel as long as possible, but Jamie, in truth, held most of the cards. With Fritz's money as her weapon of choice, she sailed into the tightest circles, raven-haired, swan-necked, and doe-eyed, dispensing enough largesse to overcome the sensitivities of charitable boards of trustees all over town. A mere million dollars got her onto a private college board even though her only advanced degree, rumor had it, was from a cosmetology school. Even less was required to open the doors to a hospital's boardroom. When she and Fritz underwrote the major costs associated with the city's annual Black and White charity ball the next year, she was triumphant. All talk of the prenup faded.

In a town as young as San Francisco, there's not much difference between old and new money. As Geoff Johnson, the Devor's board chairman, says with a pirate's grin whenever we talk about how much the Devor should ask a prospect to give, "It's all green, Dani, and for rich people, it grows like grass." Would that the rest of us had access to the same lawn care products.

"Danielle," drawled a husky voice at the other end of the phone, jarring me out of my reverie. "I don't want any hiccups in the dinner because of this…this unfortunate event. Are there any problems we need to tackle to make sure the dinner comes off as it should?"

"Good morning, Jamie," I said. "I know the King's Jar has gone missing—"

"It will show up, I'm sure. These old storerooms are always so cluttered. Is everything else all right? Rene wasn't on the program, was he? Fritz expressly said he wasn't to be, you know."

Interesting. I had not heard that before. Briefly, I wondered if it were true.

"Actually, Rene wasn't going to the dinner," I said. "The plans are on target. I'll draft remarks for Mr. McBeel soon. I'll be in New York Saturday to do a rehearsal of the program, approve the final menu, printed materials, flowers, the whole thing. Of course, I'll check the guest seating specifically with you when we get closer to the date and all the responses are in."

I was breathless when I finished, having been afraid to stop long enough in my report for Jamie McBeel to jump in with questions or new orders.

"I don't want anything to spoil this. I have reporters coming, you know, and several dear friends."

The dear friends were the New York socialites she had been courting. I knew about them because it was my job to make sure they sat at "good" tables, got VIP treatment, and met all the right (read, richest) San Francisco people. Since one of Jamie's guests actually was royalty, a distant cousin to the British throne, I was already fretting about what constituted a "good" table for her. Would the British royal cousin be upset sitting with an African ambassador whose country had ripped itself from the embrace of the British empire eighty years ago? The CEO of a multinational corporation that had recently moved major manufacturing operations from England to Korea?

I assured Jamie I was working on it, promised to show up at her New York penthouse the day before the dinner with seating charts in hand, and privately hoped Mrs. Important was finished with me for the time being.

"Oh, one more thing, Danielle," she said in her distinctive voice, causing me to curse silently. I knew we were coming to the real meat of the phone call. "Fritz was very unhappy to hear that you have invited the UN ambassador to Kenobia. You know, he was once the chairman of the Ministry of Antiquities, or whatever they call it, and interfered grossly in an important expedition my husband was supporting there."

This would be the expedition that resulted in Bouvier's recovery of the artifact McBeel was giving to us twenty years later. I wondered how to respond to Jamie. It was quite possible that the current ambassador from Kenobia was one of those bribed, or maybe he knew about the bribe and had tried to stop the sale. Either way, it would not be without precedent in the murky world of dueling research teams and cash-strapped countries with greedy leaders and byzantine political structures. Bribes were part of life at many borders. But if the ambassador's presence could embarrass them, why had the McBeels let the event plans get to this point before mentioning it?

"I'm not sure what we can do, Jamie. The board and the event committee invited the UN ambassadors of all the countries represented in the Devor's Non-Western Antiquities collection. Wouldn't it look strange to leave one out, especially the person representing the vessel's country of origin?"

"I'm sure you can manage it." And she hung up, just like that. I resisted the urge to slam the phone down and instead swore loudly.

"You called, tramp?" said a voice from the hall. Brown curls, a dangling earring, and then an arm covered in African bracelets appeared in the doorway, followed by the full body—and I do mean full—of my assistant, Teeni Watson.

I groaned. "I just got off the phone with someone who wants me to uninvite one of the guests of honor at the New York dinner."

"Oooh, I hope you told him he was a fool even to ask," she said, plopping down on a chair and running her hands through her hair.

"It was Jamie McBeel," I said.

"Oooh, I hope you said yes ma'am it will be done according to thy will."

Teeni doesn't have much direct contact with the VIP donor group, but on the first occasion when she was at a gathering Jamie attended, the latter apparently decided Teeni was a coat checker and dropped her fur coat into Teeni's outstretched hand, which Teeni had offered in welcome. Teeni didn't react fast enough and for a long, drawn-out moment the garment lay slumped on the floor between them like the dead animal it was.

Mrs. McBeel never said a word, merely arched her brows and kept walking. Teeni decided to let it go, and bent to scoop up the coat, which resulted in the rest of us breathing again.

"I can't imagine how to do it without provoking an international crisis. His office has already RSVP'd and Louise wants him to sit at the head table with the McBeels, for heaven's sake."

"Sounds like Louise didn't hear anything about this."

"Jamie said Fritz wants him uninvited, but Louise told me she and Fritz went over the head table list a week ago. If he felt that way, why did he approve having the ambassador at his table?"

"You haven't talked to Louise in at least forty-five minutes, so it's time for the phone to ring. See what she says. Maybe she can talk Mrs. McBeel out of whatever ails her, 'cause she sure has something up her you-know-what." Teeni shook her head, her earrings jangling.

People who know Teeni aren't fooled by her style. She's tough, all right, in the best ways. Born in the San Francisco projects to a hard-working single mother, Teeni took every Boys and Girls Club field trip she could. She fell in love with art during after-school trips and made a beeline for the

University of California's Berkeley campus after graduating from high school. A full scholarship and enough talent to fill a Muni bus propelled her through her undergrad degree and into the graduate program in art history. Over the past few years, she has focused on California's funk art movement and is the guest curator of an exhibit the Devor will host next year, the last requirement for her Ph.D., at which time I am resigned to losing my assistant to some savvy museum. She talks like a Ph.D. when she's with curators and foundation program officers. If she wants to be down home in our private conversations, I'm cool with it.

The phone rang. Teeni reached across the desk and picked it up. "Ms. O'Rourke's office," she said in her other voice. "Oh, hello, Mrs. Johnson," rolling her eyes at me. "I sure do. Is the florist okay with that? Wonderful. Sounds like you have everything under control. Dani? Yes, in fact, she's right here." Teeni handed me the phone and walked out of the office, waggling her multi-hued false fingernails at me in farewell. I took a gulp of cold coffee from the mug on my desk, grimaced, and began explaining our latest problem to Louise Johnson.

Plato said it best: necessity is the mother of invention. Louise and I spent the next twenty minutes in overdrive. We now had two head tables, one in the main dining room and the second in the reception hall. Louise and her husband would sacrifice their status by sitting in the second room with the ambassador from Kenobia, a couple of board members, New York's lieutenant governor, and a film actress and her rich-as-Croesus hedge fund boyfriend from Beverly Hills. Closed-circuit TV and a classical guitar player would warm up the atmosphere and there would be an extra allotment of champagne for the ambassador's table.

Louise and a trusted woman friend would engage to keep the ambassador away from Jamie before the dinner, and I would tell Jamie we were doing all we could, without saying we actually weren't doing what she demanded. I was a little leery, but agreed with Louise that our options were somewhat limited. It helped that, as far as I knew, Jamie had never met the ambassador since the controversy in question happened before her tenure as Mrs. McBeel.

I didn't have time to draw a deep breath, much less head for the coffeepot in the copy room before Tom showed up in my doorway, leaning on the door frame and frowning. "I need to give you another update."

"Walk with me, Tom. I need coffee. What's up? Your expression tells me it's not good news."

As we headed down the corridor, he shook his head. "No jar. It wasn't at Rene's house in San Francisco, which was my last hope. The police say the house was undisturbed and there's no sign of a break-in at the lab. They think it could mean it was someone who had access to the Warefield building, another researcher, or someone Rene knew. People don't lock the doors while they're in their offices. There's no security in the entrance hall once the main doors are locked at night, though, so it isn't much of a clue."

"Was anything else missing?"

"My friend says the cops asked the office assistant to help them search the lab and Rene's office. A couple of Rene's files on the vessel were missing, old stuff, the assistant said."

We filled two paper cups, stirred in sugar from packets, and wandered back up the hall. "Who is this friend of yours?" I asked. "He seems to be in the thick of the investigation."

"No, but he picks up things. Steve and I were grad students together. He did a lot of work in Kenobia himself. Not the same historical period as Rene's, but his laboratory and offices are down the hall from Rene's, so they bump into each other. He says the archaeology department is humming with gossip. Some of it is pretty unsympathetic. Rene didn't play well with others, you might say."

"Sad. Any of those detractors likely to be mad enough to whack him over the head and steal the jar?"

"Nah, these are academics. While they're capable of intense dislike, jealousy, and spite, their weapons of choice are words, not chair legs. That's what it was, apparently, a chair that the intruder grabbed from nearby."

"I don't want to know, thank you." I shivered. "What about the other members of his team? I saw the senior researcher, Oscar somebody, at Rene's lab when I went down to Warefield to talk to Rene. Isn't he the one who came to the Devor for the walk-through with you, the one who wanted to be included on several of the wall texts?"

"Oscar Shelby, major geek." Tom scratched his goatee absently. "In a way, I know what he's saying. The head of the team gets all the credit, and that's who goes into the history books. But would one of them lose his temper and hit the old man? Underneath the griping, they worshipped him. And, let's face it, they have to be worried that they could lose the grants that Rene's name and reputation brought into the lab. This Oscar's built his career around the ongoing excavations at the site."

"The jar is almost two feet tall," I said, as much to myself as to the curator. "It couldn't have vanished into thin air."

"Especially since it can't be displayed or sold openly," Tom reminded me. "Everyone in the field will know within forty-eight hours that it's been stolen."

"It's that important?"

"Yeah."

"I understand its value in demonstrating African connections to the world before slavery and colonization. The jar undermines the stereotypes about primitive people living in some kind of darkest Africa, right?"

"You got it. I'm amazed Fritz McBeel was able to buy it, even twenty years ago. Today, he wouldn't get to first base. So, if it hasn't been hustled off to a private collection where it will sit in secret for decades, it will probably show up. Preferably not in pieces in a garbage can."

On that cheerful note, Tom stroked his goatee and slumped off.

I sat at my desk, drumming my fingers for a full minute. My job doesn't usually include solving murders. But making sure the cops or the university found the treasure was critical for the Devor, and rescuing my big event was my highest priority right now. I had less than two days to try and push the theft investigation forward before I got on a plane for New York, so I picked up the phone and speed-dialed the only person I knew who might be able to help. At the very least, if I played it right, it might get me a date.

chapter 4

SAN FRANCISCO HOMICIDE Inspector Charles Sugerman is half of a team of investigators who spend far too much time in the company of people whose close, personal friends are murderers. Charlie is younger than his partner by about fifteen years, which means he hasn't seen as many dead bodies or interviewed as many nasty suspects. That's probably why he's still a cheerful person. When he smiles, his eyes shine like pale, green emeralds through a screen of blonde eyelashes.

"Hey Charlie, am I catching you at a bad time? I mean, you're not in the middle of a shootout or anything, are you?"

"Dani? It must be you. You're the only person I know who would ask a question like that." His deep chuckle sent a little charge up my spine. "Nope, no guns blazing, although I'd rather be doing that than this damn paperwork."

He sighed. "Writing reports takes up 50 percent of my time. The other half is mostly listening to bullshitters, the ones on the street and the ones who work for the city. What's up?"

"Any chance you're free for a quick bite after work?" I said, crossing my fingers.

"Good timing. We wrapped up a case a couple hours ago, and another's hit a dead end for the moment. I actually get to eat a real meal tonight. Not another break-in at your apartment?"

I still wince when I'm reminded of the strange happenings when Charlie and I met. "No, nothing like that. I need your perspective on a robbery gone bad. A scientist named Rene Bouvier at Warefield University was killed. My interest's a missing artifact from his lab that's supposed to come to my museum."

"So you are involved in another murder."

I couldn't tell if he was genuinely annoyed or simply teasing me.

"No, really. I'm simply trying to understand the odds the stolen item will be recovered."

"Weiler and I didn't draw the case. I heard Brendan talking about catching a call from the university. Weiler and I seem to get all the drive-bys and drug killings these days."

"Could we talk? Want to meet at Café Trieste in North Beach around seven? I'm up for pizza."

Pizza, advice, and then? Charlie was sweet. However, flirting and one lingering kiss summed up our romantic history pretty nicely. I was touchy about relationships, courtesy of my ex-husband. Charlie never hinted at a trauma in love. Nevertheless, something cautionary seemed to hover in the air along with the pheromones whenever we met. At first, it was probably his suspicion that I might be a killer since we met while he was investigating a suspicious death at the Devor. But when that case was closed and he asked me out, I noticed we were both easily spooked.

For good reason, I reminded myself. My husband forgot he was married, my prior boyfriend defenestrated from my office, my chances of landing Safari Man on one date weren't worth calculating, and Charlie had a twenty-four/

seven career hanging out with bad guys. And, to top it off, my confidence factor wasn't too high these days. The last time I tried to fit into my skinny jeans, the zipper got stuck.

» » »

The zipper was still on my mind two hours later as I waved away a third piece of prosciutto-laced pizza in favor of more salad and explained the case of the missing object to Charlie.

Peter Lindsey, with Tom's input, had handled the trickiest portions of the year-long negotiation to secure it for the museum's collection, and Rene Bouvier had brokered the gift because, he told me, he disapproved of important artifacts disappearing into private collections or elite organizations where access might be overly restricted.

"Scientists and the public have as much right to learn from the treasures of the past as a bunch of rich assholes," he had said in a pinched voice. The only reason the Devor got Bouvier's support for the gift was because we agreed to follow his plan for sharing it with the world.

In fact, the professor told me that he hoped the vessel would be repatriated to Kenobia some day, a possibility Fritz McBeel vehemently opposed. The billionaire was adamant that the Kenobians didn't have the expertise, the resources, or the freedom from violent political upheavals to protect something as important as the vessel. In his negotiations, Peter tiptoed around the issue.

I told Charlie all of this and about Tom's concern that it might vanish into a private collection.

"It's amazing how frequently that kind of theft happens," Charlie said, nodding his head. "I mean, you think Nazis or Napoleon's troops looting their way to Moscow. These days, from the little I know, it could be some Armani suit who's glorified in the *Wall Street Journal* every day."

"We can't let that happen," I said. "What can the police do? How can we help?"

"People talk, Dani, and the FBI agents who specialize in this have the right contacts. They also work with Interpol if they have reason to think it's left the U.S. Sooner or later, if they're lucky, the truth leaks out."

"FBI? Interpol? Are they involved?"

"Trust me, if it doesn't show up soon, they will be. My opinion? It's not likely that your pot will wind up in a trash can. I'm betting it's the reason for the murder, if it was murder."

"What do you mean 'if'?" I asked.

Charlie took a few seconds to smooth his silk tie, flecked with a green that complemented his eyes. I got distracted, wondering if his mother or someone else picked it out for him. Whoever it was had good taste.

"Maybe he wasn't meant to die," he said, thinking out loud, "but to be stunned enough to stay still while whoever took it got away. You told me he was an old man, and that could mean he was more vulnerable than the thief knew. Or, maybe they got into a fight, the victim fought back, and the thief hit him harder than he intended to."

"Jeez, you sound like the defense lawyer," I said.

"I'm just saying murder to get this artifact doesn't ring true to me. This kind of theft rarely involves violence."

Charlie's perspective helped. Who wanted the jar so much they'd panic and bash an old man on the head for it if he didn't hand it over? Realistically, who would be crazy enough to steal a priceless object from a billionaire with enough money to chase such a robber to the ends of the earth with or without the FBI's help?

"How about this?" I said. "What if the government of Kenobia wanted the vessel back? Could they have hired someone to grab it?"

"Ah, well, that's politics, and that's beyond me," Charlie said, upending a wedge dripping with cheese. "I think I could find Kenobia on a map, but that's about it. If there's an international angle to this, good luck. I doubt Brendan and his partner will be much better, either."

"Did you tell Brendan I was asking about the artifact?"

"Yup. He said there's not much you haven't probably heard or that he can share. He agrees it probably wasn't supposed to be murder. Using the chair suggests a lack of premeditation to him, too."

"Does Brendan have any ideas about where the artifact could be now?"

"He says the university people don't see it on a regular basis because it's normally locked away. But it wasn't in that locked lab room. It could still be in Warefield's storage buildings, miscataloged. Or lying around in that lab, which he says looks like a rat's nest."

"Hardly. It's big, it's distinctive, and no one who works there would mistake it for anything else."

"Brendan said the place was crawling with students."

"Postdocs," I said, "academics who have their doctoral degrees and are heavy into research. And grad students. Tom told me researchers competed to coauthor scientific papers with Rene or claim him as a mentor."

"Well, no one's been cleared yet," Charlie said, "in part because they all left fingerprints all over the lab."

"But presumably not on the chair?"

"Unfortunately, there too. Brendan says one of the guys in the lab picked up the chair and set it back on its legs and then someone else moved it again to get it out of the way of the emergency crew that came when they called 9-1-1."

"Then how do they know it was the chair?"

"Blood. That and a matching dent in the victim's skull. Autopsy results aren't in, but Brendan's betting on a fractured skull and hemorrhaging in the brain. They'll interview everyone again and check alibis in the next couple of days."

"Is he calling in the FBI?"

"Not yet. He's more interested in the fatality than the artifact, is my guess. But the university will probably insist. And, don't forget, there's bound to be an insurance policy, and whichever company wrote it will put their own investigator on the case quickly, as if we need more people mucking up the scene."

Charlie leaned forward. "Look, Dani. I hope you're not thinking of getting involved. Leave it to the pros, okay?"

"Absolutely, if you mean Rene's death. I hope you guys catch the bastard who did this, but my interest is in recovering the vessel, or determining that the Devor is out of luck. It's a unique piece of history. To lose it would be a second tragedy, as my curator put it."

"I hear you, but to lose you would be kind of a tragedy, too," he said with a smile.

Fair Irish skin gives me away. I felt a blush rising.

"I have to know if we're going to abandon or revise our new African history display," I stammered, kicking myself for my complete inability to flirt.

"This vase, it's that important?" Charlie backed off, probably thinking that's what I wanted. So not true.

"It's kind of an urn, and, yes, it's unique. I hope the police will tell us when the FBI gets called in. We can help bring them up to speed on the object. We also need to be in touch with the claims investigator for the insurance company. That's not a problem, is it?"

"Not if that's as far as you go." He looked sternly at me.

"Promise," I said, reaching over to wipe a thread of mozzarella off his handsome chin. If I hadn't been so distracted by his gorgeous jaw line and the fact that he was off duty until tomorrow, I might have thought twice before making a promise I wasn't sure I could keep.

That's called tempting the fates, my inner voice reminded me. To prove it, his cell phone rang. As he asked a few staccato questions and looked hastily at his watch, the fates laughed.

"Sorry, Dani. I was hoping we could go somewhere for a drink, and maybe take a walk around North Beach," he said as he pocketed the phone. "The case that was stuck came unstuck. The guy we're trying to nail got into a shootout over in the Excelsior neighborhood."

"Is he dead?"

"Not yet. He's headed to S.F. General, and I need to meet the ambulance there. Don't want this punk to die without confessing to my open homicide. Are you okay to get home on your own?"

"Absolutely."

He smiled apologetically, threw some money on the table, and was out the door like Clark Kent in search of a phone booth.

The waiter hovered, hoping to shoo me off so he could squeeze more people in. Stubbornly, I ordered a double espresso and some house-made biscotti and used the time to digest what Charlie said.

Who had the King's Jar now? The people closest to it, physically, were the other researchers in the lab. I remembered

Oscar as an overweight guy in Coke-bottle glasses and baggy jeans who rubbed his hands together a lot. Tom asked his opinion several times, and I had the impression he respected Oscar's knowledge. Rene didn't seem bothered by Oscar's demands for acknowledgment on the wall texts or in the printed handout. As Tom had pointed out, Oscar would hardly kill the man who made his career possible.

Who wanted it most? Not the researchers, who already had access and who weren't collectors. Not the McBeels, who already owned it. The government of Kenobia? They could petition for it openly without resorting to illegal means, although there was no guarantee they'd get it back. Anyway, how could they display it if everyone knew it was stolen and a respected researcher killed in the process?

I remembered Rene's face, twisted with dislike as he railed against Simon. Rene implied Simon played a shady role in getting the artifact out of Kenobia and into McBeel's hands. It was hard to believe Simon would risk his reputation and career now to get it back. And for whom or what?

From the outside, Simon seemed to have enough money to live the life of a jet-setting journalist and media celebrity. True, he was likely to know at least one or two ultra-wealthy private collectors of sub-Saharan archaeological treasures simply because he knew so many wealthy people. Tom told me that Simon had recounted an eyebrow-raising dinner in Dubai with an old, withered man who had created a private museum for his personal pleasure. Simon told Tom he was sure at least half of the theatrically lit, fabulously beautiful pieces were contraband, but that the collector was too well shielded to face scrutiny.

Where was the vessel? I wondered if thieves might be holding it for ransom. That had happened with some famous paintings in the past. If so, what was the price, and how would we find out?

The waiter was giving me the evil eye. I paid up and exited the toasty café into San Francisco's typically nippy night air. As I headed home from lively North Beach to the quiet of Pacific Heights, I promised myself to do some digging when I saw Simon in New York. At the very least, I would get a short list of the private hands into which our prize might fall.

And then? I asked myself. Fly to Dubai? Play detective? No, I'd turn anything I learned over to the FBI. Well, maybe to Charlie and let him decide what to do with it. Get more involved than that? Absolutely not. There was silence from my inner voice, not the comfortable kind.

» » »

First thing Friday morning, I got down to the serious work of packing my briefcase and coordinating with Teeni and the rest of the fundraising staff for the week in New York. Our PR director had set up some media interviews that we would have to think about in light of the theft. The other events would proceed as scheduled.

Charlie called to make sure I got home safely, which was sweet. Louise called to say it was pouring rain in New York City but nothing new had gone wrong. A reporter at the *San Francisco Chronicle* called to ask if I had a private phone number for the McBeels she could use on "an important press matter." Good luck.

I spent a couple of hours drafting comments for the board chair to start off the dinner speeches and to honor the McBeels for their largesse. I hedged my bets about where the artifact would be on the evening of the dinner by referring only in general to the vessel as one of the many ways Fritz and Jamie—even though she hadn't personally shown any interest in the Devor except as a social setting—had supported the museum over the years, blah, blah.

I'd sharpen it in New York, when, I hoped, I could add more information about the vessel, assuming it had shown up by then. Lucky for me, Peter wrote his own remarks, and they were always brilliant and witty.

Tom had no news about the missing piece when he dropped in, but he did say Simon was coming to the Devor to spend an hour or so in the archives, working on some footnotes for the catalog. I thought I might have a minute to say hi to him, but the day was over before I finished everything on my list.

Waiting to board the flight in the evening, I checked my Blackberry one last time, and my heart beat a little faster. My dinner with Simon was one of those untouched events and something to look forward to in all of this confusion. Nothing, I smiled to myself, not even my plan to check him out as a suspect and a source, would interfere with that.

chapter 5

SIMON WAS WAVING a big green bowl in the air and running around the museum. Rene Bouvier's finger shook as he pointed it at me and said in a quavering voice. "He stole it from under my nose."

"Excuse me, miss? Do you want coffee and a muffin?" The stewardess smiled as she leaned across the empty seat toward me. I banished the dream and sat up straighter. New MBAs try to outdo each other with tales about back-to-back red-eye flights they take across the country in search of the big deal. In all of these stories, leaving one coast at the end of a working day and being razor sharp and on your game when you arrive in the corridors of power thousands of miles away before breakfast is the implicit brag point.

Total macho crap. The red eye sucks. Stale air, cramped spaces, a total lack of privacy, and the great gift of arriving at your destination looking like you slept under an overpass.

It was still early enough on a Saturday morning that I had no trouble waving down a trolling car for hire. I watched the sky over Manhattan turn pastel as we zigged and zagged our way through Brooklyn and Queens, over the bridge, and to my hotel in midtown. Showered, soothed by breakfast from room service, and dressed in black sweater, pants, and jacket, I headed for the Pilgrim Club to meet Louise and a small army of committee members, caterers, florist's assistants, and the Club's manager.

If all worked according to plan, I'd grab a nap before dinner with a fellow museum fundraiser. It's fun to spend time with someone else who knows what goes on behind the scenes—the endless currying favor, sniffing around (within ethical boundaries, preferably) for information about people who have lots of money, the great coups and the deals that fall through for crazy reasons. You also hear gossip about which museums are hot, which are hurting, which may be about to start a poaching expedition for new directors and curators.

By late morning, I was in the thick of the latest round of seating charts that reflected the demands of people who wanted to sit at the same table as their friends, their bosses, their children, or the royal personage. The head table, where the Queen of England's distant relative would park her royal self, would have to seat forty if we were to accommodate all the "close friends" who had lobbied board and committee members in the past couple of days. Since the McBeels and Peter were already at that table along with an elderly couple who had recently signed a multimillion-dollar pledge to the museum and the personage and her husband, there were only three open spots.

"I know that seating chart crises are normal," Louise said with a sigh, pushing wiry blonde waves off her forehead. "This one is going for the record." Louise Johnson was in her sixties like I'd like to be in my sixties, trim, straight-backed, dressed in a pale green cashmere turtleneck, a Hermes scarf, and black knit slacks from Saks Fifth Avenue's designer racks. It was only when she talked that I felt the generational divide. All her life, she had been her hard-driving husband's helpmeet, the woman behind the success. Her self-confidence was fragile, easily dinged.

"I once came into this dining room with the maître d' to do a last check before we opened the doors," I said to get her laughing. "A guest was blatantly moving the place cards from his table to one up front, dumping the place cards from the other table on a sideboard where no one would see them."

Her face froze. Wrong story. "Oh, no. Remind me to get one of the committee to stand guard."

I changed the subject to the goodie bags that would sit on each guest's chair: a sample of a designer's sandalwood perfume, a Kente cloth-wrapped soap, an elegant wooden box of African bush tea, and a signed copy of Simon's last book. Not too shabby. What would be shabby would be the outright filching of extra goodies by other guests, a common occurrence at the end of black tie parties.

My cell phone rang and I retreated to the mezzanine lobby, sinking into a deep armchair. "Hey, Tom. Glad you called. I need some advice. If there are only fifty dozen apricot roses in New York City on the day of the dinner, should we risk mixing them with pink ones, or abandon roses altogether for tulips?" Silence greeted my question.

"Maybe I should call back later. You asked me to keep you up to speed and I think you need to know this. Is this a bad time?"

"Sorry, Tom. I'm giddy from lack of sleep. What is it?"

"I got a call really early today asking me to meet with the police this afternoon about Rene's death and what they now think is the theft of the Song jar."

"Damn. I hoped the Devor could stay out of this."

"Get this, Dani. The cop asked me about Simon and how he and Rene got along. From something he said, I got the idea that someone told them Simon might have had a motive to hit Rene and take the jar. With you and the boss out of town, I thought I'd better call. I'm wondering if I should put the catalog project with Simon on hold."

"Why? Do you think it might be true?" I said, surprised.

"I can't see it," Tom said. "He might try to charm it off Rene for some reason, but hit the old guy over the head and steal it? Doesn't compute."

"I agree it's crazy," I said, "but I'm as leery as you guys about the possibility of bad publicity. Why don't you call the museum's outside legal counsel? I'll let Peter know we talked and that I okayed your going on the clock with the law firm. And, remember, it's Saturday. Don't spend the whole day on Devor business, okay? You still seeing that adorable redhead you brought to my party?"

"That adorable redhead just got engaged to a banker. I'm on the loose, sad to say. Know anyone?"

I could never figure out why a woman hadn't grabbed Tom by now. He might not be handsome and he was definitely too intense about work and the Celtics, not always in that order, but I thought he was a keeper. When I got back to San Francisco, I'd have to scroll through my contact list to find a candidate for his affections. I wouldn't do it for anyone else, but Tom deserved the best.

I hiked back into the dining room, asking myself if I was 100 percent sure Simon couldn't be involved. Ambitious, yes. Full of himself, absolutely. But I'd never heard rumors about a violent history. My guess was that Oscar and the others on the team had absorbed Rene's hostility as part of their loyalty to the old man and one of them had passed it along to the cops.

My immediate problem was keeping Louise from quitting as dinner chairperson during the next several days.

As I got back to the table and smiled encouragement at her, I made a mental note to send a fruit basket to her hotel suite, along with a note from Peter, praising her for her diplomacy, patience, and leadership. My second mental note was to tell him I'd done that in case she called him to say thanks.

I was surreptitiously checking the time when the chef sent out the test meal for the several committee members in attendance and me to taste and approve. The ladies cooed over their persimmon salads accompanied by champagne and the organic beef tenderloins and broccoli rabe with California cabernet. They saved their highest accolades for the ginger chocolate mousse topped with vanilla whipped cream, served with espresso in tiny demitasse cups.

The chef was relieved, both because this was the second round of tasting for us and because he had a Club dinner to do this evening. The dining room staff was itching to start moving tables around, and soon the Devor ladies wandered off to Bergdorf's while I hurried back to the hotel to do a final review of the program script before meeting with the people who would be videotaping the party.

Given that we didn't know if the Devor would actually possess the centerpiece of its non-Western collection by the time of the dinner, I needed to develop a Plan B. As of now, 2:30 New York time on Saturday, I had none and was too groggy to think about it.

Too bad. My hotel voicemail included a terse message from Peter to call him immediately, a snappish demand from Victoria Peerless in San Francisco to call her as soon as I got her message, and a frosty request from Fritz McBeel's foundation director, Wayne Lawson, also in San Francisco, to call without delay. I ordered a large pot of coffee from room service and began with my boss.

"Where have you been?" Peter said when his assistant, Dorie, put me through. "I've been stalling. I have to return Jamie's call. That smarmy assistant of hers has called about ten times. Dorie's ready to slap her."

"Tell Dorie not to do it until I'm there to enjoy it. You could have called my cell. I've been with the ladies who lunch and just got back to the hotel. I have messages from La Peerless and Fritz's foundation director. All urgent."

"You never answer your cell," Peter said. "You told Jamie we'd take care of the table seating, right?" Peter's voice was getting that prissy tone that said he was getting stressed, not good for the people around him. I ratcheted my own voice down and kept it soothing, what I imagined a horse whisperer might do.

"Almost. I'm scheduled to meet with her here the day before the dinner, to go over the chart. Louise and I finessed the business with the Kenobian ambassador. Poor guy's practically sitting in the hall, which should make Jamie feel better. I never promised Jamie veto rights, though."

"Maybe she picked up on that and has decided to work on me," Peter said.

"That sounds like Jamie. And, having Wayne Lawson, who writes the checks, come after me fits the pattern, too. What do you want me to do here?"

Peter was silent. If anyone enjoys snaring big gifts more than me, it's my boss. If it came to it, he would tell me to lose the ambassador from Kenobia. But I needed him to make the decision, since it would not play well with Louise, and therefore her husband Geoff , the Devor's board chairman.

"I'll call Fritz on his private line now," Peter said, "and see if I can drop in to see him today, before he leaves for New York. If he's pulling the strings on this, his body language may tell me more than what he actually says. Stall La Peerless and Wayne until you hear from me, okay?"

"Will do, with pleasure. Oh, by the way, you're sending a basket of fruit to Louise. "

"Whatever you say. I'll call you as soon as I know something. Go have some fun." Good. He was cheerful again, which meant I could relax. Now, all I needed was a nap.

» » »

In light of Peter's criticism, I kept my cell phone on with the ring volume up when I left the hotel that evening. I was trying to tune out my cab driver's tirade about immigrants taking over New York City so I wouldn't be tempted to ask him about the thick Russian accent in which he was delivering his judgment when it rang. Waving it at the scowling face in the rearview mirror, I warbled "my boss," mentally thanking Peter for rescuing me on a trip that was going to take another ten minutes, given the rush hour traffic inching uptown on Park Avenue.

"Wish I could tell you something definitive," Peter said after reporting that he had met with Fritz McBeel for about fifteen minutes. "I tiptoed into the subject of the ambassador from Kenobia. He smiled vaguely at the ceiling in his typical way but didn't say much, so I finally had to ask him straight out if you understood correctly that he didn't want the man to attend the dinner."

Thanks for making me the source of the problem, I thought.

"So? What did he say?" I asked as the cabbie blared his horn at another cab and squeezed so close to it on the passenger side (my side) that I involuntarily leaned away.

"Said no, no problem. Said you might have misunderstood, that he is sure Jamie would never have suggested uninviting an important African diplomat."

"Oh, shit!" I shouted, partly because I was clearly going to take the fall for this little contretemps and partly because the cab driver had run a red light at Seventy-fifth Street, almost getting us killed.

The driver glared at me in the rearview mirror. In my country, ladies don't swear, he was saying with his smoldering eyes. *In my country, taxi drivers don't kill their passengers,* I thought but didn't say.

"Sorry, Peter," I said meekly. "Traffic scare. Thanks for going directly to Fritz. I guess that means I do my best to avoid Jamie. If she hits me with it when we go over the seating charts, I have to say something, though."

"Take the initiative," Peter suggested. "When you walk in, tell her how pleased you are that Fritz explained that you misunderstood. That has to shut her up, right?"

"Brilliant," I had to admit. "Especially if you're a masochist. I have to hang up. See you tomorrow."

Dinner with my colleague was more fun than I anticipated. I finally bailed at midnight and got a gloriously silent cab driver for the return trip to the Algonquin and eight hours of sleep.

» » »

Sunday, D-day minus five. I breakfasted with Louise, who was already panicking at the thought of the RSVPs that would come in to the Devor with Monday's mail.

"People will call with the good news that they're coming right up until it's time to get dressed," I reminded her. A few would even show up at the Pilgrim Club with brazen tales of having called ages ago, or having told their secretaries to call, or that the dog ate the invitation.

"We have a table near the kitchen set aside for them, remember? All will be well." Any places not claimed by the time the room was seated would be offered, at his suggestion, to the tuxedo-clad brothers-in-law of the second cousins of the Ambassador from Eritrea currently residing in Queens but conveniently languishing in delis close to the Club as dinnertime approached.

"My husband called last night," Louise said. "He told me the police still don't know who killed poor Rene."

I filled her in on the public version of events and pointed her to this morning's *New York Times*, which carried a ten-inch obituary and photo. "The article didn't mention Fritz McBeel's financial support of Rene's work, or that the vessel is missing from his lab."

Louise frowned. "I should have called Mary. She must be so distressed."

The non sequitur puzzled me until Louise explained. "Fritz's first wife. She took a class from Rene when she was at Warefield and caught the archaeology bug. Geoff and I always thought that's how Fritz got interested in the Kenobia project. She and Rene still keep in touch."

"Jamie's not so interested," I ventured.

"No, not at all. I think she's a bit jealous of Mary, which is foolish, of course. Mary didn't come out of the divorce very well off, you know. Fritz and his lawyers are nothing if not careful about guarding his money. But that's water over the dam."

We parted soon after, Louise to a day spa and me to take a long walk up Madison and down Fifth, a personal ritual in all but the filthiest New York weather. Madison Avenue uptown is a window shopper's delight even when the stores are closed, and the black-railinged sidewalk edging Central Park on Fifth on the way back downtown triggers hazy childhood memories. *I (heart) New York*, sang my endorphin-fueled inner voice as I turned back into the Algonquin lobby, my nose chilled and my cheeks tingling from the brisk air. I stopped at the reception desk to pick up a *Washington Post* and stood there for a minute, skimming the day's headlines. War, famine, political infighting, the usual cheerful morning topics. Nothing about Rene Bouvier.

"Hey there. Had your uptown walk yet?"

No, it couldn't be. There he was, grinning as I lowered the paper and turned around.

"Dickie?" I said, making it a question. His hair was mussed and the brightly colored muffler wrapped around his neck set off his bluer-than-blue eyes. A polished twenty-something woman in designer jeans, high-heeled boots, and pink sweater eyed him speculatively from a nearby leather armchair, her coffee forgotten in her upraised hand.

Dickie—that is, my ex-husband, Richard Argetter III, he of the fast cars and large fortune—knew how much I loved coming back to my hometown. We spent a lot of time here early in our courtship. He proposed to me in one of those corny horse-drawn carriages that pick passengers up in front of the fountain at the Plaza, a romantic gesture I privately adored even though, as a native New Yorker, I was honor bound to scorn. For an instant, I remembered how much fun it was to be in love with him.

"In the flesh. Suzy says you're going to dinner with that TV sleazeball, and I wanted to remind you to be sure you bring the pepper spray."

"Did you call Suzy to check up on me? Never mind," I said, my good mood vanishing. Suzy Byrnstein is my best friend, and loyal to me, but she thinks Dickie was suffering from high-altitude sickness when he took up with the underwear model and hasn't written him off as my soul mate. "For one thing, Suzy would never call Simon a sleaze-ball. For another, it's none of your damn business. And for a third…" I ran out of steam, or reasons. So typical of my ex to decide he had the right to manage my personal life. It was bad enough that Dickie and I lived in the same town and traveled in the same circles. Ever since he had taken a bullet for me when I blundered into the sights of a killer last year, Dickie had been acting like my personal bodyguard. Since I had no intention of being that stupid twice, I didn't need the babysitting. In fact, if either of us needed guarding, it was more likely to be him. A bachelor with a history of liking pretty girls and a large fortune attracts single women like nothing else, and he seemed at times oblivious to the little social traps they laid everywhere for him.

"Just saying. Anyway, I wanted to ask you something. Want some coffee?" He gestured to the breakfast room off the lobby.

"No thanks. You were talking to Suzy?"

"I didn't know where you were staying and needed to talk with you."

"The phone wouldn't work?"

"Better to ask in person and, anyway, New York's a small town, a drop-in kind of place, don't you think?"

"I really have to get going, Dickie. Can this wait?"

"Won't take a minute," he continued cheerfully. Cheerful was a strategy with him, I had figured out long ago, when people might not be planning to do what he wanted them to do. "You know I'm escorting Mother to the dinner, right?"

"Yes, I saw it on the RSVP list," I said, edging toward the elevators.

"Know where we're sitting yet? Mother has hinted, broadly, I might add, that she wants to be seated with the duchess, or princess, or whoever she is. Any chance of wangling that?"

I pressed the up button, groaning inwardly at the image of Mother Argetter giving me the evil eye if I couldn't deliver. "Your mother and about two hundred other guests. Louise is going nuts. I don't think I'd dare mention it to her. Seriously, Dickie, Jamie McBeel has the whole table sewn up. You're within curtseying range. I hope that will do."

"I'll make sure it does. Want to go for a hansom cab ride after the ball?" The elevator had come and he was holding the door open to the annoyance of a couple with beaucoup luggage.

"Thanks, but no thanks." I got in. He followed me. "I'm a working girl, remember?" I said as I pushed my floor button. "I have to stay to get the last guests out the door, settle with the steward, make sure no one left glasses or keys behind, yada yada. I'll be dragging by the time that's done."

"Well, breakfast tomorrow then?"

"How about the morning after the party instead? Where are you staying?" I asked, begging the fates that it wasn't the Algonquin.

"My old college roommate still owns that hideous black leather and chrome bachelor penthouse on Riverside Drive. Remember it? I'm bunking with him. Mother's got a suite at the Plaza, of course."

Of course. She was locked into a 1950s vision of upper-class status, even as the barbarians pushed their way through the gates.

The elevator stopped at my floor, and the couple dragged their suitcases out as Dickie again put his arm into the open door. I told Dickie I had to go.

"Okay," he said, as I angled past him. "See you at the royal party. Breakfast the next morning for sure." The elevator closed on his signature crooked grin, and I relaxed. Privately, my plan was to spend a couple hours at the Metropolitan Museum, walk through Central Park, and spend the rest of the afternoon at the American Museum of Natural History. Alone. A perfect New York Sunday.

I unlocked my room door and noticed the red light blinking on the house phone. Didn't I have to call Victoria Peerless and Fritz's financial guy back? No, I decided. It was Sunday and I was off duty. The McBeels could snap their fingers all they wanted. I had earned some free time. To make sure I didn't backslide, I turned my cell phone off. The newspaper and a fresh pot of strong coffee beckoned for now, high culture the rest of the day.

chapter 6

A SYMPHONY OF TAXI horns echoing off the walls outside
my window woke me up early Monday morning. I had a couple of fundraising visits to make to charitable foundations,
and before long I was striding down the Avenue of the Amer-
icas (Sixth Avenue to natives) to the first. Then, a quick cab
up to Rockefeller Center and an ear-popping ride to a high
floor for another meeting, this time in a richly decorated
corporate boardroom. In both cases, my hosts were polite
but noncommittal, which didn't surprise me. Their offices
are full of hopeful fundraisers like me, all with good ideas
that will bloom if watered with someone else's money.

I checked my watch as I finally pushed open the glass
doors to the sidewalk. Time for a quick bite, then back to my
hotel room to touch base with the staff back home.

First call was to our beleaguered Non-Western Arts curator. Tom told me in aggrieved tones that he got a call from
a Kenobian archaeologist headquartered at an Ivy League
university over the weekend, fishing for information on
the whereabouts of the star object of our upcoming exhibit
space.

Tom sighed audibly. "If the new head of antiquities in
Kenobia gets involved, this is going to get very complicated.
For all I know, they'll reopen the discussion about who owns

the jar, if only to cast blame on the former minister, the one who's now the ambassador to the UN There's bad blood there even though they're cousins."

I felt for Tom, who could see his entire career unraveling over the missing jar. "Don't think about it today," I said. "Nothing you can do right now, correct?" I wasn't sure it would help, but a verbal hug was the best I could offer.

When I reached Teeni, she reported that Victoria Peerless left a message that her boss was bringing four more guests, including a reporter for the *New York Post*'s society section, and that they needed to be seated near her table, but not too close, whatever that meant. Wayne Lawson, Fritz McBeel's financial agent, had called for me, too. I told Teeni I would call both of them as soon as we got off the phone.

The majority of the fundraising team in San Francisco was doing business as usual, Teeni said. She and two junior staffers were flying in Tuesday. They would handle the check-in table at the Pilgrim Club, which would leave me free to meet and greet trustees, donors, and gift prospects, talking up the Devor and the new exhibit. Or not, depending on what the cops found in the next forty-eight hours.

Finally, reluctantly, I called Lawson, who made it clear he was not happy I had taken so long to get back to him.

"Mr. McBeel is anxious that the museum receive the transfer of ownership papers for the artifact, and I need to know who to send them in care of, since everyone seems to be away."

"Away" sounded like a bad place to be in Lawson's tone of voice, somewhere between a bar at the wrong end of Mission Street and a cave in Afghanistan.

"Thanks, Wayne. I didn't know Fritz had signed it over yet. I thought we had an appointment late next week?"

"No, no. He completed the legal transfer, let me see, it must have been Wednesday. Yes, I recall. He met me in the morning at the Foundation to take care of a few things. It's dated Wednesday."

"The day Rene was killed. Hey, wait," I said, feeling a whiff of something uncomfortable, "that's when the vessel went missing, or at least when we learned it wasn't accounted for. How could Fritz give it to the Devor if he didn't have it?"

Although Wayne's voice hardened, his casual tone didn't change. "The artifact was transferred legally to the Devor in good faith before anyone could have known it wasn't in the university's vault, Dani."

"Maybe so, but even if he gave it to us, we didn't get it, or at least we haven't yet. Why don't you hold onto the papers until things sort themselves out a bit more?"

"Mr. McBeel wants it made clear that finding the artifact is the Devor's business, not his. He has washed his hands of it. Now, who should I send the documents to?"

Why does this feel like a game of hot potato? I asked myself. "Wayne, this is complicated. I know you see that. You can send the papers to the museum's attorney, of course. Unless the vessel shows up, there will be a lot of questions about insurance, charitable tax valuation, and the like."

His voice cut smoothly across mine, the voice of someone who has no intention of disappointing his generous employer. If Fritz McBeel said to make it go away and keep his name out of any scandal (and that was precisely the point, I guessed), then Wayne Lawson was on the case.

"Mr. McBeel wishes the Devor well in finding their artifact and knows the staff will cooperate fully with the police in any inquiries they might direct to the museum. I have another call waiting. Thanks." And he hung up.

I sat there, chewing my lipstick and wondering what to do. Something smelled about this, something more than McBeel's understandable aversion to being mentioned in the context of a murder investigation. Had he signed those papers Wednesday morning, or did he and Wayne do some creative back-dating when news of Bouvier's death reached them?

Lawson would have no compunction about fudging the papers, I was sure. He was McBeel's go-to guy and had been for more than three decades. Rumor had it Lawson had something on McBeel from their early days together, something that guaranteed him a prominent place on the payroll forever. Rumors like that persisted about anyone who had the ear and confidence of someone as powerful as McBeel, though. Usually started by someone who didn't but wished he had.

People love to gossip about the rich. Dickie and I must have kept the mills churning for a while. I didn't like to think about it, so I punched in the number for another star of the McBeels' retinue.

"Victoria Peerless," she said, answering on the first ring. I could see her, shiny blonde hair in a neat ponytail, pearl studs in place, slightly puckered lips.

And good morning to you, my inner voice snapped back.

"Victoria, hi, it's Dani. You called?"

"Saturday, I called Saturday," she reminded me. "And again this morning, early."

"Well, yes," I mumbled, thinking this was unfair, having all the McBeels' minions unloading on me at once. "I was, um, tied up. I know you've added four more names—"

"Mrs. McBeel has."

"Yes, of course. It's fine, we'll shift the seating around when we're sure we have all the changes in hand."

"That's not why Mrs. McBeel asked me to call you. She is concerned that whoever speaks about the artifact be quite accurate in explaining the gift."

"Yes?" Had she been on the phone with Lawson? Was this their coordinated way of pressuring the Devor into taking on the costs of the jar's recovery?

"Mrs. McBeel wants to make sure the program script doesn't jump the gun, so to speak. After all, the Devor can hardly be said to own the artifact if it's missing."

Huh? I was speechless, trying to wrap my head around her meaning. Maybe she took my silence for disagreement because her voice rose in volume when she spoke next.

"We're—that is, Mrs. McBeel is—adamant about this. It's fine to say the artifact will be given to the Devor, that it is a promised gift, and that the museum will be showing it soon. Under no circumstances should the script say or imply that the Devor owns it yet. I hope I'm making that clear?"

"Perfectly. Have you talked with Wayne recently? He told me Fritz signed the papers the other day and that, in Fritz's mind, the Devor does own it."

"I can assure you that's incorrect. The artifact is community property, and Mrs. McBeel definitely hasn't signed such an agreement." Her tone changed from insistent to sugarcoated. "Mrs. McBeel's sole concern here is that the Devor get the best deal, and taking ownership right now, when its whereabouts are unclear, would not be a good deal at all, don't you agree?"

I couldn't think of anything safe to say. To agree with Jamie was to flout Fritz, if both of their assistants were correct.

"Has the director signed the contract?" Victoria said into the silence.

"I don't think so. Peter's in New York by now and Wayne just this minute told me he's sending the contract Mr. McBeel signed to the Devor."

"Good. Please tell Peter that under no circumstances should he sign that gift document until he hears from us—Mrs. McBeel, I mean. Is that understood?"

"Victoria," I said, hoping the steam coming out of my ears wasn't audible, "I need to talk to Mrs.—Jamie—directly. I don't know what the heck's going on, I'm trying to manage a million details for the party, and I don't know enough to give Peter any directives. Is Jamie there?"

"She went in their jet. She arrived at her apartment in New York on Friday and she has a full schedule already. Anyway, I am, as you know, fully authorized to speak for her, and she specifically told me to pass her message to you and to make sure your supervisor received it." There was ice in her voice.

I danced around a bit, promising her I'd pass the message along to Peter, not mentioning that I would also pass along Wayne's. After some more pushing on her part, we ended the call in something of a draw. As soon as we hung up, I speed-dialed Peter's cell.

» » »

Peter, hunched over a glass of white wine in the Algonquin's bar later, was as puzzled as I had been. Squinting at his glass, he muttered, "What the hell? I can't figure the angles on this. Fritz's push to offload the vessel on the Devor I get. Everything's our problem then. But what's Jamie's game?"

I had no answers. My short-term problem was getting through the gala program without mentioning the damned jar.

"Tell the Devor's attorney not to forward the papers," I said finally.

"Right. Duck and dodge," he said, sighing loudly and polishing off the remainder of his wine. I declined his offer of another mojito.

Peter turned toward me. "This may be nothing dramatic in the end. I've been thinking. We have no involvement in Bouvier's unfortunate death. We never had the King's Jar in our possession. We'll find the money to open the exhibit without it even if Fritz reneges on his pledge. I think it's quite possible McBeel's overreacting in the moment, wanting to distance himself from any notoriety. Most of our wealthy donors would feel the same. He'll probably come around pretty quickly when the murder and robbery are solved."

"True," I said. "It did occur to me that Jamie might be trying to protect the Devor in the meantime, even if her abrasive manners make it hard to believe."

Peter merely shrugged.

"Hi," someone said over my shoulder. Peter looked up with a puzzled expression. I swung around on my bar stool to see Rene's senior researcher, Oscar, dressed in a bulky suit and running shoes, peering at me. He shoved his glasses onto the bridge of his nose with a pudgy finger and smiled tentatively.

"I'm here for the McBeels' dinner," he mumbled, looking from me to Peter uncertainly, his smile fading. His forehead was beaded with sweat, and his suit jacket was being dragged off one shoulder by a large computer carrying case.

"This is Peter Lindsey, the Devor's director," I said, waving my hand in Peter's direction. I could swear my boss flinched. "Oscar's working with Tom on the exhibit details."

"Oscar? Shelby?" Oscar supplied his name uncertainly as he held out his hand, as if he wasn't quite sure he had it right.

"Ah," Peter said. Oscar was definitely not in Peter's league and, without money, power, or a warehouse full of desirable objects, Peter's interest level in Oscar was low, but he rallied. "I'm very sorry about Rene's death. This must be a hard time for you and the other members of his team."

"Yes," Oscar said, his face crumbling and turning pink. "It was terrible."

An awkward silence fell as Oscar looked at his feet and Peter and I looked at Oscar. Peter seized the moment to signal the bartender for the check, signing for our drinks, and explaining that he had to meet the chairman of the finance committee of the board for cocktails.

"I'll catch up with you tomorrow, Dani, and I'll want to hear all about your hot date." He winked and touched my arm as he left the bar, nodding to Oscar, who was ordering a beer.

"I hope I didn't break up your meeting," Oscar said, his forehead puckering.

"Nope, we were both leaving," I said, preparing to make my own exit. "Are you staying here?"

"Yes, Fritz—Mr. McBeel—insisted." He sounded apologetic. "I'll be at the dinner?"

"Yes, I saw your name on the list as their guest," I said as cheerfully as I could. It was hard to know how to talk to Oscar. He needed lessons in how to make small talk. Maybe that didn't matter in his world, I reminded myself. Not everyone is shallow. His pain at his mentor's death was visible. I had to be nicer. "I'm glad you'll be there to see the McBeels honored. I'm sure they'll say something about Dr. Bouvier, too."

"Fritz McBeel's our biggest benefactor," he said with a frown, "and it would ruin us if he decided not to support the Kenobia project anymore." As he spoke, he looked inquiringly at me as if he expected that I knew something germane.

"Oh, he'll continue," I said casually. "It's a valuable project." I had no idea if this was true, but why make poor Oscar more anxious than he was?

"I'm the director of the project now, and it's my duty to make sure there's enough funding so no one gets laid off. The team has to continue its work." He stared at me with an intensity I didn't understand. I had the feeling I was supposed to say something, but all I could think of was *lighten up, fella,* and that probably wasn't politic and definitely wasn't kind. I itched to get out of the bar, but Oscar spoke before I could slide off my barstool gracefully. "Can I talk to you for a minute? Actually, I'm really worried about the funding now that Rene's, um, gone. I know you're an expert at this sort of thing, raising money, I mean."

"Well," I began, but he interrupted me with a hand in the air.

"No, I mean it. I admire you a lot. Really."

Once again, I couldn't think of anything to say. He was such a social misfit that I was embarrassed for him. I turned away for a moment and sipped the remains of my drink.

"I need advice."

I could imagine. It was hard to picture Oscar making the rounds at the National Geographic Society headquarters in Washington, selling his research plans with the same persuasive style that Rene Bouvier had perfected over the years.

But it wasn't grants Oscar was worried about. "Grants pay only about half of the costs to keep the research going, and the university doesn't give us much money. Jamie isn't interested in this stuff. Do you think she'll try to get Mr. McBeel to stop giving us operating money every year?"

"Well, that's between the McBeels, isn't it?" I should get involved in fundraising for another organization? I don't think so. "Look, Fritz McBeel is a grown-up and is used to being pressed on all sides by people wanting a slice of his huge fortune. If he admires the lab's research as much as ever, I doubt Jamie can stop him supporting it. Let's face it, he has enough money to support ten labs and still buy his wife a chateau in France."

"I think he should give us an endowment so we don't have to worry about how people will be paid every year," Oscar blurted, talking fast as if to get a scary idea out there before he lost his nerve, and blinking at me through his glasses.

Hah. Nice try, Oscar. You became the director a few days ago and you already want a guaranteed salary? I spend enough time in the pursuit of gift money to know that it seems like a perfect solution to have a sugar daddy as the biggest donor, and that it never is. When one person pays the lion's share of the expenses, it's tempting for him to think he also has the deciding vote.

"You should probably run that by Warefield University's development staff. Maybe they can help you write a proposal. Do you happen to know Ambassador Obarri?" I asked, changing the subject. Could Oscar have been in Kenobia when the Song Dynasty jar left the country?

"Um, sort of. I mean, he was in the government's archaeology ministry when I first joined the site crew. But that was years after Rene discovered the King's Jar. I saw Obarri around when we were working in the old museum he managed. He and Rene were tight in those days."

"Really? I wonder if he knows Rene's dead?"

"I wouldn't know," he said. Oscar's face grew beet red and he leaned in toward me. "But let me tell you something. Simon Anderson was involved in this. He was always undermining Rene, and he knows all these rich collectors who'd do anything to get hold of something as unique as the King's Jar."

Whoa. Where did that come from? "You think Simon killed him? Because he and Rene didn't get along? It seems a little extreme, Oscar."

"Maybe, but who else could it be? It had to be Simon."

"Did you say that to the police?" I said, trying to keep my voice polite.

"Yes," he said, nodding emphatically. "I told them to investigate Anderson. Rene always said he was an arrogant sneak. You watch. It will turn out he has the artifact."

"Do you have any proof?"

"No, but if the cops look hard enough, they'll find something. Who else could it be?" He slumped back on the barstool he had sidled onto after Peter made his escape. "Someone has the jar. It's not in the lab. I looked everywhere."

"So you think Simon Anderson killed Rene and took a precious historical object?" My voice rose, and my defenses went up on Simon's behalf even though, my inner voice reminded me, I had allowed myself the smallest moment of wondering about a possible motive for Simon. "You can't really think Simon would kill a famous scientist? It's more likely to have been a random robbery gone wrong, Oscar. Maybe whoever has the jar doesn't even know how valuable it is."

Oscar set the beer he had been drinking down on the bar. He picked at the label for a minute, seeming to collect his thoughts. "Maybe it was an accident." He hiked the strap of his computer bag higher on his shoulder and said, "I hope the Devor is okay with me doing that, talking to the police, I mean?" His anger—and his confident voice—had disappeared like the air going out of a balloon.

"The Devor has a lot riding on the artifact," I said, "so we want to do anything we can to help recover it. We know you and the rest of the team are devastated by Rene's death. Whoever caused it will be caught and punished. Give the police a little time. They're good at this."

Oscar's mouth puckered. Poor guy, I wondered if he was always this emotional. His body was blocking my way, and I scooted sideways. He raised his eyes to gaze at me, hands holding on to the edge of the bar as if for balance, a lank clump of hair in his eyes.

"I have to go now," I reminded him.

"Fritz asked me to come see him as soon as I got in," he mumbled. "I guess I can get a cab over to his apartment?"

Was I supposed to hold his hand? "Yup, plenty of cabs right outside the door. You have the address?"

He did and, as if to prove it, reached into his back pocket, pulled out a fat, crumbling wallet, and prepared to search through it.

"No, no, I don't need it, Oscar," I said, holding up a hand. "I only wanted to make sure you had it. I'll be going now," I said, determined to be done with Rene's protégé.

"Ah, okay, but I was hoping we might talk more?"

"Sure," I said, nodding and trying to look more positive than I felt. "I'm kind of busy for the next few days, but maybe when we get back to San Francisco." And with that, I eased away.

I made it across the Algonquin's atmospheric lobby and onto the elevator without bumping into anyone else. As I slipped the plastic card into my room lock, it dawned on me that Oscar might bump into Simon in the lobby tomorrow evening. If Oscar really believed Simon could have killed his mentor, it could get ugly. It would be smarter to meet my date at the restaurant. I made a mental note to call Simon. I thought about calling Fritz McBeel to give him a heads-up that one of Rene's assistants was laboring under a strange delusion. Since I didn't know Fritz very well, I thought better of it. I needed to know a lot more first. Where to start?

I knew next to nothing about Kenobia and its recent history other than that it was turbulent. Who was this Keile Obarri before he was appointed ambassador? When was he the chairman of the ministry of culture, and what did it mean that he moved from that post to the UN? Would he dare to take the fragile artifact back by force? I planned to ask Simon when I saw him. Until then, I needed the Internet.

After spending a fruitless half hour hunched over my laptop looking for Kenobian newspaper sites, all of which had bad URLs, I cruised two outdated websites hosted by the government and layered with lengthy, florid bureaucratic manifestos in stilted English. I tackled Obarri from the other end, searching United Nations online for his bio to no avail—just his name with a link underline. True to form, the link was dead. Whatever they might be doing right, the Kenobians were not setting any standards for Internet savvy.

I needed fresh air, an evening walk in mid-Manhattan, still bustling as if it were high noon. Maybe up to Central Park South, with its luxury apartment houses facing the heavily treed park, and west a couple of blocks to the brightly lit plaza and fountains at Lincoln Center. I wondered if the same Irish pub where Dickie and I rehashed a play we'd seen was still there, or if the Italian restaurant with the cloud-like gnocchi was still drawing a crowd of locals every night.

I reminded myself that Rene's murder, tragic and troubling as it was, was a matter for the police. The vessel was my business. I needed to know if we were ever going to get it or if I was going to spend the next few weeks and months explaining what went wrong to individuals who had made donations toward the exhibit and who might now wonder if the Devor really had its act together.

chapter 7

BY EIGHT O'CLOCK the next morning, New York was a bee-hive in full production. Swarms of people were fast-walking from trains and subways to their offices, taxis with horns blaring were flying up- and downtown as fast as the traffic lights allowed, and whoever wasn't scarfing down a bagel was talking on a cell phone. A lot of people were doing both, while balancing a Styrofoam coffee cup and a briefcase in the other hand.

I hit the sidewalk in cross trainers for my own brisk walk but, with nowhere specific to go, didn't have the motivation to keep up their pace. It was only five A.M. in San Francisco, but I was full of caffeine and curious to know what was going on in the office.

My list for today was light on chores. With the food, flowers, speakers, and staffing nailed down, only the tough problems remained. Would Jamie McBeel turn Louise's seating plan upside down when she saw it? What could the board chairman say at the dinner about the McBeels' gift if it was in limbo? For that matter, what should I write for Fritz McBeel to say? A talk with Peter was high on my list, but before I finished the thought, the phone in my room rang.

"Hey, Dani. Are you up yet?"

"Are you kidding? It's mid-morning in Manhattan. I want to know where you are on dealing with the McBeels' mixed messages about who owns the jar."

"Great minds and all that. Come on up to my suite."

As befitting his status, Peter had a separate living room, a western view toward the Hudson, and a huge spray of orchids on a table in front of the window. Until that moment, I had been perfectly happy with my room.

His laptop was open on the desk, which was strewn with oversized Excel spreadsheets. Seeing me looking at them, he made a face. "Budget time again. Why is it that every department asks for a 20 percent increase every year when we don't have a 20 percent increase in visitors or revenue?"

Because no one wants to be the department that gets hung out to dry while some other group gets some extra resources and the chance to shine? I didn't say anything, partly because Peter knows perfectly well why we do it, and partly because my budget request was up 20 percent.

"So, what happened with the transfer of ownership?" I asked as I parked myself on a plush loveseat.

"A standoff, I'd say. Victoria Peerless hasn't tried to reach me on Jamie's behalf. As promised, Wayne Lawson sent the signed gift deed, dated the same day Rene was killed, over to our lawyer. She's sitting on it, a wise move. She told Wayne we understood Fritz's wishes. However, since the object wasn't in anyone's possession and I would get back to San Francisco soon, she couldn't see any reason to FedEx the papers."

"Wayne's response?"

"What you'd expect. He wants to finish the job he was given, but he seems to have accepted the status quo for now.

I'm assuming he's reported back to Fritz, but I haven't gotten any blistering phone calls."

"So what do you want to say on Thursday at the party?"

"I'm hoping it's cleared up by then, frankly. I've worked with Fritz often enough to be sure he, not Jamie, holds the cards on this. And, he's famous for staying out of nasty situations, even when he created them."

"I heard about a promised gift he reneged on when he took an instant dislike to the organization's new president. Is there more?"

"You bet. Remember reading about the newspaper he bought in Los Angeles and ran into the ground by making it a PR tool for his other businesses? When some of the laid-off staff sued, Fritz's fingerprints were nowhere to be found."

"How is that relevant here?"

"Turns out Lawson had set up a dummy holding company and erased all the connections to his boss. Fritz left for an extended stay in Europe while the press barked crazily, and Lawson only smiled and shrugged. Believe me, if Fritz McBeel says we own the vessel, we don't have the firepower to contradict him."

"Well, what then? We thank him for it, even if it's gone missing, with the added benefit that Jamie will make our lives hell?"

"How about this. We thank the McBeels for their total giving. We praise them for their support of African research, the arts, and the Devor in particular. We show the images of the architects' renderings of the new space and some of the other pieces from our collection that hail from the countries whose UN ambassadors are in the audience, and delete mention and pictures of the King's Jar?"

"Waffle, you mean?"

"What options do we have? Today's Tuesday, the dinner's the day after tomorrow, and I'm betting the cops are looking a lot harder for who killed that poor bastard than they are for a big jar with a rhinoceros on the lid. Realistically, what can Jamie do if we take that route, other than behave badly, of course?" Peter made a face.

What, indeed. He had a point. As long as we didn't make any statement about it, we couldn't make the wrong statement.

"I think we have a more recent object from Kenobia in the collection. I'll email Tom and get him to send us an image to insert in the show and tell, so their ambassador doesn't feel slighted."

"Clever," Peter said. "I like it."

"Can you sell the idea to Fritz and Jamie?"

"Or die trying," Peter said with a rueful laugh. "I think I'll wait until Thursday, on the premise that we held out hope for a resolution 'til the last minute. No need to stir up the hornets' nest too far in advance."

"Chicken," I said. "Seriously, I think it's a good plan as long as you're the guy presenting it. Better tell Geoff, though. You know what they say: Never surprise the boss."

We fixed the length and order of everyone's comments, arranged that the visuals for Peter's speech would be in the laptop the hired techie would cue up for him, and told each other all would be well.

"Any fresh news from your cop boyfriend on how the investigation's going?" Peter said when we finished.

"Nada, although it's not even nine A.M. there. I did have a strange conversation with that dweeb Oscar after you left the bar. He and Rene's crew have decided Simon Anderson's a murdering thief, you'll be glad to know."

"On what evidence? Have they told the police?"

"On no evidence, just general paranoia. It was an uncomfortable conversation, I can tell you. And, yes, they did tell the cops. You aren't thinking of bailing on the exhibition catalog?"

"Unless someone puts cuffs on Simon, no," Peter said. "If the artifact is gone for good, it might even be interesting to add a short note about it, and the fragility of rare cultural icons. Make it a teaching moment."

"Fair enough, although Tom may freak out at the thought of adding something that could date the book if the artifact shows up in a couple of years. I'd like to know why Jamie McBeel told us that Fritz didn't want Keile Obarri at the dinner, when it turned out he didn't care. I'm getting worried about Kenobia and Obarri. I'm nervous about how we deal with him should the artifact be ours legally and be lost. If there's possible trouble ahead about who really owns it, I'd like to be ready."

Peter nodded. "Yeah, that's the deep issue. Tom and I feel pretty confident about the paper trail for the provenance. Let's hope it's only Jamie throwing her weight around."

"If I learn anything when I see Obarri at the dinner, you'll be the first to know. Unless, of course, I find out that Obarri killed Rene, in which case my cute detective gets a call, too."

"Don't even joke about that," Peter said, and groaned, only partly amused.

"Just kidding, promise. Want me to make sure you meet Obarri?"

"Sure. That could be useful. If he tries to buttonhole me about Kenobia's rights, I'll get the lawyers in to review the whole business again. What else is on your agenda for today?" he said, getting up and going over to the desk.

"Not much. I'll tally late RSVPs around lunchtime."

Peter nodded, his attention drifting to the spreadsheets in front of him. I said my good-byes, and we agreed to check in later in the day. As I was leaving, I almost bumped into a man from room service delivering a large silver pot of coffee. Poor Peter. As much money as we raised or took in at the door or in the museum store, there was never going to be enough to keep everyone happy. I was glad my only job was raising it.

» » »

Later, having written draft remarks for Fritz and Geoff that said, in essence, nothing, in laudatory prose, I emailed the computer file up to Peter. When I changed into a Donna Karan wrap sweater and pants outfit for dinner with Simon, I immediately had a panic attack. Too plain? Too much décolletage? I opened the room safe and took out my showy gold chandelier earrings and matching necklace. I didn't take Dickie's money when we split, but I'm not a martyr. I kept the jewelry.

The reflection in the mirror calmed me down. My hair was pulled into a clip that allowed wavy bits to drift around my ears. I looked, if I did say so myself, like a sophisticated, understated Manhattan woman headed out for one of her innumerable interesting dinner engagements. Good thing no one who saw me would know my pulse was racing and that I was flustered enough to leave first my coat, then my room key in the hotel room. On the way out, I picked up another key, hoping my blush wasn't too evident to the desk clerk.

The cab dropped me at the canopy of a little jewel box of a restaurant on a tree-lined street on the Upper East Side.

Amber light spilled onto the sidewalk from its windows and the discreet copper glow from the restaurant's door whispered elegance as the maître d' emerged to hold it open for me, smiling as if we were friends.

Simon was already there, looking very much the "adventure journalist" and television star with his deep tan and white-toothed smile. Even in this bastion of cool, he was attracting sidelong glances from other patrons. And to think Dickie called him a sleazeball.

The food called forth little humming sounds of joy from us both, from the *amuse bouche*, a tiny, potent cup of lobster broth, to the best crème brûlée east of the Hayes Street Grill. During the meal, Simon entertained me with stories, all told with sparkling eyes that widened in fake shock and a dead-on sense of dramatic timing. The tough schedule of a TV host expected to do a shoot at the Egyptian pyramids one month and another on a Caribbean reef the next. The real story behind the headlines about an über-rich young woman engaged in a messy divorce. I tried to muster sympathy about trudging off to the Nile twice in five years, although it was hard. He confessed he had escorted the divorcée in question to a couple of charity events, earning a small mention in her husband's legal complaint.

Simon shared gossipy anecdotes about the rich and famous people he partied with, the macho behavior indulged in by fellow members of the Explorers' Club, and a seemingly endless parade of admirers and friends around the world who were always at the ready to entertain him lavishly should he put down in their cities even for a day.

I was having so much fun listening that I found it easy to postpone my hard questions until we were sipping our espresso. Finally, unable to put it off any longer, I took a deep breath and began.

"Simon, this business with the King's Jar is getting messy."

His eyebrows rose, and he gave me a tiny smile but didn't say anything.

"The police don't have a clue what might have happened to it." I told him what I'd learned about unscrupulous collectors in general and asked him if he thought that might be behind the murderous attack.

"Could be," he said, glancing out the restaurant window, where a couple, fashionably late, was alighting from a cab. He turned back to me. "It seems improbable, though. The vessel is unique. Bouvier convinced most of his peers that it proved a sophisticated pattern of expansion and trade by a powerful group deep in Africa's interior, independent of the known Chinese trade along the coast during the Song Dynasty. But, kill for it? I can't see it. Its primary value comes from where it was found and when it got there, not from some intrinsic aesthetic or material value. Shady collectors generally want showier objects."

"Okay, I get that. But if someone were interested in adding it to his collection, any guesses as to who it might be?"

"You're asking me to name names, to accuse people of at least hypothetical theft and murder," he said. He looked down the little line of leather-covered banquettes at the newly arrived couple, who were handing off coats to the waiter. To break the awkwardness of our exchange, I did, too. At that moment, the woman, a porcelain-skinned blonde with the strangely ageless features that suggest a surgeon's skill, dressed in a couture Valentino suit I'd drooled over in *Vogue*, glanced over and flashed a dazzling smile our way. Simon's way, actually.

"The divorcée?" I said under my breath.

"No." He laughed and nodded to her and her much older companion. "A sweet girl with a wicked sense of humor. We went out for a while before she married him. I was fun. He was rich. No contest." He shrugged and turned back to me.

"Why should I point you toward anyone in particular? I'm not happy that Rene's dead, no matter how poisoned our dealings got. But I'm not about to send anyone on a witch hunt based on guesses."

We were silent as a waiter refilled our water goblets. I leaned forward. "You have my word that if I pass along names, they won't be attached to you in any way. I can finesse that, believe me. My interest is in getting the vessel back. Frankly, Simon, we've got a bit of a problem."

I paused. Telling him about the conflicting ownership directives I'd gotten from Victoria Peerless and Wayne Lawson wasn't such a good idea. Simon was a journalist, and we hadn't agreed that our conversation was off the record. And, if I paid any attention to Oscar's rant, my dinner companion was a suspect in Rene's death.

"I went online today," I said, changing gears. "I wanted to know a little more about Kenobia and the representative who's coming to the dinner, Keile Obarri. You know him, right?"

"Yeah," Simon said. "Until recently, you couldn't do anything in Kenobia related to archaeology without his say so. Everyone knows him. That's been true for twenty years." His tone suggested to know Obarri was not necessarily to love him.

"Fritz McBeel knows him, too," I said, looking for some kind of reaction.

"Sure," he said. "McBeel funded Rene's work, and Rene knew exactly what he had to do to get Obarri and the ministry to give him his permits. McBeel's contributions to the ministry were what greased the skids. No secret there." Simon laughed.

The blonde turned her head, smiling quizzically, wanting in on the joke. Her husband was staring at the menu, his head down, not the best angle from here, given his multiple chins.

"I know this sounds crazy, but could the Kenobians have taken the object back? We heard rumors of confusion about legal ownership of the vessel," I ventured.

"Yes, well," Simon said, playing with his napkin. "Times were different. Rene knew that Fritz was determined to safeguard the jar from untrained supervision, and I think the way Fritz convinced the Kenobians to sell it ate at the old man's friendship with Fritz."

"Rene thought you played some role in the...rescue," I said.

"Fritz did ask me to smooth things for the export license, yes. Didn't want to get his own hands dirty and knew Rene wouldn't do anything to rock the boat because it might come back to bite him."

"How?"

"If the research team was seen as paying bribes to one faction in the Ministry, you can bet another guy would want something, too."

"And Fritz, through you, was paying?"

"Best not to go there. Leave it that even after the Kenobians got their act together no charges were brought. I haven't picked up any gossip about MACPCA—the ministry in charge of their cultural heritage—going after the vessel now."

I tried to keep my voice light. "That's a relief. I feel like I'm playing that board game. You know, 'the butler did it in the garden with a lead pipe'? Everyone seems to have some connection with the artifact at some point since Rene dug it out of a crumbling wall. I only want to make sure it's recovered and that the Devor can keep it safe."

"So what are you trying to figure out? Who stole it, or who killed Rene?" His voice was sharper, cooler.

"Either or both, I guess. Killed Rene in order to steal it. Maybe, though, didn't mean to kill him. By the way, Oscar seems to think you might be the bad guy."

Simon grunted and threw his torso back in the chair. "That asshole. Did he really say that? I'll kill him." His brows almost touched.

"I hope that was a metaphor. He told me in the Algonquin bar yesterday. Why would he say that?"

"I have no idea," he said, his voice rising. "Those guys are twisted. They live inside Rene's little universe, listen all day to his rants and paranoia. Rene thought his was the only possible interpretation of the artifact, given where it was unearthed. But it wasn't, and over time, he got so protective of his legacy that he lost perspective."

I remembered the intensity with which Rene bombarded me with his biases and suspicions. Simon was pretty intense on the subject himself.

"So if it wasn't you, do you have any ideas about who might have killed Rene?" I said, trying to keep my voice light.

Simon opened his mouth, then seemed to think better about what he was going to say. He picked up a fork and began to play with it. "I have no idea. The whole thing is odd, hard to figure."

"Agreed," I said. "Last chance—any thoughts on where we should look for our precious object?"

Simon relaxed visibly and leaned toward me again, taking one of my hands in his. "I've got a good idea. Why don't we forget about all of this and dedicate the rest of the evening to us?" Those expressive eyebrows rose, his eyes radiated warmth, and I caved. I'd done enough pushing and prodding for one night.

"So, tell me, what's it like to be the Most Eligible Bachelor?" I asked. Simon put his head back and laughed.

His blonde friend looked longingly at our tête-à-tête, then gathered up her bag and headed our way, ostensibly on the way to the ladies room. As Simon stood, throwing a brilliant smile her way, he said over his shoulder to me, "Here's something for your parlor game. Did you know Obarri visited Rene several times after he got his posting to the U.S.? He admired Rene for championing Kenobia's rights, so I heard."

While Simon and Blondie kissed and exclaimed over the coincidence of finding themselves at the same spot, I sat there wondering about his last comment. So, Obarri knew where to find Rene. Opportunity to steal, although Simon was suggesting the Kenobian and Rene were friends, in which case the violence made no sense.

I glanced around. At least half the room was peeking our way, but not the lady's husband. Mr. Blondie and the maître d' had their heads together, poring over the wine list, which was as thick as a novel. I felt someone looking at me and raised my head in time to catch blue eyes like lasers boring into my skull from above. Ouch. Blondie was not delighted to meet me, no matter what her mouth said.

Clearly not part of the conversation that was being waged over my head, I let my mind drift back to my problem. My gut said Simon meant it when he said he didn't think the jar had been stolen for a secret collection.

Obarri would have been a welcome guest in the lab, could easily have asked to see the vessel. In spite of Simon's comment about the Ministry's lack of interest, I wondered if a Kenobian would be a hero back home if he recovered it? Surely not if Rene died. His sympathies were with the Kenobians. Maybe the attack was supposed to be realistic enough to throw off the police, but went wrong because Rene Bouvier was a fragile old man.

I decided to call Charlie Sugerman tomorrow and pass along what I'd heard. If I could wrestle Simon from his friend, I planned to relax and enjoy the rest of the evening.

I didn't have to yank on his sleeve as it turned out. From his table down the row, Mr. Blondie looked up, cleared his throat, and made the smallest gesture with his hand. It was magic. In ten seconds, his wife had sailed back to her table and was exclaiming happily over the appearance of a bottle of champagne.

The air space over our table was suddenly quiet as Simon sat down. Shaking his head, opening his eyes wide, and smiling crookedly, he lowered his voice. "That marriage won't last a day longer than it takes her to find a way to get half of what he owns." He signaled the waiter and we left a few minutes later, me smiling at Simon's friend with what I hoped was a look of well-bred triumph, pure bluff, but fun while it lasted.

In the cab, Simon turned to me and said, in mock horror, "Poor girl, she's far too thin."

Puzzled, I said, "I thought she looked great."

"Still," he said, deepening his voice, "you could give her some clues on how to look gorgeous." He took my hand. In the dark cab, his smile was seductive.

"I hope her husband appreciates her more than he showed it tonight." I sounded prissy to me, but Simon laughed easily.

"He does, to the tune of some Harry Winston jewelry that would blind you, and houses in Miami and London. Enough about her."

His smooth voice murmured on. His hand was warm, and I definitely had tingly feelings, but my defenses were up. Dickie's face swam into my brain, the face that was in the gossip pages when he and the underwear model laughed on the slopes in Switzerland and I licked my wounds on my sister's living room couch. Guys with sex appeal and money or fame get their pick. Why should they pick one? *Why*, argued the voice in my head, *would you put yourself in the same position twice?*

When we got to the Algonquin, Simon paid the cabbie and followed me to the elevator. "Want company?" he smiled, squeezing my arm as the elevator door opened. A man entered while Simon held the door open.

"Not tonight," I said, as my heart thumped. "Early day tomorrow. I'll see you Thursday night at the party, right?"

He took it in good grace. "Absolutely. With bells on. Call if you change your mind."

Still holding the door open with one hand, he guided me in with the other and leaned in to kiss me full on the mouth. A good kisser, an exceptional kisser. I might have continued my personal ratings test for some time had not a loud clearing of the man's throat behind us reminded me where we were. I disengaged and stood silent and embarrassed as the elevator rose to my floor.

I debated with myself about my decision while I brushed my teeth, but fell asleep before I found out who won the argument.

chapter 8

THE DAY BEFORE the gala dinner was frenetic. Louise and I started the day in her hotel suite with coffee and a big seating chart that we used like a game board, moving slips of paper around for an hour to come up with what we thought was a workable plan for seating more than four hundred people.

I copied the final version, stuffed the papers into my briefcase, and headed uptown to Jamie McBeel's apartment. The maid at the McBeels' settled me on a long, low red leather sofa facing a breathtaking view of Central Park from floor to ceiling windows. Silver-framed pictures of Jamie and Fritz were placed thoughtfully where visitors would see them no matter where they sat. A large oil portrait of Jamie went halfway to the high ceiling over the fireplace. Done in a style meant to be compared to the glorious society paintings of John Singer Sargent, it missed the boat and was merely blandly self-congratulatory and static. Jamie's genuinely pretty face was reduced to something generic, and the painter seemed more impressed by the diamonds he painted so carefully on her throat and wrist.

When Jamie wafted in ten minutes later, petite but muscled in black tights, a belted, thigh-length sweater and a cloud of expensive scent, it was easy to see what he'd missed. Suddenly, I felt clumsy and large.

The woman who had opened the door came back with a tray on which were cups and a silver pot.

"Coffee, Danielle?" Jamie asked in her deep voice, pouring before I could reply. I noticed sugar and milk were not options, which was understandable given Jamie's perfect figure. Her movements were quick, and she tossed her head now and then to get the mane of dark hair off her face.

It struck me that neither in the painting nor in person was there a sign of laugh lines on her face. In fact, her mouth seemed to be arranged in a permanent moue of dissatisfaction.

We traded small talk—the weather, the beauty of the Pilgrim Club, ways to thank Louise when it was all over—and then we got down to the seating chart again.

"I understand from Fritz that the ambassador from Kenobia will be there after all. You've put him in the extra room with that pathetic actress," she said. Not a question, and it seemed that she accepted the decision. Silently, I thanked my boss for taking on the role of messenger.

I pulled the room plan out of my briefcase along with four hundred little slips of paper and unfolded it. It was a chart with lots of circles radiating out from a central circle that was shaded blue. Each circle had ten little boxes arranged around it. The all-important seating chart. I held my breath as she started matching the names and numbers on the printed list to the chart. She made some changes but didn't demand a total redo. To my immense relief, Dickie's mother didn't get pushed farther away from royalty.

"Weren't you married to him once?" Jamie said as she fingered the slip of paper with my ex's name on it. "He left you for the Brazilian girl?" Her eyes glittered with malevolent enjoyment and the corners of her mouth turned up ever so slightly for the first time since we had begun her meeting.

"Swiss," I said, smiling back and meeting her eyes. "Louise and I weren't sure if you wanted Simon Anderson here," I said, pointing to a table across the room from the head table. "We realize you and Fritz might like to have him nearby."

There was a beat of silence for a few seconds as Jamie continued to stare at me. Then, she leaned toward the chart. "Why would that be?" she asked, raising her eyebrows. "I hardly know the man and I'm not sure he and Fritz see each other. He's a writer, isn't he, or a TV person?" She made Simon's profession sound only slightly more socially acceptable than trash collector.

"I thought he and Fritz were longtime associates because of their interest in Kenobia," I said, feeling unsure of myself. Was I tiptoeing into a faux pas?

"Well, if they were, it was long ago, before my time. I hardly know the man," Jamie said in a dismissive voice. I was reminded of Simon's comment that the only time they'd met, she had left a negative impression on him. I guessed it was mutual.

When she finished answering a few other questions I had about the chart, she pushed herself back into the cushions and glanced at her watch.

"Well, that wasn't as bad as I thought it might be. Louise has done a respectable job," she said. I smiled, knowing she couldn't read the thought bubble above my head that said, "*Thank you so much, Mrs. Never-praise-the-servants.*" Said not a word but moved on, telling Jamie what Peter and I were proposing for the program script. She looked at her watch again and indicated she was comfortable with that, too.

I escaped as soon as I could, pleading my need to check in with my staff. Teeni answered her cell phone right away, and we agreed to meet for lunch. After a quick salad at a Madison Avenue cafe, Teeni headed to the hotel, and I walked down to Sixtieth Street, using the time to call Louise and tell her she could breathe again. I left a message for Peter, who was in meetings, and even took time to call Suzy Byrnstein, my best friend, who had begged me to call. I held out the phone so she could hear hundreds of Manhattan taxicabs honking their horns at once, a symphony she and I admitted we loved.

Charlie Sugerman wasn't in the office, so I left a message telling him I had what might be useful information.

The rest of the day was an unending stream of negotiations and last minute instructions, less and less important as the problems narrowed down to small ones. By the end of the day, everything that could be done to make tomorrow's event successful, short of finding the eight-hundred-year-old, pale green, celadon vessel, had been done. There would be new problems on the day of the event, but those couldn't be rushed. I ordered room service and curled up with a good mystery.

Charlie called as I was dozing off, and we filled each other in. If there was anything new about Rene's death or the missing vessel, he hadn't heard it. He promised to pass along what I told him, although he didn't get any "aha" moment from the bits and pieces I collected. "It's a whole different world, that research stuff. I can't see why people get so riled up about old pieces of pottery and arrowheads. But, hey, whatever turns you on."

I was tempted to make a joke about what turned him on, but I chickened out. Charlie seemed old-fashioned, and I didn't know if he'd laugh or if I'd hear a screaming silence in response to my attempt at a double entendre. I said good-night in my most demure voice and reminded him I would be back in San Francisco on Monday.

"Uh-huh," he said as a phone near him began to ring. "Gotta go, Dani. Good luck with your party."

I pouted for a few minutes, but there's no satisfaction if there's no one present to pout for, so I let my mind wander to the excitement of rubbing elbows with a few billionaires, not to mention royalty, tomorrow evening.

» » »

Thursday flew. My only exercise was walking briskly up Fifth Avenue in jeans and sneakers to the Pilgrim Club to meet Teeni and the two young staffers from the Devor. The flower arrangements had arrived, and I went up to the dining room to see the sample table for ten. It was breathtaking, all sparkling silver and glassware, roses anchoring ornate table number stands, and the specially made Devor Museum gift bags sitting on every chair.

Teeni took charge after that, working with the staff to set out the easels with the seating charts, and the calligraphy name cards. She assured me the calligrapher we were blessed to have found years ago, a retired New York City librarian, was on call throughout the day as late RSVPs came in. The Pilgrim's staff scurried around, ignoring us as much as possible, well-practiced at this sort of event since they did two or three of them each week.

"Go," Teeni said, pointing to the stairs. "I don't need you, we don't need you, you're beginning to make me nervous."

I took her at her word and grabbed a cab back to the hotel, hoping to connect with Peter about the program remarks. As I walked through the lobby, Oscar appeared, as disheveled as the last time I saw him. The poor guy was weighed down by his computer bag and the suitcase he pulled behind him.

I stopped. "Oscar, you aren't leaving right before the party?" Knowing how desperate he was to butter up Fritz McBeel, I was surprised.

He didn't look happy.

"I have to manage some stuff in the lab before I leave for the field season in Kenobia, so I'm going back today. I was going to call you from the airport," he added as an afterthought. He didn't make eye contact with me, which probably meant he had completely forgotten the need to let us know he wouldn't be there. That didn't surprise me. So far, Oscar hadn't shown himself to be socially adept. Why start now?

"No problem. We always have extra guests we're trying to accommodate. I'm sure Fritz will be sorry you had to leave."

He shifted from one grungy sneaker to the other and mumbled something that sounded like agreement. "Thanks for advising me about Mr. McBeel," he said. "Can I call you when you get back?"

Since I hadn't been helpful and didn't see how I could, I did some mumbling of my own, then wished him a safe journey. He turned to wave and smile sheepishly at me, his shoulder bag bumping into an expensive looking armchair as he wove his way to the hotel door.

"I hope that wasn't another one of your dates," said a voice behind me.

I spun around. Of course. I guess I should have been relieved my ex wasn't at the next table when Simon and I were having dinner.

"Damn it, Dickie. I don't know anyone else who has the habit of sneaking up behind people like you do. Would you please quit it?" My voice was louder than I intended it to be.

"Sorry. I didn't mean to scare you. I was headed out the door and you're standing in the path, see?" He drew an imaginary line from the reception desk, where the clerk on duty was eyeing us, curious to know if we were going to create unpleasantness in his plush space, to the glass doors, beyond which I could see Oscar heaving himself into a yellow cab.

"Of course. You're always 'headed' somewhere. If I were even slightly paranoid, I'd wonder. In fact, while it's none of my business, why were you leaving a hotel you're not staying at?"

"Your boss. He and I met to discuss things."

"Things? What things? You didn't talk about me, did you?"

"Funny, I thought you said you weren't paranoid," my ex said, grinning broadly.

"Screw you," I said. I was tired, and that was part of it, but I was beginning to feel hemmed in by Dickie, who did not seem able to accept that I didn't want him back in my life, certainly not as a hovering presence.

"Okay, okay. No, peaches, it wasn't about you." His smile faded, and he shoved his hands into his pants pockets. "Peter wants to talk turkey with Mother about an estate gift and he knows you and she don't hit it off, so he thought it might be best to work through me. I mean, if I'm the only offspring she has and I explain to her that I don't need her money, she might be more willing to leave it to some organizations around town. Dad was big on the Devor and on the science museum, and she could get the family name engraved on something quite respectable even if she divvied up her nest egg between the two."

"And Peter liked that idea? I mean, letting half of it go to another nonprofit?"

"Of course not. He'd like it all, but Peter's realistic and so am I. Mother can get two plaques if she spreads it out a bit."

"It's awfully nice of you," I said as his plan sunk in. "I'm not sure about her net worth these days, but it has to be a lot."

"Yeah, well…" Dickie's ears got red and he busied himself with the loose knot in his cashmere muffler. After a few seconds, he looked up at me. "I have plenty, as you know. What I don't have right now is coming to me in a couple of years when the trust Dad set up for me matures."

His face brightened again and his smile returned. "And, let's face it, you or Peter will be after me then, you and every other good cause in San Francisco. Now, if you'd take some off me, for yourself, I mean, I wouldn't be such a target."

"Don't go there, Dickie," I said with a sigh. "We finished that conversation a couple years ago. Remember the prenup? Your lawyers went to great pains to explain to me, even though I said I didn't care about it, that breaking it was impossible."

He had the grace to look embarrassed. The Argetter lawyers were a hard-boiled bunch, and my own attorney told me she'd never seen a prenup as tight as the one I blithely signed before we got married. "No kids, no room to maneuver," she explained. "He has to nullify it personally, and you won't let me even bring that up."

Now, I said, partly to make him feel better, "Barring something catastrophic, I can make it on my own, particularly because your father, who may have been the sweetest man in the world, gave me a sort of reverse dowry as a wedding gift."

We stood there looking at each other for one long beat, remembering his father's benevolent presence in the early days of our romance and marriage, when only good things seemed to lie ahead of us.

"Yes, well, Dad was the best," Dickie agreed, his voice trailing off into memory. Then, shaking himself, he looked to the door and said he had to go. He had persuaded his bachelor host to come to the dinner and had promised to start with champagne and some time trading bragging rights about their separate trips to Nepal.

"You won't believe it. He's got himself a new piece of art. Perfect bachelor material."

I raised my eyebrows. His friend wasn't a bad guy, but he had terrible taste and his apartment was the setting for some trippy stuff.

"Bronze life-sized nude, more *Playboy* than classical, lying on a marble couch, eating bronze grapes. Her boobs are a teenager's wet dream, and the expression on her face is Hollywood starlet circa 1950. Takes the breath away. Of course, Harry's stoked. His dealer told him it was for the ages." He laughed and then he was off, waving at me and signaling the doorman to call a cab in the same easy motion.

I stood there for an instant, digesting the encounter, wondering what held us in the same orbit. When I looked at my watch, I jumped. *Get a damn move on, girl*, my inner voice commanded. *This party's going to start without you otherwise.*

chapter 9

THE PARTY WAS IMPRESSIVE. I always get a little nervous right before, when the wait staff is standing around tapping their toes and I begin to believe no one will come. Of course they do.

The Pilgrim Club was humming with partygoers twenty minutes after the start time. Teeni earned more than a few admiring glances for her elaborately frizzed topknot and sculptured red evening gown. She's a big woman and wears clothes that do not apologize. Teeni once told me her best friend was a fashion designer and that Teeni was her favorite model. Seeing her in party clothes, I understood why.

The African ambassadors and their wives came in brilliantly colored and draped ceremonial outfits, many of the women wearing elaborate folded cloth headdresses a *Vogue* editor would rush to copy.

Our San Francisco contingent basked in the reflected glory of the fabled Pilgrim Club with its tall windows, acres of thick, crimson drapery, and marble staircases. Dickie's mother, who prided herself on signaling her superiority to everyone at all times, went so far as to let her eyes flick around the details of the imposing architecture in open approval. The half of our guests who were New Yorkers did these things all the time and went to great pains to show it.

However, even for them, I observed, royalty in the person of a dangerously slender woman of a certain age who smiled broadly and shook hands gamely with anyone who approached her was something special. The most blasé guests seemed to be drawn like magnets to whatever portion of the reception room she and her silvery dress occupied at any given moment.

The reception ended, and people proceeded up the twin staircases to the dining room only a half hour behind schedule. The centerpieces of apricot roses and ivy strands were stunning, arranged in thick clusters in low crystal bowls so people could talk over them. The table settings were ornate, with two plates on top of each charger to start the meal, enough silverware at each place to feed a platoon in the field, and candles threatening to set fire to the beribboned menus propped up against a forest of wine glasses. The black-tie and long gown set took it all in stride, chatting and laughing with their buddies as if they hadn't seen each other two days ago.

The waiters sprang into action, blanketing the vast room to make sure everyone had wine and that the courses were served and cleared almost in unison, table to table. Unlike hotel ballroom service, there were no clanking trays on which to plunk used plates. Everything was whisked through swinging doors at a trot. Not for the first time, I realized I did not have what it took to be a good waiter. At this level of service, it was practically an art.

The ritual at dinners like this was for guests to jump up and visit other tables between courses. It was important to be observed chatting with the most important people in the room, who remained seated as a sign of rank. I noticed Dickie, who looked handsome in his dinner jacket, being urged in the direction of royalty by his mother, who had her hand on his back and appeared to be pushing him discreetly but forcefully.

Poor guy. This was pretty much the story of his life. A snooty local boys' school at first, then prep school in New England, then an Ivy for four years, followed by a mandatory MBA at Harvard. He told me once that no one ever asked him what he might want to do, even at the level of sports or reading. When we were dating, his favorite activities were sitting at home watching old movies or taking long walks in the Marin headlands.

That was fine with me. The young women in his social set weren't too happy that an outsider had her hooks into such a good catch, and his mother did all she could to brand me an opportunist who should be driven out of the neighborhood. Never mind that I had my own college degree, a job at the Devor, and knew which fork was for the fish course.

These days, I tried to stay out of the Argetters' way, mother and son. I was now in charge of the Devor's fundraising operations and had ample opportunity to cross paths with them, but could usually drift to another corner of the room when either one appeared. I didn't have to tell anyone that my heart sometimes gave a little jump when I saw my ex out of the corner of my eye, or that I could suddenly feel a pang of loneliness when I met friends at "our" local pub after work.

Tonight, for just a minute, my heart pinged when I saw Dickie push a bit of hair off his face before smiling broadly at the Queen's distant cousin. He had so many good qualities. If only...well, that was not somewhere I wanted to go.

The first course had been cleared, and the waiters were placing the entrée when Teeni signaled me that I was asked for at a table. I escorted a sweet, elderly man who needed to leave early to the foyer via the elevator. "It's a damn shame," he said, "but I'll be in bed before you finish your nightcap. Don't get old, my dear."

Climbing the magnificent staircase up from the main floor to the dining room was getting a little old after doing it about ten times. My calves vied with my toes, scrunched into pointy heels, to see who could scream the loudest, and I decided to ride up. Taking advantage of being slightly hidden from view at the spot where the elevator had been tucked into a corner, I slipped off a shoe and wiggled my poor toes.

The murmur of voices coming from the adjacent room, where we had held the reception, caught my attention. I assumed it was Club staffers until one voice lifted in volume and I recognized the deep female drawl.

"Don't ask me. How would I know?"

The other voice spoke, but I couldn't make it out.

"Of course you can trust me," Jamie's voice—I was certain it was her—continued. "It's a little late for this, anyway, isn't it? We can't change our plans. Fritz mustn't find out—"

The other voice cut in, still too low for me to pick out any words.

Jamie's voice rose. "All right, my plan. But you bought in, and I'm expecting you to be there, like we agreed. You know it's for the best."

The other voice took over the conversation for several minutes, and I heard a deep, masculine chuckle. I stood there, one shoe off, wondering what this was about. Part of me wanted badly to peek into the room. But I knew I would be visible in the doorway, and the last thing I wanted to do was let Jamie McBeel know I'd been eavesdropping on her.

The other voice got louder, though, and I realized who-ever it was, was walking toward the entrance. I panicked and pushed the elevator button. The door opened immediately but not before I saw a smiling Simon Anderson coming out of the reception room with his hand on Jamie's elbow.

Unnerved, I jumped into the elevator and pushed the up button, only to realize my shoe was still outside. As I hopped back out to retrieve it, Simon and Jamie simultaneously looked over at me. For a second, we all froze. Then, merci-fully, the elevator doors closed with me inside, mouth open, holding a shoe in one hand.

In the minute it took the elevator to slowly chug its way up to the third floor, I began to shake and feel my ears burn. I knew I was in the wrong, listening to their conversation, and I remembered my mother's warning that eavesdroppers rarely hear anything that makes them feel good. But, still. Simon had said he hardly knew Jamie. And Jamie had said—no, had gone out of her way to make sure I knew—that she hardly knew him. It didn't take a linguistics expert to figure out from Jamie's side of the conversation and from what I saw that both of them were lying.

Upstairs, I had a tough time making small talk while my brain sizzled. Between courses, everyone at these events table-hops, and I had to do my share, stopping here and there to see how people were enjoying the event so far. But my mind was elsewhere. Were they having an affair? Planning to sneak off somewhere together? It made sense. Handsome celebrity and glamorous socialite. What an idiot I was, thinking the great Simon Anderson was making moves on me.

The guests partied on. They ate sparingly and drank copi-ously, listened with the appearance of attention to Peter's excellent talk on the state of museums, and clapped loudly when our board chairman handed a heavy, engraved Tiffany bowl to Fritz as a token of the Devor's gratitude for his long history of support. Jamie, one hand on the crystal, smiled adoringly up at her husband. The irreplaceable Bill Cunningham took pictures for the *Times*, thanks to Jamie's PR person, and everyone felt important.

Fritz had altered my draft enough so that he sounded a little like royalty himself. He talked about Africa, "the most important place on earth to come face to face with our beginnings," and said a few words in mournful tones about his dear friend of many years, Dr. Bouvier, "whose death is a tragedy for his friends and admirers, and for the study of archaeology itself." At the end of his remarks, everyone applauded again, even louder, and it was over.

As the company began to drift away from their tables, I wandered, for the fourth or fifth time, to the room where the ambassador from Kenobia, Keile Obarri, was seated. He had no wife in attendance, and I could see by the fret lines on her forehead that his presence had been a burden to Louise. She was listening to something he was telling her, tilted politely in his direction, as she had been every other time I came by during dinner. My plan was to liberate her and have a chance to ask him some questions, so I plopped myself into an empty chair at their table and smiled my way into their conversation.

Louise got the hint and in no time I had the former head of the ministry of whatever all to myself, the movie star and her boyfriend having taken off before the speeches ended. We did the party chat for a few minutes: wonderful weather, excellent food, charming people, lovely setting, so important for Africa's visibility.

"Ambassador, I'm so glad you could come tonight," I finally said, wanting to get to the point. "Rene Bouvier's unfortunate accident must sadden you. I understand you were friends?" Talk about getting right into it. *High fives*, my inner voice cheered.

"Ah, yes. So unfortunate, as you say, Miss O'Rourke." His head was a graceful oblong and his dark skin was as smooth as a child's. Elegant was the word that came to mind. "All of Kenobia will grieve." He wasn't a diplomat for nothing.

"I understand you and Dr. Bouvier worked closely together many years ago when he was in charge of the archaeology team that discovered several important artifacts in your country?"

"Oh, indeed. Although he was a very great man, and I, Miss O'Rourke, was only a humble student in comparison."

"Really? You headed the ministry for so long. Didn't you work there even before you took the ministerial position? I'm sure you're too modest." I was holding my own.

"Ah, in those days, you must understand, there were no educated archaeologists from my country. We did not have the expertise, one might say, to research our own heritage. And Kenobia was such a poor country."

"Wasn't it fortunate that you, that is, the ministry, were able to get some funding through the field research permit system?"

"As you say," he said with another slight bow of his head.

"Did you have other sources of funding in those days?" I smiled and looked him in the eye to signal my sincerity.

He smiled back, his eyes glittering. "Unfortunately, Miss O'Rourke, the system of permit fees was a very limited avenue to create funds to use in the preservation and storage of the many valuable artifacts the Western scientists discovered on our soil. There weren't many other financial opportunities."

Okay, time to drill down. "That's why you, that is, the Kenobian government, were forced to sell some of the treasures in those lean times?"

He shifted ever so slightly in his chair to look more directly at me and lifted his wine glass, which appeared to be filled with water. Twirling the stem with long, slender fingers, he stared for a moment at it, then lifted it and drank a little. "What treasures might you be thinking of, Miss O'Rourke?" he said, hissing the esses slightly. "No Kenobian would consider permanently selling off singularities, although some were, shall we say, lent, to responsible foreign researchers until the country was stable enough economically to house them safely. MACPCA records are clear on this subject."

"Really? I am not that knowledgeable. I hadn't understood that," I said, alarm bells ringing at the "permanently."

"Perhaps you already know that this beautiful piece of evidence of Kenobia's history that was stolen from my dear friend Dr. Bouvier is cataloged as such?"

Whoa. "Lent"? Breaking news here. Peter will freak out. I opened my mouth to ask more about his rewriting of the history of "our" jar, but never got the chance. Out of the corner of my eye, I saw a figure descending on us.

Ambassador Obarri saw it, too, and as he turned his head, I could have sworn I heard a low growl coming from his throat. Quickly, he stood.

I turned in my chair. Shit. It was Jamie McBeel, and she looked like an avenging angel bearing down on us, her black velvet, strapless gown swirling behind her and her fists clenched by her side. She swarmed directly over to me, a small, dark cloud of beadwork and perfume. I thought she was going to call me out for listening to her private talk, and I cringed.

"Danielle, why didn't you tell me the ambassador was here?" she said instead in her deep drawl, glaring down. Caught completely off guard, I scrambled to my feet. Before I could muster an introduction, Obarri stood up beside me and spoke.

"Mrs. McBeel, it is so nice to see you," he said in a smooth, opaque voice. He even bowed slightly. "You must be proud of your husband's achievements for this museum."

Had they met? If so, that made two surprises in one evening.

She had pivoted toward him as he spoke. While she still sent off waves of fury, his tone must have reminded her not to lose her cool. In fact, I could have sworn I saw a faint blush as she tossed her hair and said, "Hello, Ambassador. I didn't know you were going to be here. I was misinformed or I would have insisted you sit with Fritz and me."

Liar, liar, I hollered, silently.

"You are too kind. I would not have missed such an auspicious occasion for anything. And I had the dear wife of your board chairman as my dining companion. We have an old friend in common."

Old friend? For a minute, I thought he meant Simon, but when I glanced at Jamie's face, I got it: the first Mrs. McBeel.

"Although," he continued, "I had hoped to hear your husband talk about the unique artifact from my country that I understood was to be displayed in Miss O'Rourke's wonderful museum. I am distressed to hear that it cannot be accounted for right now."

"Yes, yes, distressing, I agree," she said. "I'm sure"—and her eyes seemed to bore into his for a second —"it will turn up safely."

He shrugged, turning his palms face up, tilting his head to one side, still smiling faintly. "One must hope. One wants to be sure that whoever has taken possession of it understands that it is part of my country's great heritage no matter where it sits at any moment."

I stood there, looking from one of them to the other. The air crackled with tension, and I had the distinct feeling these two were speaking in code.

Teeni came around the corner then, stopping abruptly when she saw Jamie. She wheeled away, her red gown swishing as she did, and I called out. "Teeni, you needed me for something? Please excuse me for a moment. So sorry."

I beat a retreat toward Teeni, grabbed her arm, and led her as far away from the smaller room as possible. In the main dining room, Fritz was chatting amiably to the royal personage under the main dining room's massive chandeliers, the two of them surrounded by hangers-on who were absorbing the light from the two suns in their midst.

"Thank God you rescued me," I said. "Those two were throwing off sparks."

"Whatever, girl," said Teeni, shaking her head. "I came to ask if you wanted me to give the tip envelope to the head-waiter. You looked grim. Who wouldn't, with the wicked queen snapping like a piranha on the hunt? What's the ambassador like, by the way? He's a handsome dude, for sure."

"He was very ambassadorish. But he said something—"

Just then, Obarri rounded the corner and strode over to Fritz, the same diplomatic smile pasted on his face. Teeni and I watched from a distance as Obarri said something to get Fritz's attention. The billionaire turned away from the group, his hands in his pockets. Obarri held his own hand out. McBeel stared at Obarri for a long time before pulling his hand out and offering it.

"They don't seem too friendly," Teeni said. "Fritz McBeel looks like he thinks the ambassador might bite."

"Strange, isn't it?" I said, agreeing. "Actually, I think he looks like he might be the one to bite. Odd since it was Jamie who didn't want Obarri here and, if Peter got it right, Fritz who was cool with it."

After exchanging only a few words, McBeel introduced Obarri to the presence of royalty, who aimed another toothy smile in his direction. After what looked like a little polite chit-chat, Obarri bowed slightly to her and stepped back, taking hold of Fritz McBeel's tuxedoed arm and steering him a few steps away from the group. Leaning close to Fritz, he said something that made Fritz frown.

"I wouldn't mind knowing what they're talking about," I said. "Bet you breakfast at the Garden Court it has something to do with our missing artifact."

"Wouldn't take the bet," Teeni said. "I'm sure it does. What I can't figure out is who has the upper hand. I mean, not too many people could grab Fritz McBeel like that and get away with it."

"True. But it doesn't look like they're about to go *mano a mano*, thank heavens." After a short exchange, Fritz turned back to the group, and Obarri, looking as unruffled as ever, left the dining room and headed toward the stairs.

The evening dribbled to a close after that, waiters hustling to clean off tables and scoop up centerpieces and whatever was left from the goodie bags to take home to Queens and the Bronx.

Simon found me standing in the dining room doorway, put a hand on each of my shoulders, pulled me close, and kissed me with feeling. Too surprised to say anything, I stood there.

"You look stunning tonight," he said, fixing me with a bright glance and an impish smile. "That dress is a knockout, especially the back." He winked.

"Uh, thanks," I managed. Was he going to mention the scene with Jamie? Was I?

"Congratulations on a first-rate evening," he said, seemingly unfazed. "The word at my table was that it was up to New York standards, not an easy compliment to get." He added that he had to leave earlier than he planned to get back to California and promised to call me in a few days "for a good gossip about tonight. Maybe you'll be rested up by then."

I felt my face get hot at the reminder of my unpolished rejection of him the other night. I doubted the gossip would include anything about his liaison with Jamie. But I enjoyed the moment on one level because I could see Dickie, across the room with his bachelor buddy, giving Simon the evil eye. Good. He needed to understand I was a free woman.

Teeni and I waited until the last guest had been handed her coat and a quick tour of the dining room didn't turn up any stray cell phones or eyeglasses. Peter beamed as he left with a trustee and her husband, giving me the finger-to-thumb signal for perfection. Louise kissed me at least three times, telling me she never could have done it without me.

Dickie was a little subdued when he stopped by the reception desk to pick up his mother's coat. He apologized. She had asked him to drive her up to Connecticut to see some family friends and he had to postpone our brunch. "You pulled it off beautifully," he said. "The right people, fantastic food, and out before midnight. Sure you won't let me take you out now for champagne to celebrate?" I declined, in part because I was still feeling a little vulnerable to his charms, but I agreed to meet him in San Francisco when he got back. He touched my arm and started to say something else, but I got distracted by the responsibility of initialing the blindingly large bill for the evening. He faded away while I was going over the details with the manager, and Teeni told me later he had raved about her dress before he left. King's Jar or not, we had muddled through. Tomorrow, life would return to normal.

» » »

Alone at last, tired of smiling at everyone, and looking forward to slipping off my shoes for good, I stood at the sidewalk after midnight waiting for a cab. A limousine pulled up, gleaming in the streetlight, and, to my surprise, the driver got out and came around to open the back door, nodding to me.

"Good evening, Miss O'Rourke. May I drop you off at your hotel?" a voice said from the recesses of the back seat as I bent down to look inside. Fritz McBeel sat there, hands clasped loosely in his lap, looking up at me as if this were a perfectly normal suggestion. *Wow. Aren't we moving up in the world?* my inner voice purred.

"That's nice of you, Mr. McBeel, but there's no need. Cabs are easy to come by in this neighborhood." I figured he was being polite, the result of champagne and a boatload of flattery.

"Please," he said. "It's no trouble and I'd like to chat with you."

"Well, okay then," I said helplessly, ducking into the car as he obligingly slid to the other side of the back seat. We, who barely ever spoke unless it was for me to report on some small task I'd been assigned, had something to talk about? Uh-oh, was I about to get slapped down for letting Obarri enter the Pilgrim Club? Maybe I shouldn't be looking forward to the next few minutes.

"Jamie, I mean Mrs. McBeel, she's not with you?" I said, stumbling over the simplest question in my confusion.

"Mrs. McBeel left earlier. She had a headache."

I'll bet she did. Planning a rendezvous with the Most Eligible Bachelor and worrying that someone overheard you would give anyone a headache, especially if your husband was a billionaire and you might lose your share of a huge fortune if that someone ratted you out. *Breathe*, I instructed myself.

The driver eased away from the curb, and we began a slow, smooth drive through Central Park. For a minute, McBeel was silent and so was I. This was his party, and anything I said might get me in trouble. "We have a problem, Danielle," he finally said, smiling at me and shaking his head slightly.

"We do?" I said, smiling back but wondering which one of my problems had become ours.

"Yes. We've lost an important piece of history, and we need to find it, don't you agree?"

"You mean the King's Jar?" I said. What was I saying? Of course he meant the jar. "Well, it's certainly a problem for the Devor, and I assure you Peter is cooperating fully with the insurance investigators and the police."

"Ah, Peter Lindsey. Yes, I'm sure he is. But I think you and I understand that this may not be a matter for the police." His voice had dropped to a conspiratorial rumble, warm and casual, almost as if we were buddies.

"We do?" I squinted at him in the dark, wondering what he was talking about but flattered that he assumed I had a clue.

"We know people whose passions may be equaled by a less than perfect degree of, shall we say, ethical behavior?" He chuckled. "People who might find it altogether too tempting to snatch this precious object for their own purposes."

He beamed at me expectantly, like a teacher waiting for a favored student to produce the correct answer.

"I'm not sure what you mean," I said, pasting what I hoped looked like a collegial smile on my face, wondering when I'd been elevated to the status of confidante to the great man. "I don't know who stole it. I don't know who hit poor Dr. Bouvier." I heard the little whine creep into my voice. "I don't know anything, Mr. McBeel."

"Please call me Fritz. We've been working together for quite a while, haven't we? You know, I think you may have an idea," he said, the smile giving way to the smallest frown, "and I want you to know you can tell me whatever you suspect. I don't have great faith that the police will find it, and I cannot accept that it is gone. You will understand that."

"Even though your foundation director said you believe the jar is the Devor's responsibility now?"

Whoops, wrong thing to say. Fritz leaned away from me, staring out the window for another long minute while I squirmed.

"I only mean that, of course, I, we, will share everything with you no matter who the lawyers say actually owned the jar when it went missing," I rushed on, trying to fill the silence with something that would take the chill out of the suddenly frosty chat. "You've been a wonderful steward and supporter, and we value that so highly."

To my ears, it sounded like so much boot-licking, but I had a hunch Fritz was used to this kind of talk. I, sadly, was a little too experienced at it. But there were a handful of wealthy donors with whom I had developed friendships, and maybe this business of the missing jar had created a bond between the man who had protected it for decades, and me as the person at the Devor he had come to trust. I decided to enjoy the luxury of the rise in my status and the company. We sat silently for a few minutes as the car slipped through the city's always pulsing streets, past the restaurants still serving dinner and the bars with their neon signs competing for space above doorframes, and the groups of young people headed in every direction laughing and jostling each other.

After a few minutes, Fritz seemed to shake himself out of his private reflections and turned back to me. Leaning across the seat, he took my arm lightly and held on to it above the elbow. "I know I can count on you, Danielle. Will you call me whenever you hear anything, even the smallest detail, about how the investigation is going? You can reach me any time of night or day. I'll give you my private cell phone number. I want to be able to continue my financial support for the Devor. You're key to that now, Danielle, and I intend to make sure your boss gives you credit."

"Of course, Mr....er, Fritz." I looked out the window. "Oh, I'm staying at the Algonquin," I said, when I realized we were headed downtown, well west and south of the hotel district. Fritz didn't reply, and the driver seemed not to hear me. The car was dark, the west side street we were on now was industrial and deserted, the driver silent but, I felt, listening to our conversation. Fritz's hand was warm on my arm. All of a sudden, I felt nervous. What was I doing here, miles from the champagne and crystal chandeliers of the

Pilgrim Club, with a powerful man who was all of a sudden acting like my best buddy? Surely, he wasn't going to make a pass at me?

I shimmied closer to the door and took a deep breath. "I appreciate your concern, knowing how much the piece means to you even though you have formally turned it over to the Devor. But I haven't got a clue as to where it is or who took it, really. I'm not sure why you think—"

"Simon Anderson is involved," he said, riding over my nervous chatter, his thumb tapping against the thin fabric of my shawl. "I know it, and I think you suspect it. Let's be honest." McBeel's open hand chopped the air between us, and I jerked as if he had hit me. Maybe he was going to hit me. *When you're that rich, you can get away with anything,* I thought. "You know him well. You see him frequently. You had dinner with him the other night. He hasn't hinted at what happened to it?" He spoke softly and stared at me with a bemused expression, his head thrust forward.

My mouth was so dry I could hardly talk, and my brain had gone into a spin cycle so I didn't have much to say in any case. I was in way over my head, pretending to run with the limo crowd.

I snuck a peek as we rolled through another intersection. West Twenty-third, headed downtown. Pretty soon, we'd get to the Village and there were always people on the street. I'd open the door and jump out. No! I wouldn't. I'd just say I had to meet someone. *At this hour,* my inner voice sneered? This was crazy. He was a socialite, for heaven's sake, not an assassin. *Think, think,* I told myself.

"I take it your silence means you don't intend to help solve this mystery," McBeel said. Not a question, merely the disappointment of someone who had high hopes for a pupil who had failed the test. He released my arm then, absently, as if he hadn't realized he still held it, and sighed.

"I haven't picked anything up about who took it, honestly. But, Fritz, what makes you think it was Simon?" *Like, do you know he and your wife are arranging a tryst*, my inner voice added in spite of my attempt to shut out any thoughts that McBeel might be able to wrest from my brain.

"If it wasn't him, it was Obarri. One of them has it, and I intend to get it back. For the Devor, of course. Well," he said, his tone becoming more brisk, "if you can't help me, I have to respect that. Perhaps you really are unaware of the players here. Take me home, please," he said, raising his voice for the chauffeur. Then, he sat back and didn't say another word until the car glided up to the marble-faced building in which he and Jamie had their apartment.

I had plenty of time to stew about what Peter would say when the McBeel gifts dried up and Fritz let it slip that I had been rude or worse in our dealings and that his African collection would be going elsewhere as a result. I thought about trying again to reassure him, but his body language was clear—the damage had been done. And here I had been worried that he was going to try to seduce me. It was too embarrassing to think about.

"Good night, Miss O'Rourke," he said in his usual impersonal voice as he climbed out. Rats. He had reverted to my last name. He leaned back into the deep interior with another one of his vague smiles. "I trust you'll keep our little chat confidential. Richards will take you to the Algonquin." And, with that, he straightened up and walked across the red carpet to his front door. It was only later, when I was getting undressed, that something occurred to me. How had he known I had dinner with Simon?

» » »

I didn't sleep much, and when I did drop off, I didn't like the parade of images that floated around in my head—Simon holding Jamie's arm, Obarri's opaque smile, Fritz McBeel's sudden attention. In the morning, I packed, left a congratulatory message at Louise's hotel, and met Teeni in the lobby for the trip home.

Peter was staying on for a few days, heading upstate to the Dia Museum and then out to the Hamptons to call on an elderly man with a collection of Renaissance drawings to die for. Rumor had it someone on the Metropolitan Museum's board had ticked him off, which meant he was being courted by at least a dozen other museums in the U.S. and Europe who were ready to promise him the moon in exchange for the gift of his collection.

I was looking forward to getting back to my own turf, tying up loose ends from the event, and brainstorming with Tom Burns about how to proceed with the new exhibit space, minus the pièce de résistance.

I had one more thing on my agenda. The slacks I wore on the plane coming to New York were not as comfortable today heading back. Ten pounds had to go, no kidding, or I might have to call on Teeni's plus-size fashion designer friend.

chapter 10

THE OVERPOWERING SCENT of Asian lilies hit me when I pushed open my office door. The card that was almost buried in the huge bunch of flowers said, "You rule! Kisses, Peter," but I had a hunch it was Dorie's work. She's the best kind of executive assistant in the world—one step ahead of the boss most days. Never mind, I loved them no matter who sent them. After all, if I left out the private fireworks happening all around me the night of the gala dinner, it was a sparkling success.

A week out of the office brings its own punishment, as every working person knows. It took a full morning to plow through the accumulated mail, phone messages, memos, reports, and media clippings that the staff had flagged for my attention. My satisfaction at emptying the tray was short-lived. My stomach was rumbling when Teeni came in with the day's mail.

"Don't I at least get a gold star for cleaning out my in-box before you fill it up again?" I said.

"Impressive," she said. "How about a chicken Caesar salad instead of a paper star?"

"Yes, yes. Are you offering to go get me one, or do you want to go downstairs together?"

"Let's go eat," she said. "We haven't compared notes on the dinner. I picked up a few interesting tidbits about some of our prospects and I'm too lazy to write everything down. Plus, if I stay here, the work on my desk will call out to me. If I'm five floors down, I can't hear it saying, 'Read me, answer me, call me back.'"

Twenty minutes later, over the clatter of silverware and the hum of the museum's hungry visitors and staff, I brought up a topic that was bugging me. "I can't get over the suspicion that the Kenobians had something to do with the theft."

"Why would you think that?" Teeni asked, her fork stopped between the plate and her mouth. "You know Tom and Peter did a scrupulous job vetting ownership."

"Tell me. But these days, it's the hottest potential conflict with antiquities, and since the Met agreed to return the Euphronios krater, we're all on fragile ground if we claim an artifact another country wants back."

The krater was a large urn painted by a Greek artist, Euphronios, about 2,500 years ago. It was stolen from an excavation site in Italy in the early 1970s. Shortly after that, it was sold by a collector to the Metropolitan Museum for a cool $1.2 million, and graced the museum's collection for decades until Italy cried foul, coming up with proof that it was stolen property. Knowing it could open the floodgates since much of the ancient art in major museums was acquired by old-fashioned looting done before the twentieth century, the Met hung tough as long as it could. With this as the backstory, it's no wonder Peter, the board, and the lawyers were so careful with artifacts like the vessel.

"What sticks in my mind," I said to Teeni, "is the vague rumor that the sale of the King's Jar might have been tainted by corruption within Kenobia. That leaves room for a nasty fight if some new administration in Kenobia decides it's an important symbol of the country's heritage."

"Okay, fair enough. So where does Obarri fit in? Isn't he a member of the prime minister's family? Wouldn't that protect the Devor, if he was the guy who stamped the exit permit?"

"Good questions and I have no idea. I think I need to do a little research, if only to keep me from waking up at three in the morning."

"Web stuff?"

"No, I tried that when I wanted to learn a little more about Obarri. Dead end. Apparently Kenobia's way behind the curve when it comes to the networked world."

"Yeah, they're probably still focused on developing some kind of sustainable agriculture, and keeping some other country's rebels from crossing the borders into their territory." Teeni shook her head and made a sympathetic face. "You know what? You should go over to Cal—I'll get you a pass into the libraries. If there's any good information, it'll be buried there."

"Perfect," I said. We got up, and another pair of women pounced on our seats. "And it'll get me out of the office for a couple of hours. I don't think I can face another stack of papers today."

Teeni laughed. "You may change your mind when you see Doe. Doe Library," she explained when I looked puzzled. "Beaux Arts on the outside, dreary inside, the crypt where microfilm goes to die. But it's the right place to start."

» » »

Two hours later, I knew what she meant. The News & Micro section was strictly about function, but it produced. I had picked up enough information to realize that the new UN ambassador from Kenobia had quite a history.

For one thing, he was a half-brother of Kenobia's prime minister. This prime minister was a survivor of the last administration's prison system, which had served as a holding pen for all political opposition for the decade before the last prime minister was shot by a firing squad for alleged corruption and "misleading the country with unwarranted behavior."

While his half-brother stewed and plotted revenge in his tiny cell, Keile Obarri was keeping his head down as a seemingly apolitical bureaucrat in charge of the country's pathetically small history museum. From that base, the clever fellow learned how to collect bribes from foreign research teams in return for permits to conduct their field expeditions. He was also channeling his brother's political allies into low-level positions in the ministry of culture that would serve as a base of operations within the bureaucracy. Obarri used his time to develop a thick network of international connections and to play them against each other with rumors and innuendo to suit his power objectives.

When the revolution came and his half brother was "elected" prime minister, Obarri burst out of his self-styled cocoon and became the chairman of the Ministry of Administration for the Collection and Presentation of Cultural Antiquities (also known and admired as MACPCA), dispensing or withholding access to Kenobia's fertile research areas at will, subject only to the size of the "gifts" that he extorted for his brother and himself. Or, rather, in the official reading, for the good of the Kenobian people.

A younger cousin having reached the age in life where he needed a job, Obarri was promoted to the United Nations so that the younger man could assume the mantle of power at MACPCA.

Not surprisingly, there wasn't any coverage of a unique piece of Kenobian culture being sold off to a rich American. Duh. That would take place well under the radar. But I was willing to bet Obarri had had a horse in that race.

A photo on the front page of an issue of the *Kenobia Standard* caught my eye on the fiche page. A younger Fritz McBeel standing with a meekly smiling Obarri on one side and the Most Eligible Bachelor, grinning at the camera, on the other. McBeel was stiffly posed, his teeth bared in what could pass as a smile.

The paper was dated twenty years ago, right when McBeel was acquiring the treasure. The article made no mention of any purchase agreements or research activities. It said, in florid language, what a loyal friend to Kenobia McBeel was and how honored the ministry was that he visited and brought with him the renowned "scholar and journalist" and the "esteemed scientist." Looking closer, I saw a younger, almost handsome Rene hovering in the background, his arms crossed over his chest, a wide-brimmed hat casting a deep shadow on his face.

Quickly, I scrolled through the other issues of the *Standard*, looking for photos or mentions of the Americans, but there were none. I copied the article and the photo. If there was something crooked about the artifact's sale, this was the closest thing to a smoking gun a non-expert like me was likely to find. At the very least, I could use it to start a conversation with Simon. Oscar, Fritz McBeel, Obarri, or even Jamie...Simon connected with them all in ways that I didn't understand. My instinct said he was involved in this business somehow, but I wasn't making any headway in figuring it out on my own. I wished Peter would get back soon so we could talk it all through.

» » »

"Hey, Dani."

I turned around in the short line waiting to order coffee and saw Tom a couple places behind me. Was I imagining it, or were there a couple of new worry lines bisecting his forehead? "How's the new space shaping up?" I asked as we snaked forward.

"Fantastic, all things considered," he said over the heads of two people who were, by the looks of them, zoned out. And no wonder. It was a chilly, gray morning, the kind that begs for huddling under the duvet. Other than the baristas, the liveliest person in Peet's right now was the kid with the iPod, whose head jerked up and down in time with music whose beat was so loud I could hear it oozing from his ear buds.

Tom's nothing if not enthusiastic and welcoming when it comes to sharing his passion for the arts and cultures of Africa, Asia, and Oceania. I learn something new every time I slow down enough to listen as he explains the significance of an object to me. When the Devor Museum's elevator stopped at his floor, he invited me to come see the progress. It was pretty impressive, and clever, too. The Devor has been pressed for space for a decade, so adding anything has to be creatively done. The architects had taken a corridor that backed up to the extensive storage rooms and turned that wall into a long window into which boxes were set, displaying relevant items from the African collection. Half the fun for visitors would be looking into the innards of the museum and seeing shelf after shelf of fascinating masks, sculptures, headpieces, and other intriguing objects.

"Of course that means we're cleaning like mad," Tom said with a laugh. "Even though we normally work to keep things in good shape, having them exposed to the world like this has ramped up maintenance."

"More feather dusters?"

"Yeah, but it's sparked the inventory check we normally do every five years. We were behind, I admit. It's been more like seven, for most parts of this section. But I just hired an intern from Mills College who's going to do it, piece by piece, checking the acquisition numbers on each object against the last audit."

"Sounds like a mind-numbing job. I hope you're paying her well."

"Are you kidding? No money. College credit. She's an art history major."

"Good for us, but hard on her? How long do you think it will take?"

"She'll be done by the end of her semester—four months, maybe."

"God. Send her up to meet Teeni some time for a pep talk and some mentoring."

"Teeni will steal her," Tom said, smiling and scratching his head. "I'm not sure I should let my hard-won student out of the dungeon."

"Don't be mean." I sipped my coffee as we walked back to the elevator. The building was quiet. We didn't open until eleven today, and I was enjoying the sense of having my own private Edwardian mansion.

"Actually, I should be more worried about Simon stealing her," Tom said.

"Simon? I don't get it."

"Think about it. Tall, dark, and handsome TV star, smart as a whip."

"And she would meet him how?" I said, pushing the up button.

"He prowls the storage rooms when he's in town, looking for objects that will support the thesis of the book. If he had his way, we'd need twice the display space we have. Dani," Tom said, abruptly changing gears, "would the museum pay a ransom for something as spectacular as the King's Jar?"

Something about the tone of his voice caught my attention. He was looking at me intently, seeming to be scouring my face for a reaction.

"No, absolutely not," I said. "But I'm curious about the question. Have you heard something?"

He shook his head vigorously as he replied. Something about that head-shaking made me curious. Protesting too much? "It's not that. Somebody has it, and we want it. Whoever took it has to know it's worth a lot. Maybe they're taking good care of it and just want to get it back to us in exchange for money. Do you know for sure Peter won't trade?"

"Remember, Tom, there's an insurance company involved, plus the legalities of who owned it at the moment it was stolen—"

"Who owned it? Wait, I thought, I mean, is anyone saying we don't own it?" Tom said in startled tones.

"Can't talk much about it, but there has been some conversation, all very inconclusive and indirect. Nothing to worry about right now, and I know Peter will fill you in if it becomes an issue."

"That's unthinkable," Tom said, his face turning red. "I have to know. We examined that from top to bottom, Dani. Is it the Kenobians, because if someone's waffling now—"

"No one's waffling, Tom. Cool your jets. I'm sorry I mentioned it. I think the chances of us recovering it without paying ransom are decent, with the police, the insurance company's private investigator, and the FBI all involved."

"The FBI? That's something else I didn't know," Tom said, his voice rising.

"I expect you will soon enough. I heard they'll be talking to you and Peter any time now."

"Why me? I don't know anything about the theft," Tom said.

"But you know a lot about the market for museum antiquities of this period and place, and you worked with Rene on its transfer. Of course they'll want to talk to you."

The elevator arrived, and we parted. If Tom was unsettled by our conversation, so was I, although I couldn't put my finger on what bothered me.

» » »

Thank heavens for routine work. I needed something to keep my mind from veering off into useless scenarios in which half the people I knew seemed to be suspects either of murder or theft, or both. Fortunately, our annual fund director badly needed time with Teeni and me to review his plans for a mail solicitation, and our ever-patient planned gifts officer wanted approval to order one of those brochures that reminds older donors that they are, alas, headed for the great beyond and wouldn't they like to put the Devor into their wills?

Our public relations staffer reported that the media had moved on to newer crimes and no one was asking the Devor anything about missing artifacts. By five o'clock, I felt almost normal.

"Prince Charming for you," Teeni said when I picked up my phone. My heart fluttered. Most Eligible Bachelor? "Some day you'll tell me why you won't give the poor guy another chance." Oh.

"Put him through," I said. "I'm ready for anything, even him."

"Hey there, Dani," he said. Dani? I was so used to him calling me by some stupid and inappropriate nickname that it stopped me in my tracks for an instant. Did it mean he might actually be accepting the idea that we were finished?

Dickie reminded me we were having breakfast the next morning, postponed from New York. I tried to beg off, but he's the most persistent person I know when he's in the mood, and he was.

We met early at the Ritz-Carlton on Nob Hill. While he ate a caviar omelet and I picked at pastry and fruit, I filled him in on the mystery of the jar's whereabouts and the idea that an unscrupulous collector might have hired someone to steal it.

"Being rich doesn't guarantee integrity," I said.

"Maybe not," Dickie said. "But it sure can insulate you from the results of your terrible behavior." He stopped suddenly. "Um," he said.

"Yes indeed." Was he talking about his own fling? Apparently, he hadn't meant to. His face was red and he was dabbing his lips unhappily with the napkin. "That was a long time ago, Dickie," I said. "It's over."

"Not until you forgive me. But, no, I was thinking about people who use their clout but hide behind anonymity so they don't have to own up to their roles. You know, in politics, even at the local level."

He frowned and jabbed his fork in the air for emphasis. "Remember the time some folks in mansions near the Presidio didn't want a street widened so more people could drive or bike into the new park? Somehow, the plan was reversed, but no one knew quite why and the mayor mumbled something about public safety? The city opened the park up a few miles away, in a less convenient spot and a less privileged neighborhood. Well, I knew a few of those people, and I can tell you they were heavy hitters in the mayor's campaign fundraising lists. Money moves behind the scenes. You can be sure of that."

For Dickie, that was a long speech. And he seemed genuinely bothered by the actions of his neighbors. I would have been more impressed with his new social conscience if he didn't still treat the city's parking regulations like mild advisories aimed at people who didn't drive expensive sports cars with vanity plates signaling their status.

Before I could decide whether or not to bring that up, he changed the subject and began lobbying me to go with him to the Bahamas, on a trip put together by a professional photographer. He was leaving the next day but could book my trip in no time, and I could finally learn how to take something more artful than a fuzzy snapshot.

"You need a break, kiddo." Mr. Impulse Action at his best. When I said no for the twentieth time, he assured me that there were no single women on the guest list. I didn't bother to remind him that the scent of an unattached multi-millionaire guaranteed there would be attractive females wherever the group docked. We took a trip to Aspen once before we got married where I was overpowered by the sharp elbows of women shimmying up to him at a trendy bar and making not too subtle promises about how much fun they were on the slopes and off.

"You're a bachelor. Why not hang out with other single people?" I said, trying to keep my voice light. I wasn't jealous. Sisterly protectiveness? Friendly concern? I wouldn't wish the fortune-hunting piranhas on anyone, but my inner voice wondered how I'd feel if he came back with a red-headed Rhodes Scholar who worked full-time taking care of AIDS orphans in South Africa and happened to be a perfect size six? Great, I replied. Lucky man. My inner voice snorted, which I thought was unfair.

"Yes, I am single," Dickie said. "Temporarily. Dani, I've told you I was an asshole and—"

"No news there," I said, smearing strawberry champagne jam on my brioche and to hell with the calories.

"Okay, okay. But after last year I think you need someone to take care of you."

"Now there's a compliment," I said, lathering jam on so hard my brioche fell apart.

"Jeez, let me finish. You're testy this morning. Oh, never mind," he said, signaling the waiter. "Would you bring her a fresh brioche so she can kill it?" The waiter nodded and kept a poker face as he backpedaled from our table.

After that, we steered the conversation to safe topics like the right photo equipment for shooting a barracuda underwater or a sunset so brilliant it looked like the sky was on fire.

"Oh, before I forget," he said as we were sipping our last refills of coffee. "Mother asked me if you had ever met Mary McBeel, the first Mrs. McBeel."

"No," I said. "Why would your mother even ask?" Mrs. Argetter II never spoke to me if she could help it, which was fine with me since, when she did talk to me, there were barbs attached to every word.

"I'm not sure. I got the idea Mary McBeel wanted an introduction to you. But you know Mother. She can't get from point A to point B without inserting fistfuls of irrelevant information. I tune her out after a while, I admit."

Breakfast ended with me restless and Dickie focused on his upcoming adventure when he wasn't smothering me with advice. He told me he'd call me when he got back, and I wished him a good time. We even hugged. Definitely sisterly protectiveness, I decided.

» » »

Peter was due back the next day, and Dorie said she'd do her best to get me on his schedule, although we were closing in on the date for the full board meeting at which the annual budget and plans would be debated. Everyone at the Devor wanted five minutes with the boss to lobby one more time for his or her pet projects, she told me with a smile.

"Every year, it's the same. The head of European painting wrings his hands because there's nothing left for sale that he can afford. The photography curator knows she'll get what she requests because she only asks for small amounts. She's clever—she's slowly building up a fantastic collection. Security and IT come in with 50-percent-increase requests every year, convinced they have the only truly urgent needs at an art museum."

When I left Dorie, I went downstairs looking for Tom. Our earlier conversation stuck in my mind. He was too much of a friend for me to want an argument standing between us. But, it was time to probe a bit. He was in his office, the desk and a long worktable entirely covered with stacks of paper, bound reports, file folders, books, and photographs. He was tapping his teeth, staring into his computer screen, and mumbling to himself.

"Earth to Tom," I said, after waiting at the door for a full minute.

"Oh, hey, Dani. Come in, sit down." He jumped up and came around the desk, pulling a chair out from the wall, and knocking over a stack of books piled in front of it. "Oops, sorry."

The absent-minded professor to a T, I thought, watching as he re-stacked the books badly, slid the chair so it was facing the desk, and waved me over.

"I want to talk a bit about where we are," I explained. "Peter and I will probably touch base tomorrow, and I plan to check in with the police. I know everyone wants to talk to Simon since he knows so much about the history. Will you be seeing him soon?"

"This week, in fact," Tom said. "We're working around the pages on the King's Jar, trying to finish the rest of the catalog. It's hard. The text builds so much on that pivotal find that we don't see how we can cut out all references to it. We won't have a book if we do."

"Does that mean you might scrap the project?" I said.

"Don't even think like that. I may be crazy, but I think the blasted thing will turn up soon." He scratched his head.

"Funny," I said, remembering that Jamie said the same thing to me, "you're not the only person who thinks that. Why are you so optimistic?"

Tom's head was down as he rooted through the papers on his desk, but he looked up at me owlishly.

"Not optimistic, merely realistic. It's a hot potato. The thief will be notorious, an enemy of science and scholarship. Whoever took it must realize that already."

"Strong sentiments. Tell me what you're hearing from the insurance company. Any news there?"

"They don't keep me in the loop. Neither does Peter," Tom said, clipping his words and looking up at me. "I'm sure I'll only hear about it when it walks back into the museum."

I wondered if that was true. Was there a possibility Peter was choosing to keep Tom out of the information stream? If so, why?

I looked at him. From what he said, Tom understood full well the consequences of stealing such an important piece. But, knowing its unique and priceless value, would he be tempted?

"Here," he said, digging a folder from the pile on his desk. Flipping it open and handing the folder to me, Tom said, "Here's one of the photos from when it was still in Warefield's custody. Beautiful, isn't it?"

For an instant, I saw Rene's lined face as he said the same words on the day of his death, and I shivered.

"I guess so," I said. "Are you using this in the catalog?"

My eyes strayed to the folder. "KEN. CEL. JAR PHOTOS—ORIGINAL" was written in a rough scrawl on the tab line. And inside the cover, a handwritten note signed, apparently, by Rene himself.

"Ummm," he said, craning his neck across the desk, "no. That's Rene's file photo. He sent several folders with prints of photos he took of the object over the years and some of the other work in the exhibit, too. He wanted to make sure we used images that showed the rhino on the lid in high contrast since the modeling itself is kind of crude. Why are you asking?"

"This photo doesn't speak to me," I said, feeling silly for being so superficial, "but Rene described it as beautiful also. I remember how reverent he was when we looked at a photo together the day he died. Am I missing something?"

"It's old and it was buried in dirt for about eight hundred years, and we're seeing its meaning when we look at it. You're looking at a photo taken deliberately to show the condition of the surface and any small flaws. We hired a photographer to do the catalog work," he said. "Trust me, you'll get pretty. But Rene had to sign off on all photos of the artifact. That was part of the deal ever since Fritz bought the piece. So we used photos like this to instruct the new photographer."

"Did Simon take any pictures?" *Did he have access to the piece?* I wondered.

"No. I don't think so."

"Are you and Simon working on anything else related to the jar? Other than the catalog and the exhibition, I mean?"

"What else would there be?" Tom frowned.

"I don't know. Just wondered how well you know him," I said, feeling stupid.

"No, not now, although I'd love to do another book together some day if this one works out like I think it will."

I handed the folder back to Tom, who said as he took it back, "When I think that this unique piece of human history could possibly be lost for good, I get overwhelmed. I'm glad my department didn't lose it."

Tom's perspective was bigger than mine, and I needed the reminder. My job was protecting the Devor, and my instinct was that helping the police catch the killer or killers was good for the Devor, by eliminating us from guilt by association. But more importantly, the loss of the artifact would devastate scholars around the world, as it would Kenobians who finally seemed to understand the prestige and positive attention it brought to their country and to sub-Saharan Africa.

chapter 11

BY DAY'S END, I needed fresh air and silence. I checked my watch on the way home. Not too late for a walk if I got started right away. The shadows fall quickly on the wrong side of west-facing hills, and it can get chilly fast. But if I dressed for it and went out to the Presidio golf course area, I could watch the sun set from the top of the rugged cliff path and be almost guaranteed peace and quiet. Well, guaranteed if I left my cell phone in the apartment, a small but satisfying rebellion against the common belief that I was on call every minute.

My car fit into a skimpy space near the Palace of the Legion of Honor, which was still open, near the crest of the golf course hill. I zipped up my jacket against the steady breeze, and pulled a little flashlight from my glove compartment, a necessity at twilight on the unpaved track along the cliff. Two pony-tailed young women breezed by me on the road, jogging effortlessly and chatting without the slightest shortness of breath. Show-offs.

I crossed the street, left the road, and set off west, under a canopy of trees, the Pacific Ocean off to my right, sparkling and blue with the green hills of Marin County north of it. The sunshine and freshness of air scented by eucalyptus trees picked up my spirits immediately and cleared my head.

I promised myself I wouldn't think about anything except where I was for at least a half hour.

Occasionally, I met other people out enjoying the late afternoon sunshine, and we exchanged greetings and smiles. A dog romped over to me, sniffing my crotch happily while the old guy who owned it ineffectually commanded it to behave. When no one else was nearby, I heard chickadees chittering overhead and stopped to watch a hummingbird poke its long beak into a native fuchsia flower in a sunny clearing.

I hardly noticed when the path slipped deeper into the trees. The sky held reflected light from the setting sun for a while, and then, suddenly, it was gone. I heard a couple laughing and chatting somewhere in front of me. My watch said I'd been walking for forty minutes. Time to turn around even though it wasn't dark enough to require the flashlight.

The birds were quieting down, and the only company I had was the people I had heard before, tromping along somewhere behind me, although they weren't talking anymore. Probably concentrating on the trail as I was. I stopped to tie my shoe, and it got quieter. Had the footsteps stopped? I started walking again, and the footsteps started behind me. One person, I realized, not the laughing couple.

It's silly to be worried, I scolded myself. *I'm twenty feet down from a paved road. And, twenty feet in the other direction from the edge of a several hundred foot cliff*, my inner voice pointed out.

At that point, I tripped over a tree root. "Ack," I said as I fell, my arms out wide. My head brushed a tree trunk, and my thigh banged into a low boulder, but I was more confused than hurt. I brushed myself off, aware of the total silence around me. Had the person walking behind me left the path, maybe gone up to the road? I decided to try that myself, but soon realized this spot was too steep. Maybe a bit farther.

As I started to walk again, I heard the footsteps. I thought about coyotes, said to have walked across the Golden Gate Bridge to this area a couple of years ago. They didn't attack people, did they? Mountain lions? They definitely attacked people, according to the TV news. But here? No, this was too urban a setting. I hardly thought a deer was stalking me, and, while there were lots of raccoons, I was confident they didn't make that much noise when they walked. Which left a larger animal, Homo sapiens to be precise.

I stepped up my pace, looking ahead to see where the path opened up to the roadway at the spot I had entered it. The footsteps came on at the same pace. I started to jog as quietly as I could, but the person behind me began to jog, too. I looked over my shoulder but couldn't see anything.

Maybe I could hide behind a tree or a large boulder and whoever it was would pass by me. I looked around in the increasingly dark air. Wait. Closer to the ocean side. Wasn't that a small clearing I'd seen before, with an extra long wooden bench next to a jutting rock? It had some kind of plaque, I remembered, and I always meant to check it out. I swerved toward it, going as fast as I could, hoping to lie down under the bench before the person behind me reached the clearing. I dropped down and squirmed up against the bench and the boulder, glad I had on dark clothing.

The footsteps jogged past the clearing. I didn't dare raise my head, but I listened so hard I heard my pulse banging in my ears. Gone, good. But as I began to get up, back again. Damn. Shuffling in the clearing, muttering under his breath—it was a man—now coming closer.

What did I have to defend myself with? My flashlight. I could try to hit him with it, or shine it suddenly in his face while screaming. The footsteps seemed to be circling the clearing slowly. I reached into my pocket. No flashlight. I knew it was there, it had to be there. My fingers searched urgently but the pocket was empty. Did I lose it earlier when I fell?

The footsteps stopped at the opposite end of the wood plank bench. My pursuer sat down, only a few feet from my frozen body, but facing the other way. He sighed a few times, then stood up with a grunt and moved away, back to the trail by the sound of it. I heard him stamp away, his footsteps getting fainter and fainter.

I was so tense, I couldn't move at all for five minutes. Then, I poked my head up and peered around. By now, it was completely dark. I couldn't even see my watch. My muscles were stiff, and I got up slowly, brushing off the dirt and leaves that clung to me. I waited until I was sure there was no other sound but my breathing and headed back in the direction of the car, trying as hard as I could not to make noise. When I got to the place where the path meets the road, there was my car, sitting alone now that the museum was closed. There was no one else in sight. The bushes lining the street were dense, and it would be easy to hide between them, but I couldn't stand here forever. I hurried across the street and pulled out the car keys that, fortunately, had not fallen out of my other pocket when I lost the flashlight. I jammed the key in the lock, leapt into the driver's seat, and started to pull the door shut. Suddenly, a hand came out of nowhere and grabbed my arm and a voice said, "Don't leave."

I screamed, ducked my head away from the bulky shape leaning into the car, and began flailing at it with my free arm. If my car keys hadn't been in my imprisoned left hand, I could have used them as a weapon. What else did I have? I hit the horn, and it blasted once before his other arm reached in and knocked mine away.

"Stop. Stop it, Dani," the hulk said, and as I paused for breath and to take in the fact that this wasn't a random attack, a little part of my brain said, *Hey, wait, you know that voice.*

"Oscar? What the hell?"

"Yeah, it's me. I need to talk to you." His hands dropped my arms, and he stepped back but dropped his head down toward the car door. The voice was soft, apologetic.

"You need to talk to me?" I repeated incredulously as his features swam into view in the car's interior light. "You followed me, attacked me, and scared me half to death because you want to talk to me? What, are you crazy?" By this time, my voice had become loud and shrill to my ears, almost a shout. "You can't just call me like a normal person? You have to practically give me a heart attack—"

"There's no time," he hissed. "Someone's following me, and I'm afraid of what will happen if they see me talking to you." His eyes jerked from side to side as if he expected someone to jump out of the bushes and grab him, which would have served him right.

"Who would follow you? What makes you think that?"

"May I get in?" he said, sounding close to tears. "Then you can close the door and it'll be dark. I'm not kidding, Dani."

"Only if you swear you will not touch me. I'm going to start the car now, and if you do anything weird, I swear I will drive to the nearest house and crash into it." Oscar was harder to take seriously as a threat, and now that I was breathing again, I was sure I could handle him. "Where's your car?"

"Down there," he gestured with a jerk of his head toward the occupied end of the street. "I didn't want them to see it near yours."

"And they are…?" I repeated.

"I don't exactly know. But I think someone's been following me all day."

I looked through the windshield. I didn't see anyone else on foot. There wasn't a car in sight. I turned in my seat. No one behind us. Was this guy paranoid? And, if so, how long did I want him sitting inches away from me?

"Why would anyone do that?" I asked.

He was silent. I noticed his hands twisting together in his lap as he shook his head to tell me he had no idea.

"It doesn't make any sense, Oscar. Unless…" The jar. Did Oscar have the jar, or at least did someone think he did? "Oscar, tell me the truth. Do you know where the King's Jar is?" I tried to sound like my mother used to when she demanded to know if I had taken cookies from the plate left to cool on the table. Of course I had and of course I said no, so I was skeptical when Oscar did the same.

"I wish I did. It would make everything so simple." He moaned.

"What does that mean?"

"Nothing, nothing," he said miserably, now beginning to rock back and forth, still punishing his hands. "Only, everything's gone wrong since the thing went missing, hasn't it?"

I couldn't argue with that. "Why did you have to talk with me? What was so important that you felt the need to stalk me?" I said, getting back to the main point of this stupid conversation, a meeting I wanted to end as quickly as possible since my teeth were beginning to chatter and the draining away of the fight-or-flight response left me as exhausted as if I had run ten miles rather than crept a few hundred yards.

"I need to find the jar," Oscar said, releasing a long sigh. "I really need to find it, and I thought you might know if anyone, you know, the FBI or the insurance company, or anybody, knows where it is. We need it to keep the lab going. All of our research revolves around the meaning of that artifact, all the papers we're working on, all the research grants. I don't know what we'll do if it's gone for good." His voice was mournful.

"Well, I'm sorry to disappoint you, but I haven't heard a word. Neither has Tom or Peter at the museum. You might check with Fritz. After all, he's the owner of record still. I'm thinking he might be the first to hear."

"He doesn't know," Oscar said. "In fact…I was hoping you could help me. But it's no use." My bladder had joined the symphony of bodily complaints and I wanted this tête-à-tête to end right now. I offered to drop him at his car, which he thanked me for, and while he buckled up and drove off, I sat for a minute and pulled myself together. All of a sudden, I heard the sound of a car coming down the hill we had just been parked on. It seemed to be coming fast, and as I looked out the rearview mirror, I saw the headlights flick on. It passed me without slowing down, zooming off in the direction Oscar had taken.

My hands were shaking as I drove slowly into the well-lit Sea Cliff neighborhood. I made it as far as the end of the block before I pulled over, opened the door, and threw up on the street in front of what was probably a twenty-million-dollar house. What a great way to experience the peace of nature and the joy of exercise. I would be sure to come out here again sometime. As in never. And wasn't I the clever one, leaving my cell phone at home so I would be sure I couldn't call for help like a reasonable person?

The rest of the way home, I drove like a little old lady, peering ahead and checking carefully at intersections, trying hard not to imagine what might have happened to Oscar if the car caught up with him. I was beginning to think this particular treasure was very bad luck.

» » »

The apartment door locked behind me and my windows secure, I felt a little better. A glass of sugar-filled ginger ale did the rest. I dialed Suzy's number with a steady hand. Suzy did her usual thing, enveloping me in a rush of questions, concerns, offers of help, and advice. I let her wind down before assuring her I was okay. She encouraged me to tell her everything, which I did, offered to come over, which I declined since it was late, and made me promise to call her as a walking partner the next time I wanted to go out at dusk.

"Did he hurt you?" she said, almost cutting me off as I was relating Oscar's strange actions.

"It wasn't like that," I said. "Oscar is a wimp. And he was scared, really scared. He says someone's following him."

"Do you think he's right?" Suzy said. "I suppose you didn't get the make and model of the car, the license plate, anything?"

"For heaven's sake, I was too upset to think about that, and, anyway, I'm no Nancy Drew. I threw up two minutes later."

For a full minute, I considered calling Charlie. But what did I have to report? Nothing, really. Suspicions, being surprised by someone I knew who didn't hurt me, getting sick in a public road? Hardly. He'd think I was some kind of drama queen. By the time I crawled into bed, I was feeling almost normal. Not normal enough to sleep well, however, and I gave up around five A.M. as the first birds began to chirp in the eucalyptus tree outside my window.

» » »

It was still early when I hit the office. The fifth floor staff corridor was quiet except for the sound of a printer far down the hall, our dogged data entry staffer no doubt, deep into the quarterly gift report.

My message light was blinking, and ordinarily I would have let it wait until I started a pot of coffee, but I was wired this morning. I hit the playback button.

"Danielle, it's Jamie." The distinctive, drawling voice and commanding tone. "I need to give you some papers right away. Please come over to my office at the foundation first thing tomorrow. I'll be there early."

Shoot, this was probably related to the tug-of-war over the vessel. I checked the time stamp on the call. It had come in late yesterday. I wondered why La Peerless hadn't made the call. Maybe she had a day off once in a while.

I debated for a couple of minutes. Better to wait until the attorney for the Devor was available? I knew Jamie was likely to be pissed if I didn't show up, and that would translate into more hassles. I was already a bad person for allowing Ambassador Obarri to come to the dinner. Or maybe I was in trouble for seating him in the hall, if I believed Jamie's comments.

Oh, oh, the little voice in my head piped up. *What if she wants to find out what you overheard at the gala dinner between her and Simon?* I would play dumb. There weren't any other sane options. No way was I going to risk the wrath of San Francisco's most powerful woman because I might have a factoid that could undo her.

What I really wanted to do was ignore the message. However, we desperately needed to get this business with the jar resolved quickly, no matter what the outcome was. And Jamie McBeel had to be catered to while the search went on. Sighing, I picked up the black leather tote bag that doubled as a briefcase and headed out again.

The Fritz and Jamie McBeel Charitable Foundation was headquartered in an elegant townhouse in Jackson Square, a small neighborhood of antique stores, trend-setting architects' offices, and decorators' businesses near the Embarcadero. I got lucky with metered street parking right out front and filled the meter with as many quarters as it would accept.

The building's foyer was locked. I rang the bell for the Foundation's top-floor suite. Before I could get an answering buzz, a silver-haired man of a certain age bounded into the foyer and opened the door with a key.

"Want in?" he said, smiling at me.

"Yes, please. I'm expected at the McBeel Foundation," I said.

He waved me in with a sweep of his arm. "Can't keep them waiting," he said, grinning. We took the stairs by unspoken consent, he peeling off at the second floor, where a bronze sign on the wall spelled out the name of a superstar designer famously dead from an excess of good living. I continued up, embarrassed at the sound of my labored breathing.

The Foundation's glass door was closed, but not locked, and the lights in the small reception room were on. I went in and waited for a couple minutes. The place was quiet, which didn't surprise me. The Foundation was not exactly a nine-to-five operation. I thought I heard a door open, so I headed into the short corridor that led first to Wayne Lawson's office on the left. The glass door to his suite was closed, the lights were off, and his secretary's work area was empty. I knew that he had a private office beyond the main room because that's where I went to pick up the checks Lawson signed on behalf of the Foundation. Fritz McBeel didn't have an office here, preferring to work from their house high on a hill in Pacific Heights, but Jamie and Victoria Peerless shared the suite to the right at the end of the hall, so I continued down the corridor.

Their glass double doors were open, and I could see the lights were on. "Jamie?" I said as I entered. Tall, east-facing windows funneled the bright morning light into the space, highlighting the rich tones of Oriental rugs and the tawny wood of the antique furniture. Victoria Peerless usually occupied a large L-shaped desk to the right of the door, but she wasn't there now. Shading my eyes against the bright sun, I looked at Jamie's own regal table under the windows, clear of papers as it always was. I remembered the layout from previous meetings, so I turned left, where an alcove hid filing cabinets and electronic equipment that would otherwise spoil the luxurious impression created by Jamie's interior designer.

That's when I saw the feet. Feet in Laboutin red-soled heels, my mind duly noted. Chic, very expensive. But feet lying down. Not a good sign. From where I stood, Jamie's back was to me and she looked pretty normal, except for the fact she was lying on the floor, which was, in my experience, not the kind of thing she would do.

"Jamie?" To my own ears, I sounded like a scared little girl. I peeked farther around the corner.

"Ohmygod, ohmygod," someone said. Me, I realized. Then, a soft, "Help, help," as I saw San Francisco's richest trophy wife flopped on her side beside the copier machine, her elegant sweater and slacks set off by a brilliantly colored Hermes scarf around her throat, her eyes half open and her face a curious shade of pink. A stroke? Maybe she just fainted? I dropped to my knees.

"Jamie, Jamie, are you okay?"

She was not paying any attention to me. I grabbed the hand I could reach and began to pat it. The pats became little slaps.

"Jamie, wake up," I said, raising my voice. When I let go of her hand it flopped to the floor, and the sound made me want to throw up.

I jumped to my feet, looking around frantically. Somewhere, I heard a door close, and I ran back into the corridor.

"Help, help. Whoever's here, come quickly. Jamie's unconscious," I shouted. No answer, and the lights in Wayne Lawson's office were still off.

I ran back into Jamie's room and checked. Still there on the floor. The phone on the fax looked way too complicated to operate. I ran over to her desk and dialed 9-1-1 with shaking fingers. When the operator answered in a slow voice, I interrupted her to tell her to hurry, hurry and get someone here right away, no kidding, something awful has happened. The slower she talked, trying to calm me down, the louder and faster I got until we were talking over each other and I thought I would scream.

"You don't understand. It's Mrs. McBeel, Fritz McBeel's wife," I said. Maybe the operator didn't run in those social

circles, because she was unmoved. She assured me that the
police and an EMT truck were on the way. At her request, I
gave her my name. She wanted me to stay on the phone until
they arrived. I was too freaked out to think, and I dropped
the phone and ran back to Jamie. Shit, shit. No change. I
groaned.

I thought about putting my ear to her chest, but I would
have had to turn her onto her back and, anyway, the pounding of my own pulse was so loud I wouldn't have heard the
Blue Angels bearing down on us in Fleet Week. There was
no sign of blood, thank god, although her tongue protruded
a bit, which didn't look right for such an elegant person. One
arm was pinned under her torso and the one I had patted
was partially under the copier stand. The bottom drawer of
the four-drawer file cabinet closest to her was open. Maybe
she tripped over it and hit her head as she fell.

Kneeling next to her, my mind spinning out random com-
mands to move, stay put, do CPR, or scream, I noticed a file
folder under the copier, partly hidden from view. She must
have dropped it when she fell. Without thinking, I pulled
it toward me and gasped. Handwritten on the tab was a
clear reference to the artifact I had come to think of as the
Devor's: "NEXT STEPS, CEL.JAR." I flipped open the file,
but it was empty. Well, almost. A small key was taped to the
inside of the folder, next to a scribbled note. "Can Simon
trust Tom?"

"Tom"? Tom Burns? Dedicated, honest Tom?

I heard sirens outside the window and slid the empty
folder back under the copier. *Wait*, my inner voice screamed,
fingerprints. If the "Tom" was my friend and the Devor's
curator, he'd be a prime suspect even though I couldn't
bring myself to think seriously that he was involved. Anyway,

that note could pull the Devor into something nasty. Without more thought, I snatched the folder back and scrambled to my feet. In three steps, I was in the center of the room, shoving the empty folder deep in my oversized tote bag, where it joined a couple other folders I had taken home the night before.

All this time, Jamie was as still as the wilted flowers on her worktable. The sirens were silent, too, which meant the emergency personnel were probably here. A cop barreled into the room, stopping short when he saw me.

I pointed to the alcove. "She's there. I think she tripped over the file cabinet," I said, hoping I sounded helpful and not like a key thief.

At that moment, the young EMT crew, their walkie-talkies alive with static, poked their heads into the room and followed the cop's arm wave into the alcove. As they went into high gear, ripping open supplies and barking out next steps to each other, the cop stepped back into the main room and came over to me.

"You called this in, ma'am?"

"Yes."

"Is she a friend of yours?"

"Not exactly. She's a benefactor of the organization I work for. She asked me to come over. I don't know why."

"What's her name?" he said as the drama behind us continued.

"Jamie McBeel. Mrs. Fritz McBeel?" I didn't have to ask if he recognized the name.

"Hold it," he said, and turned away, pulling a cell phone off his equipment belt.

I looked at the EMT guys, who were also talking into their equipment, passing along information to someone somewhere. They had electric paddles out and had started to turn Jamie on her back when one of them shouted, "Officer, over here. You gotta see this."

The cop, still talking, walked over to see what one of the crew was pointing to. I didn't budge from my spot. No, thank you, I did not want to see how she died. I did not want to know that she was dead, in fact. If I thought I could get away with it, I'd run like a bunny from this horrible scene. *Why me?* I asked the universe. I hate this stuff, really I do.

"I'll be damned," the cop said to no one in particular. Then, to the EMTs, "Don't touch anything unless you need to for life-saving purposes."

"She's way gone, sir," one replied, looking up and shaking his head.

In spite of myself, I peeked over from where I stood, while the cop got back on the phone. I heard him say it looked like a homicide. All I saw was Jamie's face. The EMTs had pulled her scarf away from her throat, spoiling her impeccable outfit and exposing a funny-looking, pinkish line on her neck. All of a sudden, I needed to sit down, on the floor if necessary. My legs felt like jelly and my hands started shaking worse. My mouth was so dry I could hardly speak. "Officer," I breathed, "I'm not feeling so good."

As I hit the rug, one of the techs leapt up, and I saw, through spots, the cop turning in my direction, still frowning. Then, to my great relief, it all went black.

chapter 12

TOO SOON, I swam back into consciousness, the EMT waving something sharp-smelling in my face, the cop standing over us, his thick-soled, polish-black shoes a few inches from my face. I was tempted to close my eyes again, but they had seen me squinting at them. The EMT recommended I stay where I was for a few minutes, but the policeman was looming over me. Better to look him in the eye. I struggled to my feet, agreeing to sit at Victoria's desk.

"If you're up to it," the cop said, "let's get some of the basics out of the way while we wait for Homicide."

Homicide was coming? What if it was Weiler? I'd had enough of his suspicious nature during my only other involvement in a murder. Worse, what if it was Charlie? I cringed, thinking of the expression on his face if he found me here, especially after his warning to stay out of the investigation of Rene's murder.

I produced my driver's license, my business card, my boss's name and title, a promise to let the police hear the message on my office phone from Jamie, and everything else I could without telling the cop about the key or the folder. I would think about why I was holding back when I was a little less stressed, say in a month or two.

Damn, damn. It was Weiler's voice floating down the hall toward us. I distinctly heard him say, "...bigwigs will be all over this one." He strolled in, tugging a small notebook out of his jacket pocket. I closed my eyes, willing him back out the door.

"Holy shit," he said. "Not you again." Maybe he meant the cop. Maybe he had it in for one of the EMTs. Maybe if I never opened my eyes, all this would magically disappear.

"Dani, what the hell? Are you okay?" Ah, perfect. Of course he would be here, too. They're partners.

"Dani, what's wrong?" The second voice was a lot closer now and there was no help for it. I braced my hands on the desk and opened one eye to peek. Yup. Same green eyes, same square jaw, clenched at the moment, same broad shoulders, now leaning in toward me.

"Hello, Charlie," I managed, clearing my throat and reluctantly opening the other eye. Sure enough, Inspector Weiler was planted in front of the desk, his shapeless sports jacket open, skinny tie skewed to one side as usual, every bone in his wiry body radiating annoyance and suspicion. "Hello, Inspector Weiler. I can explain—"

"You better believe you can explain, Ms. O'Rourke," he said. "As in right now."

The uniformed cop saved me. He probably wanted to show that he was on top of things, and so he jumped in with a report. Weiler squinted hard at me, but left me, moving over to the alcove with the cop. The EMTs were packing up their equipment, and other people were arriving, some in uniform, some not. The space was getting crowded. Charlie told me to stay put for a minute and joined everyone else peering down at Jamie's crumpled body.

I sat with my head in my hands, unwilling to cope with the knowledge that San Francisco's most powerful social-ite was dead. It would be a huge scandal. How would Fritz react? I didn't see him sitting around waiting for the police to figure out what had happened. With his bucks and influence, I could see him taking the investigation into his own hands. My imagination was conjuring up black-clad men with sunglasses and ear wires when a sharp voice jerked me to attention.

"What is going on? Who are you people? What are you doing in my office? What's wrong?" It was a lot of questions, fired like arrows at the people clustered in the room, and Victoria Peerless sounded as if she expected answers to them all immediately.

The cop who had arrived first moved swiftly toward her, his arm outstretched to keep her from seeing into the alcove. He didn't know La Peerless. She simply ignored him, marching into the center of the room, and spinning on her heel to see what was happening, her briefcase swinging wide as if it were a weapon.

The men tried to block her view with their bodies. She must have gotten a glimpse of Jamie's body because she dropped the briefcase and let out a piercing scream, then another, and another. Charlie jumped to her side, taking her arm and forcing her back in my direction, murmuring to her all the time. I jumped up to give her a place to sit. I don't think she even knew I was there. Her eyes were huge, staring straight ahead, her face white.

She dropped into the chair, not screaming any more, but breathing hard. "No, no, this is not happening," she whispered. I knew how she felt.

"Dani, do you know her? Who is she?" Charlie asked me, urgency in his voice.

"She's Victoria Peerless, Jamie's personal assistant," I said, crouching down next to her. "Victoria, it's me, Dani. Try to breathe slowly, okay?" I grabbed her hand, and she jerked it away, not looking at me. She was staring hard toward the alcove, leaning forward slightly, straining in that direction.

"Ms. Peerless," Charlie said. "Ms. Peerless, I'm going to need your help. Can you focus on me for a minute?"

She turned her head slowly, blinking as if she was waking up. "Danielle," she said in a small voice, "what are you doing here? Where's Jamie? Why isn't Jamie here? She said she'd be in early."

I looked up at Charlie, raising my eyebrows. What was I supposed to say? I guessed she was in shock.

"Ms. Peerless?" Charlie said again, motioning me to move as he drew up a straight-backed chair, one of several lined up across from her desk, and sat facing her. "I need to ask you some questions. Would you like a glass of water? Dani, I mean Ms. O'Rourke, can get you one."

I looked around the room and didn't see a source. Maybe it was in the alcove, in which case, no way could I get her a glass of water. I shuddered at the idea of going two steps in that direction.

"Water. Here," Victoria said, swinging a limp arm toward the credenza behind her. Thanking the interior decorator gods, I found the discreetly tucked-away fridge, handed her a chilled bottle, and gulped from another. I wanted brandy, but right now I had too much to worry about to muddle my thinking with a strong drink. Sooner or later, Weiler would come back to me. In the meantime, Charlie might want some answers.

I was burning to give Peter a heads up on the situation. I didn't know if Jamie's death had anything to do with the Devor or the missing artifact, although coming on the heels of Rene's death, it was pretty likely, even without that cryptic note in the folder. Whoever killed her wasn't likely to be a jilted social climber who didn't get invited to the McBeels' A-list Christmas party.

Charlie asked Victoria for some basic information and if she had a number and address where Fritz could be reached right now. The noise level around us rose as two men and a woman walked in with black boxes. A cop called out to Weiler to say a florist was downstairs demanding to deliver an arrangement to the suite. Weiler sent someone down to get his name and interview him.

I didn't hear much of what Victoria was saying in almost a whisper, but I did hear someone else order people to move away from the body. I shuddered again, wishing myself far away from this place.

Glancing at the door, I saw a few curious faces peeking in, including the guy who let me in the building earlier. He was staring at me. Building tenants, I figured, wondering about the commotion. Charlie said my name, and I turned back.

"Dani, I'm sending two guys over to the McBeels' house right now. Is there anything I should know about him or his household before we hit him with the bad news?"

I shook my head. "They don't have kids. A butler and a housekeeper live there, and there's usually some help around. You should call Wayne Lawson, who heads up his charitable foundation. I think they're pretty close. In fact, Wayne's office is in this suite, across the hallway. Has he come in yet?"

"No one else who works in this suite has come in yet," Charlie said, glancing down at La Peerless. Her body was rigid, her hands clutching the plastic water bottle. As I watched, a tear slid out of one eye and trickled down her face. All of a sudden, I felt the tragedy from her perspective. Her behavior always suggested a fierce loyalty to her boss, identification with Jamie's wealth and power, and pride in her position as Jamie's closest aide.

I walked back around the desk and put my hands gently on her shoulders. She stiffened a little, but this time she didn't pull away. "Victoria, I'm so sorry about this. Is Fritz back in San Francisco? They need to tell him what's happened," I said softly.

"No," she said, in a voice that threatened to break. "He didn't come back in their plane when she did."

Charlie nodded and went over to confer with Weiler, then left the office.

"They had an argument," Victoria said in the same whispery voice, almost to herself. "She told me to book her into Rancho la Puerta for a weeklong spa session. 'That'll keep him out of my face for a while,' she said. I was going to do the booking this morning. I only needed to know if she wanted the same villa this time." Victoria exhaled raggedly.

I was still absorbing this when Charlie got back. He had just begun to speak to us when Weiler called to him.

"Hey, Sugerman. Over here. You should see this." A tall, lanky woman with a gray ponytail rose to her feet. She had gloves and booties on and in one hand she held a small piece of paper, which she showed Weiler and Charlie. She pulled a transparent bag from a box and dumped the paper in it before handing it to Charlie.

He surprised me by bringing it over to where La Peerless and I were parked.

"Either of you know a guy named Simon Anderson?"

His eyebrows shot up when both of us gasped.

"He couldn't be involved," I said with conviction.

"He wouldn't hurt anyone," Victoria said at the same time in a wavering voice.

"So, I guess you both know him," Charlie said. "The card says 'Explore! Television,' so I'm guessing he's the smooth talker with the pith helmet I see on the Discovery Channel when I'm eating my dinner? Are you ladies fans or do you actually know the guy? Dani?"

"I know him," I said, moving around to the other side of the desk and sitting in the chair Charlie had vacated. "In fact, we had dinner in New York last week."

Victoria looked at me with more focus than she had previously shown. A frown line on her forehead and a pursed mouth comforted me in a funny way. She looked more like the Peerless I knew.

"Where did you find his card?" I asked Charlie.

He was being a cop, which means you never answer anyone's questions. I remembered now. Until further notice, I was a suspect.

"Do either of you ladies know where Simon Anderson might be now?"

We shook our heads in unison. Then I remembered.

"He said he was coming back to San Francisco after our gala dinner. I don't know when."

Simon's business card in Jamie's office didn't make him a murder suspect. The baggie routine was serious, though. It must have been on the floor in the alcove. Could it have fallen out of the file folder that was, um, in my tote bag at this moment? Could I go to jail for evidence theft? If I could go to jail for an empty folder, what punishment might I get for pocketing the key?

Weiler was deep in conversation with another man who had shown up and who was kneeling next to Jamie. They both looked hard at me, Weiler folding his lips in and out and squinting. He called Charlie over, and the tones of their voices suggested they were arguing. Weiler finally shrugged and turned back to the other man, and Charlie walked the few steps back to us, frowning.

After asking me to give him the precise time of my arrival and what exactly I did from the moment I entered the building, Charlie told me I could go for now, which actually made me feel more guilty. He said he needed Victoria to help the police search the office to see if anything was missing, if she was up to it, and to review her appointment book and phone messages. Uh-oh. Would she realize a key was missing? A folder? I had a monster headache, a lump in my throat, and a parking ticket when I reached my car. All before noon. Taken together, a bad day that I knew was going to get worse as word of Jamie's sudden death got out.

» » »

By the end of the day, it was big news. Peter called an emergency meeting of the board's executive committee, which I jointly staff. The police had warned me not to make any comment about the murder scene, and Peter agreed to protect me if anyone asked questions. He invited Tom Burns, who was looking frazzled, to sit in.

Peter confirmed that the FBI was now involved in the search for the vessel, as was an investigator hired by the insurance company. Apparently, McBeel's foundation had insured it for five million dollars.

I did a brief report on the Devor's outstanding business with Jamie and Fritz. Geoff Johnson, the board chair, reported that his wife, Louise, our brave dinner chairperson, had called the McBeels' house and confirmed that Fritz was still in their New York apartment. McBeel planned to fly back to San Francisco as soon as his private jet touched down in New York to pick him up.

All San Francisco was buzzing, and why not? I could see the headlines—LEADER OF HIGH SOCIETY MURDERED IN DOWNTOWN OFFICE. Even Teeni, never Jamie's greatest fan, was shaken. Sitting in my office after the meeting, she said, "Somehow, you think people like that are protected, you know? It's not like they're going to get caught in gang cross-fire while they're walking back from the 7-Eleven. Who had what in for her? Leave out the small stuff—jealousy of her position, irritation at being outside the charmed circle. That African ambassador looked angry, but I'm betting he's keeping his comfortable United Nations seat warm today."

"Agreed," I said. "She could have interrupted a burglar. Frankly, my biggest fear is it's related to Rene's death and therefore to the missing jar."

"Why do you think that?"

I couldn't tell her about the title on the file folder, much less about the key. "Too much for coincidence," I said, shrugging. "Think about it. She and Rene traveled in the same circles for one reason only—Fritz's interest in and support of African archaeology. Within a couple of weeks, the vessel's gone and they're both dead."

"You may be right. I don't—"

My phone rang, and I waved Teeni away as the attorney for an elderly man considering a six-figure gift began quizzing me on annuity payout rates, not my strength. I could have put him off or routed him to the planned giving officer, but it was a relief to have a conversation with someone who didn't start by asking me for gossip about San Francisco's number one news item. Anything that took my mind off the scene in Jamie's office for even a few minutes helped.

When we finished going over the pros and cons, it was after six. I set the office phone to take messages, grabbed my tote bag, and joined other staffers headed down in the elevator. I was so intent on getting home fast so I could look at my stolen clues that I didn't see Charlie until I almost bumped into him. He was leaning on my car in the lot behind the museum.

"Where did you come from?" I blurted.

"Thought I'd waylay you privately," he said. "We need to talk."

"Okay. What about? Want to come to my apartment?" I blushed. "That came out wrong."

He laughed. "I knew you were only being polite. Anyway, this is business, as you probably guessed. Let's take a walk." He steered me out of the parking lot and toward Mission Street. We didn't speak again until we were across the street and on the paved path in Yerba Buena Park, the Martin Luther King Jr. Memorial waterfall noisy in the background.

"First," he said, "We're pretty sure you're not a suspect. You haven't strangled anyone lately, have you?"

"Is that how Jamie died? How horrible."

"It is, and if you tell a soul, I will personally arrest you and throw you in jail with San Francisco's most aggressive ladies of the night."

"Promise," I said, although the picture he painted was intriguing, like a piece of conceptual art. Even thinking like that was evidence that my brain was skittering around stupidly. *Focus*, I told myself.

"Okay, then. We need you to give us a minute-by-minute rerun of your visit to the foundation office, and I do mean detailed. It was too crowded in there this morning to conduct a thorough interview."

Jamie's distorted face floated in front of me, weighing me down almost as much as my dishonesty did.

"I already did that twice, once for the first policeman who arrived and again for you," I said, not thrilled at the idea of recalling the scene in detail all over again.

"Weiler wants to be there when I go through it with you, to make sure I don't miss anything. Frankly, I think he's unhappy that we've seen each other a few times. Like I'm going to get so distracted I miss something, which is, of course, ridiculous."

Indeed. I had been trying my best to distract him for months. I could have told Weiler he had nothing to fear.

"We'd also like to borrow what you're wearing today to make sure you didn't contaminate the scene, or it contaminate you."

"Fine," I said, beginning to panic. Would they ask me if I took something? Would La Peerless realize the folder and key were gone? Was I about to commit perjury? What had I done, and should I confess all to my green-eyed hero?

"I told Weiler we could count on you to help." I looked away, at the banners advertising YBCA. If anyone can sense a guilty look, a cop can. I'm sure they get training for it. I lamented having left my sunglasses in the car, although, since the sun had disappeared over the hills to the west, wearing them might have made him suspicious.

"Do you want me to go home now and change?"

"Yes, we'd appreciate it. If you'd put your clothes and shoes in these separate plastic bags, and I'll take them to the station. Oh, we'll need you to come in tomorrow, too." He handed me the small package he had been carrying.

"Somehow, I feel like a suspect."

"We need to go over what you saw and did again. It's routine. I thought, frankly, that you wouldn't be happy having us come to your office. You know, gossip?"

"I know gossip," I said. "Thanks. I don't think anyone there sees me as the killer type. I appreciate it, though. I might have to shift a meeting or two if you want me in early."

We walked back to my car. His was parked nearby and he followed me home, waiting outside while I bagged up my slacks, jacket, and shoes.

It was dark, and the air smelled sweetly of jasmine when I came out of my building in sweats and sneakers. He was leaning on the car, smiling.

"Here you go," I said, wishing I had the nerve to invite him up for a glass of wine. He'd probably say he couldn't drink on duty or something. There was a touch of Dudley Do-Right in my green-eyed cop, darn it. So I was surprised when he looked around, ducked down, and kissed me almost furtively. A nice kiss, longer than friendly, over way too soon.

"Bye," he said, grinning. "See you tomorrow," leaving me in a minor state of shock.

When I had replayed the romantic moment as many times as I could, I gave up trying to figure out what it meant and settled into the couch with the folder and the key at last, determined to wrestle some useful information out of them about the missing vessel. "NEXT STEPS, CEL.JAR" sounded promising. I flipped open the folder. There were the light pencil markings that led me to grab it: "Can Simon trust Tom?" I looked all over the folder, but there was nothing else, only this little bit of script.

Whose question was it, and what did Simon need to trust our curator about? Simon and Tom were coauthors of the catalog, although I wasn't too sure what that translated to specifically. Tom was the scholar, and I figured he had the major role in developing the theme and the scope of the coffee table volume. Simon was probably better at writing for non-scholarly audiences, and he had great instincts about how to get people excited about science. The note might refer to the issue of editorial control if the two of them didn't agree on how a topic should be covered.

Tom hadn't given me any clue that he and Simon were having problems working together. He was obviously upset about the artifact being missing, but I hadn't gotten the feeling he was holding anything back in our discussions about it.

I remembered him asking about paying a ransom, however. For some reason, that hadn't felt right. The Devor's curator and I were on the same team when it came to getting the treasure back it, weren't we?

I thought about calling Simon but first I needed to think about how I wanted to handle it. I could hardly say I found his name in a folder I stole from underneath Jamie McBeel's body.

I turned my attention to the key. It was too small for a door lock, and it had a four-digit number stamped into it. Nothing else, no key manufacturer's name or logo. Could be a bank safe deposit box, a padlock key, or a locker key. The obvious suspicion was that it was the key to a storage place where the jar was hiding. Without more information, though, that didn't help much. Could be anywhere in the world—San Francisco, New York, an African airport.

Who owned the key? Rene? I remembered Rene's face, twisted with anger, as he blasted Simon. If Rene were going to spirit the jar away, he'd hardly ask Simon, so the notation wouldn't fit. Jamie? The folder was in her office. If Jamie stole the jar, she might involve Simon, especially if they were lovers. In a worst-case scenario, the reference to Tom could explain his comment about a ransom. But the Devor hadn't received a ransom demand and, anyway, Jamie hardly needed money.

I considered talking to Tom directly, but the fact that two people with some connection to the King's Jar had died already was a powerful warning. I'm no super hero. I brake for cats, and I faint easily.

I promised myself that I would get the key and the folder into Charlie's hands quickly, preferably without having to say that I took them from the crime scene. If I could deliver answers at the same time, I'd feel less guilty. Friends or not, there was no way I could ask Fritz why Wayne insisted that the Devor accept the gift formally on the same day Rene Bouvier died. But Victoria Peerless, being Jamie's personal assistant and self-described right hand, might know a great deal about her boss's reasons for giving us the opposite directive.

Time to make Victoria Peerless my new best friend.

chapter 13

IT'S NOT POSSIBLE to sleep when you've seen what I saw in Jamie's office. I got up a dozen times during the night, mostly to escape the onset of nightmares that even the memory of Charlie's sweet kiss couldn't overpower. I finally fell asleep as the sky was beginning to get light. The phone woke me.

"I know it's early, but please, please call me," Suzy's voice said into the machine when I didn't pick up right away.

Dragging it from the bedside table, I mumbled, "Hey, Suze, no need to shout. I'm here. What's up. What time is it, anyway?"

"It's after eight. I honestly thought you'd be up by now. I heard you found Jamie McBeel dead in her office. I can't believe it."

Suzy would have gone on for a long time like that if I hadn't sat bolt upright and yelled into the phone, "What do you mean you heard that? Where?"

"On the radio, the top of the hour local news, just now. Why? Isn't it true?"

"No. Yes. I mean, that's not the point. No one told me they were going to make that public," I shouted. Had someone from the Devor leaked it? Who would do something like that to me?

"Suzy, I'm sorry. You surprised me is all. I'm still groggy. Didn't sleep well. And I never thought anyone but the police and a few people at the office would know. This is awful."

"Okay, calm down," Suzy said. "Talk to me while you make coffee. Are you okay, I mean physically? You didn't have to fight off a killer this time, did you?"

The reminder of my last disastrous blunder into a nasty scene made me shudder. "No way. I didn't even know she'd been murdered until...oh, wait. I'm not supposed to say anything specific, Suzy. Charlie—"

"Charlie Sugerman's involved? Your Charlie?"

Before she could go on, I interrupted, promising to call her back once I was showered, coffee'd, and at my desk at the Devor. She wasn't happy, but she promised to keep her cell phone handy and told me to stay safe.

As I pulled the front door of my condominium building shut behind me forty-five minutes later, it occurred to me that Simon hadn't been in touch since news of Jamie's death went public. Odd, since he loved gossip. I wasn't sure what I wanted to share with Simon or how to bring up my questions about his possible involvement in the business of the missing artifact, but he'd probably call soon, so I had to think about it right away.

I turned to walk down the steps and did a double take. A white panel truck with the logo of a local TV station was parked across the street, its roof-mounted satellite dish lording it over the line of cars. As I watched, a woman reporter I recognized walked around the truck from the back, smoothing her dark hair with one hand, juggling a microphone and an earpiece with the other.

She must have heard I was the person who found Jamie. We met on the steps as the satellite truck for another station pulled up and parked at the fire hydrant. The young man who jumped out, shrugging on a sports jacket as he loped over to us, wasn't any happier to see her than she was to see him. Their separate cameramen lumbered up, equipment balanced on their shoulders, chatting more amiably with each other than the reporters.

With two microphones in my face and cameras recording my hair blowing around my head, I tried to look compassionate and serious instead of how I felt—nervous and off balance. The reporter did her best to trip me up and get me to say something about what I saw. I didn't even confirm that I was at Jamie's office, only that her death was a tragedy and the police were investigating.

By this time, the neighbors, the dog walkers, and the passing cars had become an audience. Yvette, my charming French Canadian neighbor, was not at home or a new TV star might have been born, which probably would have saved me lots of trouble unless she got excited and told them about my previous brush with criminals. I finally extricated myself, mostly by being so unresponsive to their questions, and succeeded in driving away.

The rest of the day was a blur. Peter and I met for thirty minutes so I could brief him on the media chasing me. We decided he needed to send something to the entire Devor staff directing them not to talk to anyone about either of the McBeels and call Geoff Johnson to alert him to the new media attention. We agreed I'd be escorted by a Devor security guard to and from my car for now. I even got a VIP parking spot close to the private entrance, which only proves that every cloud has a silver lining.

Someone from Inspector Weiler's office called and asked me to come to the station the next day instead of right now.

I could pick up my clothes then. Whatever. How likely was it that I'd choose them ever again? ("Oh, I think I'll wear this great outfit I was wearing when I found a dead person.") The caller also told me they had some new information and would appreciate my assistance evaluating it. Great, now I could worry myself sick about the key and the folder. The new information might be Victoria Peerless saying she left the folder right on Jamie's desk. Could I be in any more trouble?

Simon finally called as I was scowling at an upbeat report on the progress of the annual fund. He was eager to know what was going on, and there was drama in his voice as he told me how horrified he was to hear Jamie was dead. He told me he would have called sooner, but he had been under the gun to sign off on a script for next season's TV show so the production team could begin scouting locations.

I told him I'd been under siege and we agreed to meet at a tacqueria deep in the Mission District where we were unlikely to bump into anyone with a microphone and a news deadline.

» » »

By six o'clock, I was dragging. Simon met me with a crooked smile and outstretched arms, hugging me close. "Poor Dani," he murmured, patting my back. It was tempting to be "poor Dani," but something in me rebelled. Pulling away, I smiled and shook my head.

"Poor Jamie. Poor Rene. Poor Peter Lindsey, wondering what will happen to his expensive archaeology exhibit. I'm only the hired help, hoping we get the prize back in one piece. And," I added, "poor Fritz. I understand he wasn't in town when it happened."

We took our places at the end of a line of restless gourmets waiting for one of the city's best-rated cheap meals. In less than a minute, we weren't the last in the line that shuffled forward eagerly.

"I talked with him this afternoon," Simon said. "He's back already."

"Uh-huh. The private jet. How did he sound?"

"You know. Same old Fritz. Slightly distant, rambling a bit, doing his best stiff upper lip thing but without the British accent."

"Have the police told him anything?"

"If they have, he wasn't sharing it with me. He did say the funeral will be at Grace Cathedral. Invitation only, I gather."

"Are you invited?"

"Of course." Simon turned to me, eyebrows arched in fake surprise.

"Wonder if the Devor staff, well, Peter and me at least, will get the call. I'd like to pay my respects and see if I can substitute a more dignified memory for the one I have."

"It will be quite an event. Fritz said they're flying in the Westminster Boys Choir." He did that thing with the eyebrows again.

"You're not serious."

"Yup. The whole team working in Africa's on its way back, too. Fritz wants a major show of loyalty, I think."

"Loyalty to…?"

"Him, probably, as their benefactor."

We had reached the order counter and, as I always do, I ordered far more than I could—well, should—eat, the aroma of fresh chopped cilantro making my mouth water. We picked up our beers and beat out another couple for a tiny table in the corner. I sat facing the wall in case the reporters who tracked me to my house got a sudden urge for fajitas and black beans.

"Fritz says you—" he leaned forward and lowered his voice, "found the body?"

I took a huge bite of my burrito and used the chewing time to decide how much I should tell Simon. One, he was a known gossip. Two, his name was in the folder. Three, he was a journalist. But he was a friend.

My honest self told me I had killed any possible future with Charlie and couldn't unburden myself to him now. My dearest friend Suzy was loyal but loved to share everything she knew, which meant, realistically, I couldn't confide in her. Teeni was great but, bottom line, she not only worked for me, but for the Devor. I'd put her in an ethical bind if I shared confidential information with her. I needed to think out loud with someone, and my cat wouldn't do.

"I'm not sure how Fritz knew. We haven't spoken."

"I guess the cops told him. He asked if you were doing all right. Are you?"

"Simon, if I tell you something, you have to promise it's off the record and that you won't tell anyone, and I mean anyone, what I say." I fixed him with an I'm-serious frown and felt a dribble of hot sauce work its way down my chin.

His eyes gleamed as he reached across the table to wipe the sauce off. "Word of honor, Dani. I'm good at keeping secrets."

Ah, yes, the scribbled note on the file. If I could figure out how, I'd ask him indirectly about that. So I told Simon about the scene at Jamie's office, leaving out the folder, the key, and the marks on Dani's throat since Charlie had threatened me with jail time if I gave that information out. I described Victoria Peerless's shock, the arrival of the homicide team, and the total unreality of seeing the powerful, energetic Jamie lying so still and defenseless. The burrito sat neglected as I slid back into that place and time. At some point, Simon reached over and held my hand.

"You knew her, didn't you?" I said abruptly. "You told me you didn't, but that wasn't true. You had some kind of relationship." I was remembering vividly his hand on Jamie's arm as they came out of the Pilgrim Club reception room, and the closeness it implied.

Slowly, Simon sat back in his chair, releasing my hand and frowning slightly. "I knew her, of course. Their foundation was an underwriter for the TV series. You knew that."

I shook my head. "No, actually, I didn't. I thought you said you met her only once. So, did that mean you got to know Jamie through the TV show?"

"I'm not sure what you mean. I didn't know her well. We— Jamie and Fritz and I—met for dinner once. He wanted to talk about Kenobia, where he had his great adventures. She had zero interest in his tales of Africa, but she pressed me for stories about the filming I did in exotic locations. Stalking lions at night, stuff like that. Her only interest in Fritz's experiences in Africa was how much his prize purchases were worth. At least…"

Simon's voice trailed off, and he took a long swig of beer. When he set the bottle down again, his eyes didn't meet mine. Instead, he checked his watch.

"Hey, I'm sorry. I have to leave soon. I have a conference call with some guys in New York."

"Fine," I said, "but first, finish that sentence. At least what?"

He glanced up. "Sorry, Dani. I was about to give up someone else's privacy, and I wouldn't be much of a pal if you couldn't trust me not to share something you told me in confidence, right?" The eyebrows sprang into action.

"This is serious, Simon."

"I'm going to be grilled by the detectives tomorrow. I'll tell them anything I think is relevant to their investigation. But I'm not ready to be cross-examined by anyone else, much less someone I consider to be a special friend."

I couldn't decide whether to be flattered or suspicious that he was trying to soften me up. After a few seconds, I opened my mouth to argue, but stuffed in a couple of chips instead, reminding myself I wasn't here to pry into a murder.

"Fair enough," I said. "But I'm worried because the jar is still missing, and the Devor has to do something. We're in an awkward spot, and I don't believe for a minute that Rene's and Jamie's deaths are coincidental. If his was related to the theft of the artifact, so was hers. But how? And is it possible she knew where the jar was—where it still is?" There, I got the question out, even if it was kind of indirect. I needed to pick up some kind of clue about what the little key opened.

It was Simon's turn to hide behind a mouthful of food, his eyes drifting past my shoulder to the noisy scene around us. After he swallowed, he focused on my face and there was no more sparkle in his eyes. His words were clipped, and he exhaled sharply.

"Listen, Dani. It will turn up. It's too valuable to be destroyed, too singular to resell, and too arcane to interest the big time antiquities crooks. You'll get it in the end. But," he said, his voice rising along with his hand to silence the question I was about to ask, "for now, I suggest you go back to chatting up little old ladies about their wills. Stop playing detective and stick to what you know best. Take my word for it and don't get messed up in this stuff. Now, I really do have to go."

And he was up and out of the restaurant before I could think of a suitable reply. No good-bye hug, not even a smile. I turned to look for him, but he had already disappeared.

The excellent burrito was a lump in my stomach as I headed home. He had hurt my feelings with his comments about my job. I didn't much like him saying I was "playing" detective, either. Something I said had triggered his anger, but what? It had to be my question about Jamie knowing where the missing jar was. I was onto something, maybe the meaning of the cryptic note on the file folder. Interesting that Simon wanted me to stop pursuing the subject.

Which brought me back to the key I couldn't tell the police about. If I couldn't talk to anyone about the key, what good did it do me to have it? If I couldn't provide any useful information along with its return, I was scared to let Charlie and his partner know I had taken it in the first place. I had to figure out the key's secret quickly and get it into the hands of the police without incriminating myself. Victoria Peerless might know the key was missing. If she did, I'd bet my Jimmy Choos she knew what it was for.

Meanwhile, could I manage to get a little private time with Fritz McBeel to see what, if anything, he suspected about the coincidence of his wife's death and the disappearance of the King's Jar? I'd say that Jamie's conflicting instructions about signing the papers still needed to be resolved.

The picture of Fritz and Obarri with their heads together at the New York gala dinner came back to me. Were they arguing about the jar? I might get some hint by mentioning to Fritz that I'd seen them together.

Good. I had a couple of items to check out. Little old ladies, hah. If Simon thought that was all I could handle, he was in for a surprise.

» » »

Never mind raising money for the museum. My checklist now included taking Victoria Peerless to lunch, getting face time with Fritz McBeel in his hour of grief, and seeing if the key I found was anything like the one I had for my own bank deposit box. I still had to go to the police station for a repeat of my account of the morning of Jamie's death. But first, I had to talk with Peter.

Teeni brought a stack of newspaper stories that darkened my mood. None mentioned the lost treasure, thank heavens. Peter had given a flattering quote about Jamie to the local paper, and they included most of it with a photo of him, Jamie, Fritz, and Geoff Johnson at a party we held last year. Innocuous. Not quite as innocuous when it came to "Devor executive allegedly found body."

Fortunately, at least for me right now, San Francisco, once a great newspaper town, was limping along with one understaffed morning paper.

Peter's assistant called to say the great man was ready to see me. "Hey, Peter," I said as I entered his office. In an alcove where he could lift his head at any moment and gaze at it was one of my favorite Diebenkorns. Actually, all of Richard Diebenkorn's paintings are my favorite Diebenkorns. I nodded at it and turned my attention to Peter. "I don't know how you get any work done with that killer painting doing its thing over there."

"Hmmm," he said, his head bent over some papers. He scribbled his signature on a couple of letters, ran his finger down the margin of a spreadsheet before initialing it, and swept a small pile of pink message slips to one side, all in a ⸱ matter of seconds.

"Come, sit," he said, jumping up and waving me over to a group of sofas and chairs bigger by far than my living room, with window walls that faced north. If there hadn't been an ugly, metal-clad high rise in the way, I could have seen the top of Nob Hill and more of the blue sky framing the city.

Dorie walked in, her high heels clicking briskly, to pick up the letters and ask if we wanted croissants and coffee.

"I'm headed over to North Beach to be grilled by the cops about Jamie's death," I said, shaking my head. "The last thing I need is a caffeine and sugar rush to make me more nervous than I am already."

Peter looked at me. Running his hands through his wavy brown hair, he said, "What do you have to be nervous about, Dani? You aren't involved." His handsome face contracted in mock horror, or, at least I thought it was mock.

"I am, in a way. I found her, for God's sake. And I had an appointment to meet her." *And stole important evidence from her office that might implicate one of our senior staff members*, I added silently.

"Well, that's not personal, not really. I mean, it's not like you were friends." He put verbal quote marks around the word.

I reported on the media interest, leaving out any suggestion I hide under my desk or in Croatia for a few weeks, but making it clear the Devor needed to distance itself from the murder quickly.

"Here's the thing, Peter," I said, "Jamie's death isn't our business except that she was demanding we not accept the gift, remember? And since we haven't had time to debrief from the New York dinner, I haven't told you about the hostilities between her and Kenobia's ambassador. I'm sure it had something to do with who owned the object. The last thing we want is to find ourselves in a pissing contest with a poor but noble African country that wants its heritage back."

Peter shook his head. "That cannot happen. Oh, I meant to ask you—was Lawson there when you found Jamie?"

"No, at least not when I arrived. Why do you ask?"

"I'm remembering that his office is across the hall. If he'd been there, maybe this wouldn't have happened."

"Um," I answered, suddenly remembering the sound I had heard from somewhere else in the suite that had made me think someone might be around to help. I had to tell the police about that. "I was too shocked to pay much attention when I left, and the place was crawling with cops. Why? Has he called you?"

"Nope, nada. Good point. I need to call him. I'll do it right away. Do you think Tom Burns would slit his wrists if we cancelled this exhibition?" Peter said, hunched over his plate, crumbs dropping from the corners of his mouth.

"No, but he'd leave the Devor faster than you can eat that pastry. Are you kidding? It would start a whisper campaign in the museum community about our management of donors and our capabilities to take care of important materials. No way."

"Okay, okay, I was kidding," he said, his voice rising and taking on a nasal edge. "I'd better talk to Tom, to see what he recommends doing at this stage. Please don't tell me it's too late to make changes? We'll have to revise the show and the catalog if the piece doesn't show up soon."

"You're sure you haven't gotten any hints that someone has it?" I said. "Nothing from the FBI or the insurance people that would give us hope we can get it back somehow?"

"Not a word, scout's honor. You're thinking ransom? Yeah, so was I. The FBI's coached me on what to do if I do hear from someone, but they haven't picked anything up, and I give you my word there's nothing like that happening here. I wish it was that easy."

I nodded. "Thanks for sharing. About the catalog, I'm sure it will cost, but we'll do what we have to when the time comes if we have to. Maybe you need to meet with Tom and develop a Plan B?"

"I'm hoping Simon's around, too," Peter said. "I'd like to talk to him. I still have a weird feeling about how Fritz wound up with this significant object. You're scaring me with your talk about unhappy Kenobian diplomats. I know the lawyers have signed off, and Tom says he hasn't been warned off having the Devor accept the gift by his peers in the archaeology museum community. And, Tom says, as of today, the field team from Rene's group is en route to the dig in Kenobia, so we can't ask them to revisit the history."

"Most of the crew is too young to have been in Kenobia then," I said. "Simon is in San Francisco, though. I saw him yesterday. In fact, he told me the American crew's on the way back from Kenobia. Fritz wants everyone at the funeral. You going?"

"Of course. You?" he said, glancing up from his pastry and flicking off a crumb.

"I wasn't invited," I said.

"Oh, sure you are. You're coming with me. Well, hold on. Maybe not with me. I saw the Channel Three news story."

"Ouch," I said, my head throbbing. "I'm hoping it will blow over since we're not commenting at all."

"Fair enough. Let's wait 'til closer to the day to decide if you come to the funeral, though. Meanwhile, give me Simon's cell number. I'm assuming you have it?"

"Sure, but what do you think any of these people can or will tell you that you don't already know?"

"Simon talks a good game, but I always feel he's not telling the whole story. I'd like to ask him some tough questions about the time he was in Kenobia with Rene's team."

"Yeah, well, I tried that when we had dinner in New York and it went nowhere," I said. "What is it you want to know?"

"Were papers forged to get the thing out disguised as a less important artifact? Was Obarri paid off to look the other way? Does the prime minister know? All the things that can come back and bite us should this issue get any hotter."

"Not too much, huh? I don't see Simon answering any of those questions if they might implicate him. Are you suggesting Simon might have been party to a scandalous international theft?"

And, if so, I asked myself, *had Rene also been part of the same scheme to smuggle a prime artifact out of Kenobia while Obarri was guarding the store?* Even if I knew the answers, it left the big question unanswered. Did Jamie, who wasn't even in the picture in those days, know something so dangerous that someone killed her?

"No, at least I don't think so. Any chance you can have another dinner and dig more?"

"I'll try. No promises. He did say he'd call in a few days."

"So call him," Peter suggested, cocking his head and giving me a cheerleader's face.

"I said I'll try, Peter." It would be easier for me to call him on Peter's behalf, but still hard, given our last conversation. "Want to come along?"

"Nah. I think he's taken with you, Mata Hari. I saw him smooching you at the Pilgrim Club. You'll do better on your own."

I opened my mouth to protest, decided it wasn't worth the hot air, and left my boss scooping up a batch of spreadsheets to go over with the finance VP, who hurried in as I walked to the elevator.

chapter 14

TWENTY MINUTES AND two extra-strength Tylenols later, I wedged my car into the packed garage next door to the police station at Powell and Vallejo streets and threaded my way past the doubled-parked police cars that littered the pavement outside headquarters. The street was like this day or night, given that the station was wedged between Chinatown and North Beach, two of the most congested and tourist-filled neighborhoods in the city.

I was feeling the signs of stress as I mounted the outside steps, everything from pounding temples to sweaty palms. Part of me wanted to unburden myself of my illegal actions at this meeting. That part had put the folder and the key, retaped where I'd found it, into my tote bag with the goal of explaining what I'd done in some way that wouldn't result in jail time. The rest of me had a hundred reasons to hold on to it for now, including avoiding jail time. Victoria—and what she identified as missing—were the biggest reason to hold back or to fish it out of my bag when I saw Charlie.

The desk sergeant told me Charlie was due any minute. In the meantime, Weiler had told him to have someone escort me up to their office. A uniformed policewoman whose battle against extra weight was going even more badly than mine marched me down the dirty corridor to the elevator without a word. Stabbing the floor button with a thick finger, she looked down at the elevator floor until the doors opened again and shouldered her way out in front of me.

"Inspector, you wanted to see her?" she said as she leaned into the crowded room. Before I could thank her, she was clumping back to the elevator.

"So," Inspector Weiler said, "you're mixed up in a murder again. Why am I not surprised?"

"'Mixed up' is hardly the right term for it," I said, forcing myself not to sound bitchy. "Shaken up, horrified, sad that a patron of the arts has been brutally killed, yes."

He gestured me into the same stuffy little conference room I'd been in before, squeezed into a corner of the four-person office. Weiler offered me coffee and tossed his notebook on the plastic tabletop as he eased into a chair.

"Okay, then, if you're just an outraged citizen who happened to be on the scene, you won't mind running through what happened so we can find the real bad guy."

I couldn't tell if Weiler was being sarcastic or giving me a hard time for the hell of it. I tried not to show my impatience as he walked me through everything again, from the time I got the phone message to the moment he arrived at the McBeel Foundation office. I've seen enough cop shows to know they look for inconsistencies, and I was careful to tell it the same way I did the first time, especially when it came to withholding the fact that I took evidence from Jamie's office. I was fast realizing how hard this was going to be. Not to mention that, if I admitted what I'd done, Charlie and I would be history. Not that we were news right now.

Charlie walked in as I finished repeating my story.

"Good news," he said to Weiler. "They picked up the guy we were looking for, trying to sell a quarter bag to an undercover over on Ashby Avenue. He's on his way back to the city right now, courtesy of the Berkeley cops."

"Excellent. After we're finished here, let's see if he still says he never leaves the Tenderloin."

Charlie nodded as he pulled out a spindly metal chair and wedged his six-foot-two self into it. "So, have you already told Dani why we need her help?"

Was there a chance I could trade my help for amnesty on the folder?

"Here's the deal," Charlie said, smiling at me with those mesmerizing eyes. "We seem to be running in all directions. There's the researcher's murder. There's a missing piece of history, may have been stolen, which is not, strictly speaking, Homicide's problem except that Fritz McBeel is leaning on the chief for help in that investigation, and the chief leans on us. Then, there's the FBI, and they're good at leaning, too, when they're not leaving us out of the loop. To top it off, Mrs. McBeel is killed right in our backyard, and the media's all over this one."

I nodded, listening for where I came in and hiding my shaking hands in my lap.

"By the way," Charlie added, his face serious but his eyes sparkling, "you did good on TV except for the way you were glaring daggers at the reporter."

Weiler stirred in his chair. "Now," he said, "it gets kinky. McBeel's telling us he thinks some old acquaintances might have killed his wife. Turns out we've got to look at a couple of Africans from a country that doesn't have a local consulate. We're trying to coordinate with the New York City police, but they could care less. No crime on their turf, and they're always going twenty-four/seven with their own stuff."

"What's this got to do with me?"

Weiler spoke first. "We figure you or someone at the Devor must know something about the place the thingama-bob came from. We need to know how to reach these folks. McBeel is telling the chief he thinks the Africans might be pissed at him and his wife for not offering to give it back to them."

This was exactly what Peter and Tom didn't want to hear.

My mind flashed back to the tense conversation between Jamie and Ambassador Obarri at the New York dinner. Fritz could be right. If Obarri believed Jamie knew who stole the King's Jar from Rene, he could have sent someone to threaten her. The key, though, had been in a folder so near Jamie's body that anyone would surely have seen it and grabbed it. That is, if he had the time before I scared him off.

But he could have taken the contents of the file. I hadn't stopped to consider what might have been in the folder. If people were planning to steal the artifact, they'd hardly incriminate themselves by creating a folder to document the crime.

"Ambassador Obarri is easy to reach through his delega-tion, and he's the only Kenobian contact I have. I'll email his secretary's number to you as soon as I get back to the office," I said. "I noticed Obarri and Jamie weren't exactly friendly at the black-tie dinner. They mentioned the King's Jar, and Jamie said it would turn up, but neither said anything spe-cific. He was smooth and she was frosted, but what about? I don't have a clue." I repeated as much of the short conversa-tion as I remembered.

"All right," Weiler said, tapping his plastic pen on his notebook. "That could square with what McBeel said."

"Maybe," I said. "But I saw Obarri and Fritz in close con-versation a little later. They seemed on unfriendly terms, too."

"Any idea what they were talking about?" Charlie said.

"None. I was all the way across the room."

"Okay," Charlie said. "It's a starting place for us, anyway. Anything else you can tell us about any of this?"

An opening. I looked into those green eyes and couldn't do it. Talk to Victoria first. Then, I promised myself. So I gave them something else.

"I'm sharing this in confidence. The donors would ream me out if they knew I told you."

Both men nodded.

"There does seem to be some conflict about the Devor's legal ownership." I told them about Victoria Peerless and Wayne Lawson and how each claimed to represent one spouse, and how they were at odds over when the Devor should claim the gift.

"I'm sure it means something," Charlie said with a sigh. "But I'm damned if I know what. What do you make of it?" He turned sideways to look at Weiler, who was chewing his lip and doodling in his notepad.

"We'll need a copy of the contract," Weiler said. "Maybe something will stick out. I'm trying to figure out who's on whose side, to tell you the truth." Hah, my thoughts exactly. Had the same interested parties been chasing the artifact all along, first at Rene's lab, then in Jamie's office? "The artifact is the football in this game," he continued, "but I'm beginning to think it's a little like our gangbangers."

"How's that?" Charlie said.

"Well, think of this as teams. Let's assume, in spite of the confusion over who owned it when, that Mr. and Mrs. McBeel are on one team. The Africans and the old man are on the other because of some idea Africa should get it back.

A guy on one team gets killed, and bang—retribution. A guy on the other side gets killed."

"And they get killed because…?" Charlie sounded skeptical.

"Each side wants the ball, the thingamabob," Weiler said.

"But," I said, "who actually has the thingama—the jar? I mean, isn't that what we—I mean you—need to focus on as the clue to why people are being killed in the first place?"

Weiler shook his head. "Our job is to catch murderers. Sometimes motives help steer us to the bad guys. But the DA makes the case. We look for the perps."

So, I was on my own. Maybe I had been right to hang onto the folder after all. "That reminds me," I said, "did you find fingerprints on the chair? That would be an important piece of evidence."

They both looked at me as if I were a not-too-smart kindergartner. Neither spoke for a moment. Silly me. Had I really thought they were going to share crime scene evidence with me merely because I asked?

"Don't forget Joe Safari," Charlie said, changing the subject. "Him, I don't trust. I don't know where he fits in, but he's too smooth. I guarantee he knows something he's not telling."

Simon again. Maybe men didn't like him because he was so obviously an alpha male. "Simon said you were going to interview him. Have you asked him these questions?" I said.

"He'll be here in a couple of hours," Charlie said. "Don't worry. He'll get a chance to tell us everything he knows about this business."

"Let me go back to the big question," I said. "Why? I mean this was all supposed to be a wonderful piece of generosity, a way to ensure the future stewardship of an important part of history. The McBeels were both enthusiastic when we started talking. We were assured the Kenobians weren't a problem. Why has everything gotten so ugly?"

"Hey, I thought you were here to answer our questions." Charlie threw his notebook on the table. "Maybe we need to start all over with this investigation, get the files from the Bouvier death, and go back to McBeel with another round of questions."

"You think you can do that?" I said. "He's a powerful person, and he likes his privacy."

"He wants his wife's killer found, doesn't he?" Weiler said, his voice rising.

"Of course," I said. "But no one in his position wants to be dragged into the public spotlight of a police investigation."

"Too bad," Weiler barked. Charlie had made it clear that Fritz had clout with the police chief, though, so I would bet on Fritz in a showdown with Weiler.

"Another question for you," I said. "Peter and Tom have to meet with him as soon as possible about where we go from here with the gift. And I need to talk with people on his staff. Peter and I will be at the funeral and at the McBeels' house after. All that contact isn't a problem, is it?"

"Nope," Weiler said. "But don't discuss our conversations. In fact, I'd prefer it if you didn't mention we've been talking to you other than to take your statement. Sounds like you're not too fond of Mr. McB."

The last came out like a question. I wasn't sure how to explain my reservations about Fritz and Jamie. They were good to the Devor. Jamie had always been rude to me, but she was rude to almost everyone who wasn't royalty or writing for the society pages of something. Fritz was aloof until the evening of the gala, but polite—even if he occasionally used the royal "we" in conversation. And now he was drawing me into his circle of trusted advisors.

"No, he's all right," I said to Weiler. "But I'm a business acquaintance."

Weiler nodded.

Jamie's face, unexpectedly, swam in front of my eyes, and I was weighed down with guilt for having stolen the stuff from her office while she was—I shuddered—lying there dead.

"You chilly?" Charlie said.

"No, just thinking about finding Jamie. I don't think I'm over the shock yet."

Wayne Lawson's name had been bouncing around in my head since I mentioned him and I was seeing the empty office suite again, but remembering a feeling someone else was there. "Wait," I said. Both men turned.

"I can't remember if I mentioned this to the police at first. I have a slight—and I do mean that—impression that there could have been someone in the suite after I got there. The police arrived so quickly, and I forgot it in the confusion."

"It could be important," Charlie said.

"It wasn't anything I saw. It may have been the sound of a door closing. I know it was before I called 9-1-1, because I ran to the door and yelled for help when I heard it."

"And you didn't see anyone?" Weiler said.

"No. I can't even swear it was a door. It could have been a fax machine starting up, or even something outside the suite. Not much, I know."

After an awkward moment in which they both looked expectantly at me, and I sat there, trying to look more helpful than I felt, the three of us left the little room, Weiler heading to his desk by the window, Charlie and I to the elevator.

He pushed open the door to the street, and I ducked under his arm.

"Charlie," I said, drawing a deep breath, "have you found any papers or other things in Jamie's office that might be important?"

"You mean for solving the murder or finding your precious object?"

"Either, I guess. I was wondering if Victoria has been able to help figure out, you know, if anything's missing?"

To my ears, I sounded phony. Charlie didn't react.

"She's pretty undone by Mrs. McBeel's death," he said. "I'm seeing her again today. We need to determine who might know Mrs. McBeel was there early that morning."

"Could it have been a random killing?" I asked, trying to ignore the swooping butterflies that filled my stomach. "I got in without Jamie's help, thanks to a man who was coming to work. Maybe something like that happened and it was a robber."

"We know about the guy who let you in. He freaked out at first, thought you were the killer."

"No way. Are you serious?" I said, my voice rising to bird pitch.

"Indeed. We checked every person who had an entry key to the building and no one else let a stranger in. It's possible the vic—Mrs. McBeel—let the killer in."

"That's beyond horrible," I said. "It makes me sick."

"Well, it happens a lot. People get killed by people they know, even people they love and trust, more than you might guess."

"So," I said, realizing suddenly how far away from my question Charlie had steered us, "did Victoria notice anything missing?"

"You do keep at it, don't you?" Charlie said, grinning at me. "If I didn't know otherwise, I'd think you were a reporter. You know I can't answer questions about the investigation. We never know this early in the game what's going to be important. We're in strict gathering mode, Dani, no exceptions. Well, obviously, some exceptions because I did a bad thing and told you how Mrs. McBeel died."

"And you have my word it won't go any further."

"Still," he sighed, "nothing more. I appreciate your coming down," he said as we walked down the steps.

I cleared my throat. "It's probably not a great idea to have dinner again while this is going on, right?"

"Probably not." He turned to me with a mock frown. "If we're ever going to get beyond a first date, you need to stop showing up where people are getting themselves killed."

First date, said my inner voice. *He wants to get beyond the first date.* On another level, his comment made me realize that I have had far too many connections with people who have died in the past year. How bizarre and sad. I guess it showed on my face.

"Hey, I was only kidding," Charlie said, ducking his head a little to look at me. "I'll call you as soon as we get whoever did this, and we'll do something special. Promise."

I badly needed to unload my guilty secret and get back to my day job. Every minute I delayed confessing made the job harder, but I couldn't seem to start. My head felt like it was in a vise by now, and my hands were like ice. It was now or never. I took a deep breath. "Charlie, I have to tell you something."

A passing uniformed officer called out hello to him, and Charlie answered with a friendly insult.

"I'm not sure how to explain this," I began again, "but it's something I should have told you a lot sooner."

He looked down at me. "Sounds serious. Go ahead."

"Well, it's about—"

"Charlie, you old sumbitch," a loud male voice said practically in my ear. I jumped, and Charlie spun around.

"Frankie, I'll be damned. Where'd you come from, you old horse's ass?"

Charlie and a weather-beaten man who looked about eighty slapped each other's backs and hooted with manly laughter. They exchanged news for a minute, ignoring me until Charlie glanced my way and explained he had to escort a witness to her car.

"Sure thing, Old Green Eyes," the guy said, winking broadly. "I'm headed upstairs. See you in a few minutes."

"He's the man," Charlie said, laughing as the guy, bow-legged but spry, trotted up the steps. "Homicide cop who has come out of retirement twice to save our asses on tough cases. Knows the local drug trade better than anyone. We're using him as a consultant on a nasty double homicide near Army Street a few weeks ago. A Mexican gang, we think."

He stopped. "Oh, I interrupted you, I'm sorry. What were you saying?"

"It wasn't important," I said, trying to smile. "I'd better get back to the office."

"Yeah," he said, squinting up at the roof of the building across the street, "me, too."

The adrenaline that had been making my hands shake had evaporated, and I didn't have the strength to go through with it. I needed more Tylenol and a new plan. Jamie's face in death and the key in my bag threw a dark curtain over everything. As I huffed my way up several flights of stairs at the garage, I checked my watch. First, a visit to my bank. I wanted to know if the key was the same kind that opened a bank deposit box. Then, as soon as I got back to the office, a call to Victoria to set up something masquerading as a social visit.

» » »

Yes, the bank officer I spoke with in the Laurel Heights branch of my bank told me, it could be a safe deposit key, but not theirs. And, no, she had no idea whose it might be. "They're all alike, I think," she said.

I needed to go at it from the other end, from its owner, or its owner's agent, a.k.a. Victoria Peerless. I was a fool to think I could withhold something as important as the key from the police. I didn't have the skill or resources to track the clue down, and I was convinced it would lead to the prize, which was far more important than my own ego.

I couldn't bear to say I deliberately took it from under Jamie's dead body, like a hardened criminal. I had spent too long trying to think of a white lie that wouldn't mislead the police, but would excuse what I did. I had settled on saying I must have picked it up when I picked up my car keys, which I had dropped when I saw her body. But in the light of day, with several cups of coffee increasing my jitters, it sounded like a weak plan. It would arouse less suspicion if I could get the key back to Jamie's office, but, for that, I had to persuade Jamie's assistant to help, and that might be tough.

I needed to know if Victoria even knew the key was missing. If she knew, it might mean she knew where the jar was, or at least what was going on between Jamie, Simon, and Rene. Why wasn't she answering her phone?

Stepping off the elevator onto the Devor's fifth floor, I reminded myself it was time to put the mystery aside for a while and take care of business. Teeni, chewing on a red pen that was as bright as her lipstick, looked up from her desk when I wandered into her office and frowned. "I'm running on empty here," she said. "You know I'm supposed to be doing the final edit on the program for the Funk Art show?"

"Which happens to be the companion to your dissertation," I said. "Not too much pressure."

"Well, we're behind on planning that series of dinners you and Peter dreamed up. The first one's supposed to happen in eight weeks, and I'm out here trolling for a guest list. But I can't be spending this much time on it, Dani. I've got too much riding on my own work."

I apologized, knowing my involvement in the jar's disappearance was creating problems in the office. "I'll assign someone else to start work on the first two dinners, how about that?"

Headed back to my office with a cup of coffee, I continued to obsess about the mess I had created by taking the folder. I now believed the writing on the tab was Rene Bouvier's. It looked like the writing on the file folder I had seen in Tom's office. Tom's friend had told him an assistant said some files were missing from Rene's office. Okay, then, the file folder I stole wasn't Jamie's to begin with. How did the folder get to her office floor, and why was it empty? If Rene's killer brought it to confront her, he surely would have taken it with him when he left. Unless my arrival interrupted him.

I stopped in the hallway, frozen. Had the killer heard me? Did he know who I was? Did he suspect I might have the folder and the key?

Teeni called to me from her open door. "If you're planning on moving again, Victoria Peerless is on the line for you. Can you pick up in your office?"

I shook off the scary thought and got back to merely embarrassing ones, like asking her to help get me off the hook with Charlie.

"Have you heard anything about the police investigation?" she said after we exchanged hellos. "Do you think the police have any idea who did this horrible thing?" Her voice wobbled a little at the end, but she didn't give in to it.

"Don't know anything. How about you?"

"I had to meet a policeman at the office yesterday. They wanted to know if anything was missing, and who Mrs. McBeel saw the day before she died."

"And was anything missing?" I said, keeping my voice as casual as possible.

"Impossible to know," Victoria said. "Nothing obvious. The display of ancient Grecian rings was still on the wall in its frame, and her checkbook was in the safe. She doesn't keep a lot of valuable things in her office."

"How about stuff related to the King's Jar?"

There was a short silence. "Why would she have anything about that in her office?" Victoria said sharply. "What sort of things did you mean?"

"Nothing specific," I said hastily. *Only files and mysterious little keys*, my pesky inner voice added. "It's just that there's been violence associated with it and it would be quite a coincidence for this not to be about the stolen piece."

"The police asked the same thing," Victoria said. "But Mrs. McBeel didn't have any interest in it, as far as I know. Well," she continued when I didn't speak, "other than making sure the museum actually got the gift, as you know. She didn't like the idea that the McBeel Foundation's lawyer was so quick to decide finding it wasn't their problem as long as Mr. McBeel got a write-off for the gift."

Nice of Jamie, I thought. Since when had she cared about the Devor? "Look, Victoria, I know this is hard for you. But if it wasn't connected to the jar and Rene Bouvier's death, and it wasn't a robbery, what could it be?"

Silence again, this time punctuated by the sound of a long intake of breath. "Could we meet?" Victoria said in a voice unlike her usual commanding tone.

"Sure," I said, worried that maybe she did know about the folder and the key, maybe knew I had them and wanted to confront me directly. "I'm game for dinner some night, actually. Anything specific you want to talk about?"

"Yes, but not on the phone. Tonight, maybe?" Her speech was hurried, but the imperious tone was gone. In its place I detected anxiety. We settled on a time and place and said our good-byes.

A minute later, Teeni poked her head in the door. "Forgot to tell you that hottie, Simon Anderson, must have called you three times in the last hour. Says it's urgent. Call the man back, please, or I'll have to stop answering the phone."

Maybe to apologize for his curtness the other day? I was prepared to be gracious.

Simon answered his cell phone on the first ring.

"First, *mea culpa*. I was beyond rude last time we met. I'm worried about you getting too deeply into what looks more and more like a nasty, convoluted business. What I meant to say was, let the cops and the FBI and the insurance company track down the artifact. They deal with bad guys all the time. You're much too nice. Please forgive me?"

He gives good apology, I'll say that. After I told him I understood, which I did at least somewhat, he told me he had to go to New York for a few days to meet with his TV producers, who were pushing him hard to finish mapping out the next season so they could hire writers, directors, and crews. "Every day of delay getting started adds expense at the back end, especially when we're headed to monsoon country."

I murmured understanding.

"You haven't heard anything about the police investigation, have you?" he said. "Clues? Suspects they're questioning?"

"No," I said, wondering where this was going. "You met with them. Right? Have you heard something?"

"Nothing. I'll feel better when they arrest someone for killing poor Jamie."

Victoria had been quick to say Simon couldn't have killed Jamie when Charlie showed us Simon's business card. The bottom line: was he such an adventurer that he wouldn't hesitate to break the rules if it was to his benefit? Or, to put it another way, were my instincts about people so poor that I would consider kissing a murderer?

chapter 15

"*I KNOW WE'RE ALL* terribly distressed, and I hate to bother you, Dani." It was Louise, and it was after five. I hoped this would be a short call.

"This should be a time for you to celebrate. Having the duchess there was a huge success. I'm sure it was why there were so many pictures in the society pages afterward. And poor Jamie looked so happy in the photographs."

I made the right noises, wondering what Louise wanted.

"You remember me mentioning Mary McBeel, don't you? Fritz's first wife?"

"Yes," I said, clueless as to the direction Louise was taking.

"Well, she'd like to meet you, and I thought coffee at my house might be nice. Could you come over tomorrow morning for a little while?"

"I'd like to meet her, Louise. This is a particularly busy time—"

"A short visit. I'm sure you'll like her. Say nine-thirty?"

"I'm not really sure I—"

"It's about the King's Jar, the one that's missing," Louise blurted. "Mary wants to tell you something. But it's vitally important to be discreet, you see. Please say you'll come?"

"Is this something the police should know?" I said. "Shouldn't you be talking to Peter at least?"

"I only know she wants to meet you specifically, and that she doesn't know where it is. Let her tell you herself, please."

"Of course," I said, wondering why me. But I had to admit I was curious. The first Mrs. McBeel was never mentioned in the social columns, lived quietly as far as I could figure out, and seemed to have accepted her reduced status. Was she bitter? Resigned? About to accuse her successor of theft? I agreed to be at Louise's house in the morning, intrigued by what she might have to tell me and what I might see for myself about another woman who had been cast aside.

» » »

I wasn't ready to take a long walk by myself yet after my scare and couldn't whip up any enthusiasm for a visit to the gym, where they had probably forgotten who I was by now. So, I worked until it was time to meet La Peerless. The neighborhood bistro we had settled on was one of my favorites, on the edge of Pacific Heights with a steady clientele who treated the place like their own dining room.

"You don't look so hot," I said as we sat down. "Are you sleeping all right?"

"I like—liked—to get in early so Mrs. McBeel had everything she needed for the day arranged on her desk when she arrived. It's a habit now." The effort of saying that much apparently wore her out. She slumped a little, fingering the menu but looking past me with unfocused eyes.

Fortunately, the waiter arrived, I ordered a bottle of spicy red wine and a plate of bruschetta without asking my guest, and made small talk until the wine put a little pink in Victoria's cheeks.

When she was a little more herself, I brought up the day of the murder, although I was careful not to use the word.

"Victoria, I know the police wanted you to look at the office and see if anything was missing."

"Yes."

"And?"

Silence. Victoria was looking at me with more curiosity than I'd seen all night. "Why are you asking? You were there first, weren't you?" She was getting agitated. I wished I hadn't poured her the last glass of wine. "I need to know if you found anything, Dani," she said, locking eyes with me. "It's important."

"Me? Found anything?" I was stumbling, caught off guard by her turning the tables on me. "Why is it so important?"

Her face crumbled then, and she cupped her hand over her eyes.

"She wanted me to find it, I know she did," she almost whispered.

"Find what?"

She fumbled in her jacket pocket, came up with a tissue, blew her nose, and nodded.

"I have to tell someone but I've been afraid I'd tell the wrong person. And I don't think she'd want me to talk to the police. I think she was trying to keep something from the police, in fact."

I realized I was holding my breath, waiting.

"You have to promise you won't tell anyone."

"But what if it will help find who killed her?" I said.

"Well, talk to me first, okay? Promise."

I did, although I silently added an addendum that would get me off the hook if necessary.

"After Rene died, Mrs. McBeel was behaving oddly. She was nervous. Before she went to New York, she had me call you to say you shouldn't sign the papers for the Song jar yet, and she told me she was going to put some important information someplace safe."

"What information? Where?" I said. "This is important. Where did she put it?" I found I was leaning so far forward that my chest was pushing the silverware across the table. *Down, girl*, warned my inner voice. *You'll scare her away.*

But Victoria was rushing on as though a dam had opened and all her anxieties were pouring out. "I don't know. It's killing me."

"What about asking Fritz McBeel?" I said.

"No." Her voice was loud enough to make a woman at the next table turn her head for a moment. Victoria lowered her voice. "She didn't trust him," she said. "She wanted a divorce."

I was speechless. Why on earth would the social climbing Jamie McBeel want out of the marriage that was her key to huge wealth and status?

"They were staying apart as much as possible," Victoria continued, unaware that the bombshell she just dropped left me with my mouth hanging open. "I even wondered if he killed her. But he was still in New York. That's why I need to know if you found anything when you got to the office that morning, Dani. Something that might help me find whatever she wanted me to know."

Fish or cut bait time. The key was a burden I couldn't bear alone any more and its importance seemed to fit with what Victoria described.

"Okay," I said. "Here's the deal. Yes, I did find something, although I have no idea if it's important." I fished in my handbag and brought out the key. "It was taped inside an empty file folder on the floor."

With a sharp intake of breath, Victoria took the key from me.

"I think it has something to do with the jar," I said. "The writing on the folder referred to the artifact. Do you know anything about that?"

She looked up from her examination of the key. "I think this is a safe deposit key. In fact, I'm sure of it. She had four or five for her jewelry. She stored her collection at several bank locations as a precaution."

"Does that mean you can locate the box?"

"I can try. I think whatever she was talking about is in this box."

"Not the jar?" I said, my voice probably giving away my disappointment. "Admittedly, it's pretty big for a normal safe deposit box, but I was hoping there were big ones in some banks."

"I don't see how she'd even have it, Dani. Why on earth would she?"

"I don't know. Grasping at straws, I guess. Look," I said, "my interest is in recovering the jar. I feel terrible, frankly, for taking the key. I don't even know why I did it. If it isn't going to lead to the artifact, I don't want it. There's a problem, though. I can't tell the police I took it. They'll be furious, especially because they've interviewed me twice and I haven't given it to them. So if you want it, you can have it, but only if you promise not to tell on me."

"I have an idea," she said, sounding much more like the La Peerless I knew, "I'll go around to the banks where Mrs. McBeel's jewelry is. She used to send me to get pieces when she planned to wear them for special occasions, so they know me, and my signature's already on file. I'll see if any of them holds the key number in her name and if they'll let me into the vault. Maybe I'll find the message she wrote. I'll do it right away. If not, I'll turn it into the police, say I found it lying at the bottom of a file drawer. Oh, I'll wipe off our prints first."

"Brilliant," I said, feeling a huge weight lift from my shoulders. "I'm so grateful, Victoria. I was stupid to let this get out of hand."

"There's one other thing, though," Victoria said. "Simon could know what the key opens. Maybe we should ask him."

Simon? How did he get into the picture? I asked her as much.

"She asked me to set up a meeting with him the day after Rene's death. I wasn't there because it was late and I had to be somewhere else, but I know he came."

Victoria didn't know what the meeting was about, but suspected it had something to do with her divorce plans.

"Why did you think that?"

"Not a strong reason, more like a guess. She had a list of things she wanted me to do that day, and it occurred to me most of them could be in preparation for that. You know, jewelry valuations, invoices from redecorating the house, odd things like that. I don't know why else she would have asked for that kind of paperwork except if she and a lawyer were beginning to catalog assets."

"Did you ask her?"

"Of course not. I knew she'd tell me whatever I had to know at the right time. But she had told me earlier she was thinking about a trial separation, at least, and swore me to secrecy, so I figured that was it."

"And you thought Simon's visit had something to do with her divorce?" I said, seeing his smiling face as he and Jamie came out of the deserted Pilgrim Club reception room. "Were they friends?"

Victoria's face got pink. "You mean were they having an affair? I don't think so. But they met again the next evening. I know because his card was on her desk where it hadn't been when I got in the morning after that, and there was an empty bottle of champagne and two glasses on the table. He's so handsome, don't you think?"

Handsome and dangerous. It meant he knew where her office was, knew the layout, and could talk his way in if he wanted. Was there something in that office he had to have, maybe something that implicated him in an illegal transaction?

"Think back, Victoria. Was there anyone else Jamie saw or talked to in the last few days who might have some connection to the jar?"

"No, not that I know. A lot of the work we did was to follow up on her contacts from the Pilgrim Club dinner."

"Like what?"

"Well, she sent out a lot of personal thank you notes to people who came. I prepared letters for her signature. But those were all 'Mr. McBeel and I' so they didn't have anything to do with her divorce."

"How about Ambassador Obarri from Kenobia?"

"Yes, he was on the list."

"I'm kind of surprised," I said. "I saw them at the Pilgrim Club and they were pretty hostile. And you recall she was adamant he shouldn't be at the dinner. Did she send the same message, you know, 'Mr. McBeel and I'?"

Victoria thought for a minute. "I'm sure that's what I printed out. But on a few, she wrote something at the bottom to personalize them. She might have done that with his and sealed it herself. I was constantly asking her to let me copy notes like that for the files, but she'd laugh and tell me I was obsessive."

I had other questions, but I could see she was fading fast. So was I. Way too much drama for one day. But I had to pursue one other idea.

"You shocked me with the news that the McBeels weren't getting along. Can I ask, did you work with her divorce lawyer at all?"

"Oh, no," she said, shaking her head. "I'm not even sure she had one yet, or that Fritz McBeel knew what she was planning. I'm not even sure she would have gone through with it."

"What happens now? I mean, will Fritz McBeel keep you on to help manage the foundation or the charitable projects Jamie had started?"

"Wayne asked me to stay on for now. He wants an inventory of her papers and things. Actually, I'll have to turn over the keys to her safe deposit boxes and a list of what's in them as part of that job."

"Well, we don't know that the key I found is hers, so I don't think you need to include that in the inventory," I said quickly.

Victoria yawned. "No, and my check of the banks will be done by the time I finish the inventory, anyway. I'm tired, Dani. But I promise I'll call you as soon as I tell the police about the key I found in the file cabinet."

As we parted in front of the restaurant, I impulsively reached over and gave her a hug. She might be hurting, but this Victoria Peerless was a lot nicer than the La Peerless who had run interference for her high-handed boss for years.

» » »

I had to park two blocks from my apartment. The math is simple: houses that once sheltered a single family and had one garage have been broken up into two or three flats, some of which have two or three flat mates, all of whom have cars that compete for curb space every night. It's a quiet, residential neighborhood, and I usually felt safe, but after my scare on the cliffside path, I was jumpy. I hurried to the door of my building, my keys out.

I was so nervous that I imagined the large hydrangea bush beside the steps was moving. I stopped in my tracks and stared. No, only a stiff breeze. But as I put one foot on the step, a large shape jumped at me from the darkness. I spun around, yelping. A hand grabbed my arm, a light flared in my eyes, and I was blinded.

"Be quiet," a man's voice whispered.

Not likely. I opened my mouth to scream, but his hand immediately covered the bottom half of my face.

"Stop," he said in an urgent whisper. "Cut it out. It's only me."

What "me" did I know who would grab me from behind? Wait. I pushed against the arm that was only holding me lightly now.

"Ouch," he said in an aggrieved tone as he tangled with a low hanging tree branch behind him. "That hurt."

"Oscar?" I said, panting hard. "Not again. What on earth are you doing?" I was going from scared to furious in nanoseconds.

"Shhhh," he whispered. "I have to talk to you, but they're following me again."

A middle-aged man walking a poodle looked at us curiously as he passed by on the sidewalk, but made no move to step in and rescue me. Chivalry is dead, as, apparently, is the impulse to help a stranger in trouble. Although, by now, I was standing on the sidewalk, arms on my hips, really pissed at Oscar's idiotic way of getting my attention.

"You scared me half out of my wits," I hissed as soon as the man was out of hearing range. "You remind me of my ex, sneaking around like this. If you do it again, I'm going to call the cops, understand?"

"I didn't know what else to do," he said in a pleading tone. "There's no one I can talk to about this, and you seem like such a smart person. I really like you. I thought you could help me. Can we go into your house?"

Part of me was ready to say he was paranoid, but the memory of the car that came out of the park the other night made me wonder. What if he was right? "So, you got home okay the other night? No one ambushed you?"

"No," he mumbled.

"Say what you have to say here, Oscar."

"Okay, okay," he said, "but I can only stay for a minute." He sat next to me.

"I thought you were in Kenobia."

"I was on the way, but Mr. McBeel made me come back," he said, a nasal whine creeping into his voice.

"The funeral. I heard the whole team is coming back."

"I'm screwed," he moaned, holding his head in his hands. "I'm totally screwed."

"You want to explain? And you might tell me what this has to do with me while you're at it. Fast, too. I'm tired and I have to get up early tomorrow."

"Okay, but I can't tell you everything," he said, jumping up and beginning to pace in front of me. "You'd never believe me. That's the problem."

"But why? You're not making any sense, Oscar. Calm down."

"See? You don't believe me. I need your help," Oscar said, looking at me through his fogged-up glasses. "I don't know what else to do. I want you to keep this for me in case something happens. You're the only person I can think of."

He pulled a folded envelope from his pocket and held it out to me. Sealed and taped shut with packing tape, it was thick enough to hold four or five sheets of paper.

"What is it?" I said, not ready to agree.

"Something I want the police to get if anything happens to me," he said.

"The police? Does it have anything to do with the King's Jar or why you think you're being watched?"

"Yeah. Everything. And more. I know who killed Rene."

I stopped breathing. The hair on my neck prickled, and all of a sudden I wasn't sure I wanted to know.

"It was an accident," he said.

"How do you know?"

"Never mind. I just do. Remember, this envelope is only for the police and only if I'm dead. Don't tell anyone you have it. I have to trust you not to open it, okay?"

We had been sitting in the dark, alone in the late night except for the poodle walker. A car drove slowly past us. Oscar stepped into the shadow of the tree until the car turned at the next corner.

"Oscar, if you're in trouble, you should be talking to the police, not me. If you think you know who killed Rene Bouvier or Jamie, you should tell them right now. There's nothing I can do. Please, go see Inspector Sugerman, okay?"

"I can't," Oscar said, fiercely. "Keep the envelope, all right, and don't tell anyone about this? I'll call you."

And before I could say anything, he shoved the envelope at me. Reflexively, I took it, and he left, walking fast along the sidewalk in the opposite direction from the corner where the car had turned.

I sat there with the envelope in my hand, feeling like Alice in a weird wonderland where people talked in riddles and jumped out of bushes and disappeared into rabbit holes and had secrets, lots of secrets.

Oscar's paranoia was contagious. I made sure every window was locked, drew the drapes tightly closed, and seriously considered putting the envelope under a layer of kitty litter in the cat box, except that it would be too gross to reclaim it later.

I didn't owe Oscar anything and had decided by the time I went to bed to talk to Charlie first thing in the morning. If Oscar had said the location of the King's Jar was revealed in the envelope, I would have opened it in a heartbeat. But it sounded a lot more dangerous than a missing artifact and I wanted no part of it.

chapter 16

MARY McBEEL WAS a surprise. She had to be at least six feet tall, for one thing. Lanky and slightly bowed at the shoulders, she unfolded herself from Louise's flowered sofa easily and stuck out her hand.

"Thanks for coming," she said in a deep voice, smiling. "I was in Montana when I heard about all of this and wanted to talk with someone who was closer to the action, so to speak, than I am."

"I'm a lot closer than I'd like to be," I said. "Montana—is that where you live?"

"A good bit of the time, yes. I like the stillness. You know, I see at least twenty species of birds from my front porch every day and nowhere near as many automobiles." She laughed as she stirred sugar into the coffee Louise handed her.

I had pictured someone a lot more like my former mother-in-law, ladylike, a little prissy maybe. Mary McBeel was dressed in pressed khakis and a crisp white shirt, and the only makeup I could see was a slash of pink lipstick. On her right hand, she wore a large turquoise ring with silver beads circling the stone.

"I understand you've traveled to Kenobia," I said, looking for a thread that would explain why I was here.

"Oh, my, yes," she said. "I go over every year or two to check on the work my foundation is doing. Schools, a women's center, mainly. That and the antiquities museum project."

"I didn't realize," I said, "I mean, that you're so active there."

"When Fritzie and I split, he made a generous settlement on me, generous considering we had signed a prenuptial agreement that could have left me with only the clothes on my back."

I filed away "Fritzie" for a moment when I could savor it. "Oh, you had one of those, too," I said without thinking, meaning my own.

"You mean, like Jamie? Sure did. Armor-plated—no kids, no money. You don't think a billionaire's going to risk losing half of his kingdom to a community property marriage? Anyway, what we settled on was more than enough for my needs, so I used the rest to set up this foundation to continue what I had been doing in Kenobia when we were married."

Louise jumped in, eagerly. "I told Mary that I was going to sit with Ambassador Obarri at the New York dinner," she said, "and she asked me to pass along her good wishes. But then, he asked me to bring her back a message and after what happened…" Her voice trailed off awkwardly.

"Yes, Louise, it's all right," Mary said, reaching over a long arm and patting Louise's hand. "Look," she said, turning to me, "I've been fretting about poor Rene, wondering what could have happened. And, I was worried sick about the celadon funerary jar until I got this odd message from Keile, the ambassador. Tell her, Louise."

"He told me quite sternly that I was to tell Mary to keep going with the museum project in Kenobia. He said someday

it would be the home of Kenobia's most glittering archaeological prize, that she could count on that."

Mary cleared her throat. "I'm sure he means the jar.
There's nothing like it that's been found in Kenobia, nothing
as significant or valued. But every time since then that I've
tried to reach him by phone to clarify it, his secretary in New
York tells me he's away. I don't know whether he's out of the
country or ducking me. But something's up."

"And you think I can help?" I said. "I've only spoken with
him once, that night, and I give you my word, I don't know
where on earth the artifact is at this moment."

"Oh, my dear, I didn't mean that. Of course you don't.
But Jamie's death is deeply disturbing, and I can't sit by
while people are dying if something I know might help."

"Mrs. McBeel—"

"Mary, please. Let's let Jamie be Mrs. McBeel."

"Mary, is there something you know that might help us
find the jar? Should you be talking to the FBI, or the police,
or Peter Lindsey, my boss?"

"I hope to stay out of this publicly," Mary said, "especially if it may affect where it eventually winds up. You
see," and here she paused for a moment, frowning at her
clasped hands, which were resting on her knees, "it belongs
to me."

"The King's Jar? To you?" I was stammering and I sounded
like a bad echo, I knew. But Mary McBeel's declaration was
so not what I was expecting to hear, and I was floored. I
set my coffee cup down carefully, cleared my throat, and
looked at this plain-speaking, seemingly open woman. She
was smiling ruefully at me.

"I know, dear. You thought it was Fritzie's. Most people
do. But Rene knew the truth and so does Keile. In fact, it

was Keile who set it up that way, in part to help us get the fragile object out of Kenobia safely."

"But Mr. McBeel has represented it as his to the Devor. His lawyer even gave us the sale papers that proved its provenance."

"Ah, that would be Wayne Lawson. Wayne's loyal to my ex-husband, and if Fritzie wanted papers that proved he owned the jar, Wayne would produce them. But I have the original documents, and I believe I must share them with someone."

"Rene agreed to this, too," I said, trying to remember as much as possible about the legal issues as I could since I had not been deeply involved.

"Actually, Rene agreed to something else entirely, and that's what's worrying me," Mary said, waving off the offer of more coffee from Louise. "Rene had copies of the same papers that he kept hidden away, in case he needed them to protect the King's Jar and its future. He and I talked about this at great length, and we both communicated with Keile, although he needs to stay under the radar if he wants to keep his job—or even his freedom from retribution in his country."

"What was the plan, then?" I said, still reeling from this complication.

"The Devor takes over for Rene, protecting the King's Jar for twenty years, during which time the Kenobian museum is completed, assembles its own staff and archival storage facilities, and is mature enough to properly care for it."

"But I don't think anyone at the Devor knows about this, and I can tell you Fritz—Mr. McBeel—specifically wrote into the gift agreement that the Devor was to have the jar in perpetuity. It was not supposed to be repatriated. Although,"

I hastened to say, "our director and the board will respect any legitimate claims for repatriation in the same spirit that other major museums have agreed to."

"Which is not very encouraging," Mary said with a short laugh. "Patrimony claims can get tied up in the courts for decades, as you know. But never mind, Danielle. I don't have a quarrel with the Devor Museum. The reason I wanted to talk with you is, first, to give you a heads-up that the ownership question will have to be addressed at some point, but also to ask you if you think poor Jamie died because of the King's Jar? If my ownership of it somehow is involved, I need to decide how to proceed, and who to trust. There's one extra complication that I'll explain if I have to."

I sat silent for a moment, thinking. I liked Mary and didn't want to play games with her. "Truth is, I don't know for sure, but my gut says yes. I've talked to Jamie's assistant, and she doesn't think Jamie had any interest in the piece or who owned it. But, Jamie did instruct Victoria to tell the Devor not to sign the gift papers until it was recovered, which was the exact opposite of what Wayne Lawson told us to do. I told that to the police, by the way," I added.

"I wonder," she said slowly, "if Jamie knew, and how she knew."

I flashed on the empty folder, the supposedly old files missing from Rene's office. What if they were Rene's hiding place for a duplicate set of documents proving Mary's claim of ownership? If Jamie had them in her possession at some point, they would be a powerful piece of ammunition in whatever game she was playing.

Mary continued. "I didn't care as long as it was under Rene's supervision at Warefield University. And I don't even mind Fritzie taking the credit for giving it away as long as the terms are what I agreed to. He loves being seen as the owner of things, and as a great and generous soul, which, alas, he is not. But here's the complication, and this is in strict confidence for now.

"You see, I wanted to own the jar only while the threat of coups threatened the fragile government. It is so vital that sub-Saharan African countries take responsibility for protecting their own heritage now that colonialism is over. I am fully committed to that, and the King's Jar is a powerful symbol."

She paused to drain her coffee cup.

"But I didn't fully trust Fritzie to adhere to the agreement should Rene retire and have to give up his oversight. So I stipulated that, if my ex-husband reneged on the agreement, it would nullify our prenup. His lawyers hated it, but Fritz agreed because he wanted to get rid of my annoying presence and thought his lawyers could win me over with money in the long run."

"Could Fritz have told Jamie about that?"

"Hardly. It might give her ideas of how to get around her own prenup. What I can't understand is why Jamie would put herself at odds with Fritzie over the ownership in any case."

I debated how much I should tell Mary. After all, Jamie's desire for a divorce was a private matter, and I only had it on hearsay. I looked over at Louise, listening to all this with interest.

"Do you need to talk to Mary in confidence, Dani? I understand," Louise said, jumping up. "After all, I'm the board chairman's wife and the last thing I want to do is find myself torn between Mary's interests and the Devor's. I have to make a few phone calls, anyway. I'll be in my study." And with that, she hurried out of the room.

"A good soul, isn't she?" Mary said, smiling at Louise's retreating back. "You're lucky to have people like her and Geoff around. They're top-flight." She turned back to me.

"Please, please keep this in confidence," I said, hesitating. "Victoria will probably tell the police, but I don't think anyone else knows. Jamie and, er, Fritz weren't getting along. Victoria thinks Jamie was preparing to ask for a divorce."

"Oh, for heaven's sake," Mary said, startled. "After all that work to get the job?"

In spite of myself, I laughed. I'd never thought of it quite like that.

"Sorry," she said, "I didn't mean to be disrespectful, but think about it. She wanted all of that so much. Why on earth would she consider giving it up?"

Mentally, I saw again the Most Eligible Bachelor walking out of the Pilgrim Club's reception room arm in arm with Jamie. "Maybe she didn't think she would have to give it up," I said, doubtfully.

"You mean, maybe she'd settle for something much smaller, like I did? Hardly. My tastes were always simple, and I didn't much care for the social life. But Jamie? She relished it. Did it better than I ever did, to tell the truth."

Mary looked at me and said, "If you're thinking he killed her, but you're afraid to say it out loud, I'll put it out there to shoot the idea down. Fritzie was afraid of getting too close to life, if you know what I mean. He might wish for things to happen, but act personally? It was one of the reasons we drifted apart after I realized that even the thrills of African safaris and giving money for exciting projects didn't turn him on. He preferred to view the world—and still does, I'll bet—from the safety of a high mountaintop."

In the end, Mary offered to get me copies of the papers that she said proved her ownership of the jar and where it was to be housed ultimately. I was free to share them with the police, with Peter, with anyone but the media.

"I assume Rene's copies of the documents are with his other papers, so it will come out in the end. Best not to stir up a hornets' nest with Fritzie, at least not on your own. We'll let the police decide what to do there."

She also said she'd keep trying to reach Keile and, with his permission, tell whoever needed to know more about the circumstances of the King's Jar leaving Kenobia twenty years ago. "The export documents are dicey, frankly. With enough notice, Keile can work up a cover story. But there were intermediaries, and money changed hands, and, at the time, I honestly believed it was the right thing to do. It was a glorious find, and I want its story to be a positive one, not tainted by death," she said emphatically as I got up to leave.

"Those intermediaries," I said, as I shook hands with her, "was one of them Simon Anderson?"

Mary McBeel smiled. "I haven't seen Simon in ages and wouldn't for the world get him into hot water. Let's just say he was there, understood the Kenobian system, and seemed to be on everyone's side at once. He liked being helpful, and whatever he did, it wasn't for money. He liked being in the thick of things."

» » »

I had already left two messages for Charlie at police head-quarters and was trying to concentrate on work long enough to reduce the pile of papers in my in-box to a reasonable stack when Teeni buzzed me from her office.

"You're summoned," she said.

"By?" Seemed to me I was being summoned a lot lately. I hadn't even had time to decide if I should be reporting everything that had happened in the last day to Peter in addition to Charlie. My boss was going to freak out when he learned the true provenance of the jar.

"Your friend Wayne Lawson," Teeni said, "he of the deep, if borrowed, pockets."

Ah, Fritz's lawyer and foundation head. What was it Mary had said? Loyal to Fritz at all costs? "Hello, Wayne, how are you doing in these sad times?"

"These are tragic days, certainly," Lawson said, sounding as if he were reading a soap opera script. "We are all deeply, deeply shocked by Mrs. McBeel's death, no one more than I."

"I expect Fritz is pretty upset, too," I said, immediately regretting the sharp edge I heard in my reply.

"Of course, of course. He's a remarkable man, Danielle. In the midst of this tragedy, he's asked me to set up a meeting with you to discuss where we are regarding the gift of the King's Jar. He wants to make sure the charitable intent isn't compromised by this unfortunate…" He paused.

"Tragedy?" *Behave*, scolded my inner voice, *if only because he has power to withhold foundation funds from your employer and you do want to keep your job.* "Of course," I rushed on. "It's so kind of him to be concerned about the Devor at a time like this. Have you talked with Peter about a meeting?"

"Mr. McBeel thought it might be more productive to meet with you, at least first, to assess where we are. Then, if need be, he and the director can talk."

Which probably meant if I didn't do whatever Fritz was going to suggest, he'd make sure my boss knew about it.

215

No matter. I'd run up to Peter's office the minute Lawson and I hung up.

"Where would Fritz like to meet and when?"

"His office. His home office, and if you were free sometime today, that would be most convenient."

Before the funeral? Why the rush? Maybe he needed my advice. After all, Fritz and I were on the same team, both trying to bring back the famous jar. We set a time later in the afternoon, and Lawson added a few more funereal notes before hanging up. Peter wasn't available when I called upstairs to alert him to my meeting with the billionaire widower, but Dorie promised she'd get a message to him.

Dorie was bugging me for some concrete plans for the dinner series Peter was to attend, and everything I drafted was under par. Every time the phone rang in my office, I jumped, hoping it was Charlie and wondering if I was doing the right thing by ignoring Oscar's instructions, or that it was a particularly crafty reporter wanting the gory details of Jamie's murder. I was in a crummy mood. The staff knew it and stayed as far from my door as possible.

» » »

Parking is not a problem in this part of Pacific Heights for the same reason it is at my end of the 'hood. The mansions here may have six and seven bedrooms, but there are frequently only one or two people living in them. Garages are more common, too, since the lots are easily double the size of almost anything else in San Francisco.

As I walked up the paved path to the portico, I remembered hearing that people who were part of the McBeels' social circle greeted the McBeels' butler, Gerard, by name, almost as if he were a friend. In spite of Fritz's recent behavior, I wasn't and didn't. The butler put me in a dark room near the entrance hall. I was left to appreciate the sixteenth-century tapestry that covered one wall and the similarly aged, deeply carved table that spanned almost the length of the opposite wall. A huge arrangement of white calla lilies and greenery dominated the table. To me, the effect was gloomy, but deep gloom was appropriate today.

While I stood, hands clasped in front of me, staring at the dumpy matron stitched onto the canvas sitting sidesaddle on a fat white horse whose foot was raised above the head of a tall-eared, grey rabbit, I rehearsed what I wanted to say.

"Mr. McBeel's free," Gerard's voice said from behind me. We walked without conversation from the tapestry room through the hall and into the large living room. Everything looked like it always did. The house seemed calm, unperturbed by the death of its hostess. Gerard kept walking and gestured me through an alcove and into Fritz's study.

Although I'd been to the house several times, I had never been in this room. The walls were paneled in a dark, warm wood that glowed where the light from table lamps reached it. Small sculptures nestled into bookcases, cuddling up to matched sets of leather-bound books. It didn't take an expert to see that the silk Persian rug underfoot was a best in class. A miniature, armor-clad figure perched in a niche was lit to show off its studs and hinges to perfection. Fritz stood behind his desk when I came in, seemingly backed up by his famous father in the form of a giant oil painting.

"Ah, Danielle, thanks for coming. I hope it wasn't too much trouble?" he said, holding out his hand. His handshake was languid. Poor guy probably wasn't sleeping any better than I was.

I assured him it wasn't and offered my condolences. He commiserated with me for having been the one to discover his wife's body and talked about the funeral plans. He asked if the police were being courteous and if they were thorough in their questioning. All the while, I tried not to think of Mary calling him "Fritzie." Gerard brought tea. I shut up, sipped, and waited for the real discussion to begin.

Good thing I had swallowed my tea because I would have shamed my mother by snorting it out my nose when he said, still in the same calm voice, "I must know where the Song jar is. Please tell me right now."

"I have no idea where it is, truly. I—we, that is Peter and I—were hoping you might have some ideas," I said, stumbling over my words.

"Of course I don't. If I did, you would have heard from me," he said, some animation coming into his voice now. "Remember, we agreed that you'd share any information you had with me? And I hardly need say, it is in danger if it is not being kept in a professionally managed environment."

"I assure you I would," I stammered, caught off guard. "I'm so sorry you have the impression I know something about the disappearance, but I can't imagine why you think I might."

"Was there nothing in my wife's office that day that might suggest where it is?"

Maybe a key? I kept my face blank, although suddenly I remembered Dickie telling me I should never play poker. "I assure you, Fritz, er, Mr. McBeel, the Devor is cooperating with the police and the FBI, as well as with the insurance investigator. But no one's contacted us about a ransom or anything. Have you have received some hint of that yourself?"

He fixed me with a look that would have meant serious dungeon time in another age. I understood I was not making him happy. I remembered Mary's comment that he didn't like to engage with people, but preferred to keep the world at bay. Both his face and his body language screamed that, now that I knew what to look for. His hands were clutching the arms of his chair, his body was motionless, and his chin was lifted, as if to gain more height over me. The camaraderie of the late night car ride in Manhattan was over.

In the bookcase to one side, the little figure glowed like a tiny bodyguard, ironclad and severe. "Ransom? Someone wants to ransom it?" His voice was icy now. "Who would that be?"

Ironclad. All of a sudden, I knew. Well, thought I knew. And I had no intention of sharing my theory with him. All I wanted to do was get out of there and run straight to Charlie Sugerman.

"I have no idea," I said hastily. I couldn't decide if I should put the cup down so it wouldn't rattle in the saucer, or hang onto it with two hands and try to appear normal.

"Then why did you propose it?" he said bluntly. I didn't like the tone of voice or the way he was staring at me now. I put the cup and saucer down on the little table next to me and began to babble.

"Well, it's only that there's no other reason for someone to take it, is there? I mean, unless perhaps the Kenobians wanted it back and felt they had a right to steal it."

"Yes," he drawled. "It's possible someone from Kenobia hired an assassin to take back the treasure, but the Kenobian government will never be able to prove they can care for such a priceless piece of history and they must not be allowed to have it."

"I heard they're building a new museum," I said tentatively.

"Hah, a pipe dream. The government is unstable, the people in power are corrupt. It's out of the question."

"But," I said, thinking I might as well test the waters of Mary McBeel's theory, "if you've given it to the Devor, that won't be an option any more, right? I mean, it will be the museum's property then."

Fritz shook his head. "There's always a way, where bribery and dishonesty reign. And Rene didn't help by encouraging that Obarri fellow to think it might get returned. Obarri has no place in this country, ought to be sent back to Kenobia."

That was consistent with what had looked to Teeni and me like his side of the conversation at the Pilgrim Club dinner.

"I can't speak for Peter or the board about that, but I'm confident that the magnificent jar will be properly cared for while it's at the Devor. Tom Burns is tops in his field." About as vague a statement as I could manage, considering I felt he was pushing for something.

"Burns, yes," Fritz said, shifting his weight in the chair. "Trustworthy man."

My mind skittered back to Jamie's office and the note on the folder—could it have been Fritz's writing? *"Can Simon trust Tom?"*

"Have you met with the homicide inspectors to tell them you think Kenobians may have had a hand in killing Dr. Bouvier or Mrs. McBeel?" Fishing again. I knew he was trying to convince the police that Obarri had masterminded at least the theft.

"Of course. They're not competent at this sort of thing. Local men, not terribly bright. I imagine drug dealers are more their speed. I want to make sure they don't dismiss my suspicion merely because it would be more work for them to investigate properly."

Hey, he was criticizing the man I would have liked to date if I hadn't stolen evidence from his crime scene. I was working myself up to some kind of reply when McBeel popped up from his chair.

"For now, if you're sure you don't know where it is, we have no further need to talk. But please understand I expect to be informed immediately of any developments in locating it. I will want to examine it personally when it does reappear."

Pretty high-handed, especially since the object wasn't even his if Mary McBeel was telling the truth. Fritz McBeel was behaving more like the man I'd known from a distance for so long, and I expected this was the last time he'd invite me over to ask for my help with anything. Pity. I was getting up my nerve to call the butler by name.

Clearly, I was dismissed. Only when the door closed behind me did I let my breath out. Ransom. Of course.

» » »

I should have guessed. Charlie was out of the office. I left an urgent message for him. I tried to reach Victoria, but the office phone didn't answer and I didn't have her home number. I was beginning to connect the dots and, while I had no idea where the jar was, some of the seemingly random bits and pieces of information I had been collecting were turning into a story I could sell to myself.

Teeni was at the printer when I got back to the office. "What did the great man want?" she said, scooping up a pile of color copies and walking with me to the coffee room. "How's he taking his wife's death?"

"Got me. He seemed pretty businesslike talking about it. It was too weird, though. He seems to think I know where the jar is, although he never said why he thought I'd know."

"Man's probably not thinking too straight, you know?" Teeni said. "First his friend, then his wife. His treasure stolen. I feel sorry for him."

I hadn't told Teeni about the late-night Manhattan car ride, in part because I couldn't figure out what it meant. But Peter was about to get it all dumped on him.

chapter 17

PETER LISTENED TO my recounting of the limo ride, today's visit, and, last, my tea party with Mary McBeel intensely, sitting forward on the sofa in his office, elbows on knees, fingers interlaced under his chin. After the first few words, I had his whole attention, and he didn't interrupt until I got to Mary's surprise announcement, at which he said, "What?" and threw out his arms.

"The oddest thing is how sure he seems to be that I know something about the jar's whereabouts. I mean, he's pushed me hard, twice now. Where could he get that idea?" I said.

"If he thinks Simon's involved, and it sounds like he does, and he knows—creepy, I agree—that you and Simon saw each other after the piece went missing, then he may be putting two and two together and getting five," Peter said. "I wonder if he's putting pressure on other people, too."

"You mean, rattling cages to see what happens? You could be right. Oscar is behaving strangely. He came to see me the other night in a panic." I wasn't sure I ought to tell anyone but Charlie about Oscar's statement that he knew who killed Rene. And the envelope was a hot potato I couldn't wait to hand over to the police.

"I wonder if Tom Burns has gotten any pressure from McBeel," Peter said, going over to the door that I'd closed when I came in. "Dorie, would you get Tom Burns up here ASAP?"

"About Mary McBeel's claim?" I said. "What do you think?"

"At this point, I'd give that blasted artifact to anyone who asked for it," Peter said, rolling his eyes. "Seriously, there's no way we're going to resolve that one right away. Sounds like an ugly remnant of a divorce fight. Maybe she's still feeling like the woman scorned."

"I don't think so," I said. "If you met her, you'd understand. But what if it's true and, in the end, the Devor has to give it up some day?"

At that point, there was a rap on the door and Tom came in, as disheveled as ever. Peter waved him to a chair and asked him if Fritz McBeel had been in touch recently.

"With me? No, why would he?" Tom said. He looked tired and sounded tense.

"He's been after Dani to tell him anything she knows that might help explain what happened to the King's Jar," Peter said. "I wondered if he'd been pestering you, too."

"I've only met him the time he came in to tour the space with you," Tom said. His red hair made his face look even redder than it was.

"Since you work with Simon," I said, "we thought he might be quizzing you about Simon."

"Why would he do that?" Tom said peevishly. "I'm just the water boy in this game, anyway. Nobody tells me anything."

One of the things I like about Peter is his ability to turn on the charm. Now, he sat across from Tom and smiled. "You probably know more than I do. This is a fast moving situation and we're all getting surprised every day."

"I thought you might have talked to him," I said, "because McBeel said something about you being trustworthy. It sounded as though he knew you."

"I tell you, I've barely met the man," Tom said, his voice rising. "What is this? An inquisition?" If his boss hadn't been sitting there, I'm sure Tom would have slammed out of the room.

"We're trying to make sense of a lot of strange conversations," Peter said. "Dani had another odd one with Oscar Shelby, Rene's lead researcher. You remember him?"

"Sure," Tom said. "Bouvier's protégé. I haven't seen him since Rene died. Is he taking it hard?"

"On an emotional roller coaster, poor guy," I said. "He was determined to convince me Simon killed Rene, in fact."

"Simon kill Bouvier?" Tom said and laughed abruptly. "Why, if the world worships at your feet, would you batter a distinguished scientist and throw it all away?"

"Good point," Peter said. "Makes me wonder why Oscar would even suggest it."

"I can guess," Tom said, running one hand through his hair. "Loyalty. Remember, he's been with Bouvier for at least a decade, his trusted assistant. Whatever Bouvier said, I'm guessing he believes. So, jealousy, his own and inherited from Bouvier. A non-scientist getting all that attention, money, celebrity based on talking and writing about other people's discoveries. I remember…"

He stopped, threw his large body back onto the sofa cushions, and looked at his hands in his lap.

"What?" Peter said, curious.

"Nothing important."

"If it might help us untangle this, you should tell us," I said.

"Look, it's nothing," Tom said. "When I was a new Ph.D., I cowrote a paper with Rene."

"What was the paper about?" Peter said.

"The famous celadon funerary jar, of course," Tom said in mocking tones. "It was about the blasted piece that's gone missing."

"I never knew that," I said, intrigued. "Rene never mentioned it, either."

"It didn't turn out well," Tom said, grimly.

"And?" Peter prompted.

"Nothing. The paper had some flaws and we had to withdraw it. I'm an art historian, he's an archaeologist. Made for some bumps in the research area. It has nothing to do with anything that's happening today, I promise you." Tom got up. "I'd like to get back to my exhibit now. I'm already behind schedule for opening day, and we're rearranging things to cover for not having what was going to be the highlight of the whole exhibit. My poor intern's spending all of her time tracking down whatever we have in the storage rooms from settlements at Great Zimbabwe and Mapungubwe, although both are farther south and had documented coastal trading, so they're not quite as spectacular, historically."

Peter nodded and Tom left. "Well, that was interesting," he said, looking at me. "Mapungubwe is on the Limpopo River, did you know that?"

"I didn't. Thank you, Peter. Could we possibly get back to our big problem?"

"Okay, sorry," he said, the brief smile on his face disappearing. "I've been doing my homework. Any idea what Tom's explanation was about?"

"No, but when he's calmed down a bit, I'll see if I can get more information. I have a call in to Charlie Sugerman. What do you think—should I mention this to him?"

Peter frowned. "If it brings more negative attention to the Devor, I would vote against it. Unless you think it has something to do with Jamie's death?"

I protested that I had no way of knowing and, given the theory that was brewing in my head, I didn't think it did. But I hated the thought of having more secrets, so, when Peter said I should use my judgment, I was relieved. We parted with me promising to keep him in the loop.

» » »

Charlie had left a message that he'd come to the museum by the end of the day, which was getting close. I called Victoria to see what she had learned. This time, she answered and told me the phones hadn't stopped ringing all day. It seemed Jamie's status as San Francisco's most important socialite hadn't diminished. Victoria said everyone wanted invitations to the funeral.

"I thought I could get to the bank branches where she has boxes, but it isn't going to happen. Tomorrow, I promise," she said. "Are you coming to the funeral?"

"Not sure," I said, unwilling to explain I might be a public relations risk. "If I can come, do I need a printed invitation?"

"I'll put you on the family list," Victoria said. "You could sit with me. I'll be by myself."

I was digesting the realization that Victoria, so closely tied to Jamie professionally, wasn't quite family and wasn't a friend of Jamie's friends, when Charlie poked his head in the door. I waved him in and told Victoria I'd talk to her later.

"Have you solved the crime for us?" Charlie said, smiling slightly as he pulled a chair up next to my desk.

"I doubt it, but I have information for you, plus a thought. First, are you aware Jamie and Fritz were having personal problems, that she was even talking about divorce?"

"Vaguely, although I also picked up that it was probably nothing. McBeel denies it, by the way. Don't tell me you think he killed her in a lovers' quarrel?"

I didn't tell him it could have been jealousy if Fritz knew Simon was arranging a liaison with Jamie. "No. But I started thinking about Jamie walking away from all that money and power, and I wondered if she'd do it."

"I suppose she'd sue for half of everything. Isn't that what keeps fancy divorce lawyers in gold cufflinks and Jaguars?"

"Not if there's a prenuptial agreement. See, if she signed a strong one—an ironclad one," I said, reminded again of the little figure in Fritz's office, "she could lose almost everything."

"I would be surprised," Charlie said, shrugging. "As I said, lawyers are always breaking those."

"Not always. Take it from me, some are impossible to break," I said and immediately wished I hadn't.

"Oh, that's right," he said, looking into my eyes. "Richard Argetter the third. You would know about these things."

Heat rose in my cheeks. "Not that I tried, believe me. I didn't want anything to do with his money after....Well, anyway, what if Jamie took the jar so she'd have a bargaining chip for a divorce? What if she hid it somewhere and now that she's dead, no one knows where?"

"Wait. Have you talked to Fritz McBeel about this? Has he said something to you? Weiler will eat your heart for lunch if you've been messing around in his investigation."

"Of course not. I did ask if he'd been contacted about a ransom payment—"

"Damn it, Dani, are you out there trying to be the Lone Ranger or something?"

"No, not at all. Anyway," I said, miffed at his response, "he didn't know anything about ransoming. In fact, he asked me if I knew anything, which is silly since I'm not even involved."

"Oh, really?" Charlie said, slapping his notebook down on my desk. "Could have fooled me. Look, this is already a sensitive case, and McBeel is all over the police chief with his complaints about how we haven't solved his wife's murder fast enough. Suggesting a new line of investigation to him on your own isn't going to help. Especially a dumb one like that."

"It's not so dumb," I said in protest.

"Yeah, it is. Think—are you saying the queen of high society killed an old man, stole a priceless artifact from a prestigious university, tucked it away in a shoebox, then committed extortion on her own husband, who happens to be powerful enough to crush her? And," he continued, talking so fast I couldn't get a word in edgewise, "does that lead to the conclusion that he strangled her to get it back?"

"Well, I haven't worked out all the details," I said, beginning to feel uncomfortable.

"You can say that again. Have you figured out where this object is?" He sounded as though he expected me to say no, which I did. By tomorrow, he might have the answer in the form of the key, but I had to hold my tongue now and let Victoria check out the banks and, if that didn't pan out, to bring the key and her story to Charlie.

"I suppose you don't have any proof of your theory?" he said.

"Nothing specific," I said. He started to get up, but I said, "Wait, there's more."

"Jeez, Dani, you're pushing it here. I think you should leave this investigation to trained cops and the FBI. These hunches of yours are more than a little far-fetched."

I reached into the bottom drawer of my desk and pulled out my handbag. From it, I took the bulky envelope Oscar had given me, still taped, and held it out to him.

"What's this?" he said.

"A confession, I think."

"To what?"

"I'm not really sure. I didn't open it, and I'm not even supposed to give it to you unless something happens to him."

"To whom? Fritz McBeel?" His voice radiated skepticism.

"To Oscar Shelby."

"And he would be…?"

"Rene Bouvier's associate, the senior researcher at the lab. He says he knows who killed Rene."

"Oh, yeah, the fat guy. And he gave this to you and said it was a confession?" Charlie's voice rose. "You're kidding, right?" He started to take it, then pulled his hand back and said, "Put it down on the desk, then give me a clean sheet of paper, please."

He used the paper like an oven mitt, peering at the taped flap and squeezing the thickness. "You'd better tell me everything."

So I did, at least everything about Oscar. How he stalked me on my hike, how he had hidden outside my house, his belief he was being followed and would be killed, and what he had told me to do with the envelope.

"And you weren't tempted to open it, Ms. Amateur Detective?" Charlie said, looking up from his notebook, where he was scribbling.

"Tempted, yes. But in spite of what you say, I'm no fool. I debated keeping it, like he asked me to, but what if I was holding it and he was killed and I could have prevented it by turning it over to you sooner?"

"All right," Charlie finally said when I had told him everything I could remember about my contacts with Oscar. "I need to get downtown with this right away. And we're probably going to have Oscar picked up. If he calls you, say nothing about this, and let me know he was in touch. If he asks you if you have the envelope, say yes. Understand? Don't mention Oscar to anyone, anyone at all, until we have him in custody."

"Will you tell me what's in the envelope?"

"Probably not, at least not right away. It may be nothing, but if it has real bearing on either of these deaths, it will be evidence that may not be public for some time."

"And if it tells us where the jar is?" I said.

"That'll be up to people other than me," Charlie said flatly. He left soon after that, without so much as a thank you for my help.

It wasn't until I had simmered down and swallowed my disappointment at Charlie's annoyance with me that I realized I hadn't even mentioned Mary McBeel's astonishing news or Tom Burns' old association with Rene. As I turned off my office lights and headed out, I nursed my misgivings about turning Oscar's confidences over to the police. Had I done the right thing after all?

» » »

An hour later, locked in to my apartment once again and somewhat comforted by a large bowl of pasta with fresh pesto and a salad of tomatoes and buffalo mozzarella, I patted my lap to let Fever know it was his territory for a while.

The poor cat hadn't gotten much attention lately, and no one can make me feel guiltier than Fever when he stands frozen in one spot near my ankle, looking at me with his big round eyes and a hurt expression. "C'mon up, big guy," I said, and he did, immediately turning around in a circle and making a nest of his own body.

He didn't even have to move when my cell phone rang, since my bag was next to me.

"Hello," I said, not recognizing the number.

"Hey, cupcake, how're you doing?"

"Dickie? Where are you? Aren't you in the Bahamas?"

"Yeah, isn't it great?" His voice had a funny warble to it. "I'm on Skype. The boat captain has it on his computer."

"Has what? You mean you're calling me from a boat?"

"Yeah, sort of…" His voice faded out and I waited, "…rainbows and unbelievable fish…almost drowned…and you should see the…" Gone again. "…glad I brought the big lens…"

"Dickie," I shouted into the phone. "Wait a minute. I'm not getting everything you said. Are you okay?" Why was he calling me?

"Great, it's all great. But I wanted to tell you I'm heading back early. Don't like what I'm hearing about Jamie McBeel's death and your part in it…"

"Part in it?" I shouted. "I have no part in it. That's ridicu—"

"What? Can't hear too well. I'm not going to let you deal with this on your own, kiddo," he warbled back at me. "Checked the airline and I should be…" Gone again. I waited, getting madder at his arrogance by the minute, but all I heard was what sounded like the song of the universe in my ear, snatches of notes and syllables, and waves. I finally gave up and broke off the connection, steaming. The nerve of him.

I didn't want him back here, getting involved in this. He didn't know what I had done with the evidence, or how intense Fritz was. Dickie would only try to take over my life again. I tapped my foot furiously, which made Fever pull his ears down in disapproval.

The phone rang again. Taking a deep breath, I picked up the receiver and waited for whatever satellites were involved to make the connection. Finally, I heard a distant, "Hello."

"Do not come back on my account," I said in a loud voice, determined to make my point before we lost the signal. "Do not make a mess in my life again. You made your choice when you and Betty Boop went skiing and I've made mine. We're divorced, remember? You'll never be the kind of man I want in my life, not even with your millions of dollars, in fact specifically because of your money. And you confuse me—I mean things—and I can't stand it when you hover, and I don't need rescuing by you, Dickie." I paused for breath.

"Hello?" said the voice again. "This is Ralph. Were you looking for Richard?"

Fortunately for me, the line went dead at that moment.

chapter 18

OSCAR DIDN'T CALL that night to check on his envelope, for which I was grateful, but I didn't sleep much. Between my embarrassment at what Ralph must have told Dickie (and who else?) and my worry about Oscar's probable reaction to my having betrayed his confidence, I mostly stared at the ceiling and counted my troubles. When I did drift off, I had one of those dreams where you're falling and know you'll hit the ground sometime. But you never do. You keep falling through space, which is pretty much how I felt the next morning when the ringing phone jarred me awake.

It wasn't Oscar. It was Charlie. "You should know, we're looking for Oscar, so if he calls you or gets in touch, it's essential you let us know. You can call 9-1-1, in fact."

"It sounds bad," I managed to say as I struggled with the sleeves of a bathrobe and tried in vain to find a slipper that must have walked itself under the bed. Fever stood up from his nest on the duvet, stretching and complaining at having his sleep disturbed.

"Yeah, well, that's not the half of it. But I can't say anything more and it's critical you don't tell anyone—I mean anyone, Dani—about that letter he left with you. Not your boss, not your best friend, not Safari Man, no one. Do you understand?"

"Now you're scaring me," I said. "Oscar seems more pathetic than dangerous. Are you sure he's not mixed up, maybe stressed by everything that's happened around him?"

"I can't say, but you were right to give it to me. I'm headed in to a meeting, but I'll be at the funeral. If you see me, don't do anything to show that you know me or mention that I'm a cop, all right?"

After he hung up, I tried to think clearly, but my brain refused. Coffee, it said. A long shower, two cups of strong black coffee, and a buttery croissant I picked up at a shop next to the Devor, and I was beginning to function again by the time I got to the museum.

"No business as usual today," I said to Teeni as she rounded the corner into my office with a stack of folders. "There's the funeral this afternoon—oh, no, I forgot to ask someone to send flowers."

"Are you kidding?" Teeni said, raising her voice an octave. "Of course we sent flowers. Peter sent flowers. The trustees sent flowers. My guess is San Francisco cornered every calla lily in the state yesterday. Victoria Peerless will be writing thank you notes for a year. But did you hear the latest?"

She leaned over the desk, her hands on the edge, and lowered her voice. "No body."

"What?" I clutched my large takeout coffee cup in one hand and held what was left of the croissant in the other.

"I heard from Dorie, who said Peter told her, that the police haven't released Mrs. McBeel's body yet since it's a homicide and they don't have the perp."

I raised my eyebrows.

"I learned that from *Law & Order*," Teeni said. "So, the coffin will be empty."

"Oh, yuck," I said. "This is something I don't want to know. Please, Teeni, keep everyone away, will you? I feel like crap."

She frowned. "You do look done in. Anything I can help with? Want me to hold your calls?"

I started to say yes but realized Oscar might call. I would follow Charlie's directions, but talking to Oscar on the phone to find out where he was couldn't be dangerous and might help the police. Maybe I could even calm him down. "Could you take messages, but give me the messages as soon as they come in. I know it sounds crazy, but there's a reason, I promise."

Teeni didn't argue, a sure sign that I looked bad. The proof was when she showed up at the door, saying nothing but putting a huge chocolate chip muffin and another cup of coffee on the corner of my desk. The last time I got on my complicated scale, it informed me my body fat index was in the wrong territory. Screw it, this was a crisis. Two people were dead, a priceless artifact was missing from my museum, and someone I knew might be a killer.

I must have looked at my watch a dozen times, at the little Devor Museum commemorative clock on my desk a dozen more, and at the standard issue wall clock behind me twice. An hour passed, then another. I wandered downstairs for a salad as if that would offset the calories I'd already eaten today, and then to Tom Burns' office. He wasn't there, although the department assistant down the hall said he was in the building somewhere.

Then it was time to leave for the Cathedral, my boss having decided I could go since the fickle media had moved on to a new scandal. Peter and I took a cab over together, neither of us in the mood for small talk. As we guessed, the streets around the cathedral, at the top of Nob Hill, were crowded, and people in black streamed up the Cathedral steps. A few tourists even turned their cameras on the crowd, probably convinced it was a celebrity's funeral. I recognized a few mourners but saw no sign of Charlie.

Peter peeled off to sit with Louise and Geoff Johnson near the front. Victoria was standing at the entrance with her checklist, but I wanted to sit where I'd be totally inconspicuous. As I drifted back along a side aisle, I heard my name hissed from one of the pews. Fearing an ambush, I turned away, but the voice hissed again. When I looked, I realized it was worse than a reporter. It was my former mother-in-law. She was beckoning me, all the while pushing an annoyed mourner farther down the row to make room for me. No sign of Dickie.

If I hadn't been so distracted, I could have come up with a better way out. As it was, I smiled feebly, gestured my inability to sit with her and be grilled ruthlessly until the service began, and almost ran the rest of the way back, slipping out the side door as the organ opened up and what sounded like a hundred prepubescent boys began to sing.

Ushers were closing the doors. The coffin—empty—must have been up front already. I sat on a low wall on the quiet side of the Cathedral's property, hidden from any latecomers or the press, wondering if I could get away with not going back in at all. When I heard another hiss, I jumped up. Could she have followed me out of the church? I looked around wildly.

"Over here," the voice said hoarsely. I squinted into the privet hedge that separated the cathedral from the building behind it. A head rose above the bushes, eyes peering in all directions.

"Oscar?" I said. "I don't believe this. Didn't I warn you not to ambush me from the bushes one more time? You're worse than Dickie and you're driving me nuts." I marched over to him, losing control over my temper with every step. Charlie might think the guy was dangerous, but I couldn't see it. A total idiot, yes.

"I told you I'd get in touch," he said in his nasal voice, lumbering over to me as he brushed leaves off his jacket.

"You said you'd call. This jumping out of the landscape has to stop."

"Yeah, well, I couldn't call. But this is better, isn't it? I mean, we can talk now. Everyone's in there."

"Don't you want to go in?" I said, although his clothes were rumpled and he looked like he hadn't shaved since I'd seen him in front of my apartment.

"Go in?" he said, looking up at me as if I had suggested he audition for the San Francisco Ballet. "I can't go in. I'm the reason she's dead. I...I killed her." He plunked down on the steps and grabbed his head, groaning softly.

Okay. He was speaking metaphorically, I assured myself. In a manner of speaking. Not literally killed her. I looked closely at him. If he had combed his hair this week, I'd be surprised. Ditto changing clothes. He was squeezing his hands together so hard that I thought they must hurt. Was poor, nerdy Oscar having a nervous breakdown? I'd never seen one in action before, but this must be what it looks like. I looked around, but we were alone in this quiet spot.

Charlie's warning rang in my ears. Maybe he was at least partly right. Oscar was falling apart. "Oscar, how about we go see my friend at the police station? You can tell him about this. He can help."

My friend, alas, was probably in the cathedral right now. I stood up to see how far it was to the curb, where I thought we could catch one of the cabs doubtless waiting for the service to end.

"No, no police. He said it was the only way to save it, that only we'd know about it," Oscar said, his voice breaking. He had begun to rock, snuffling sounds coming from behind his hands.

Oscar's laments sounded less and less metaphorical, but I was holding onto my deep desire that he was imagining some responsibility for Jamie's death. Anything else was unthinkable. And, while part of me was screaming to ask who "he" was, the sensible part was telling me I might be sorry if I knew.

"Mrs. McBeel warned me. She said she'd made sure we wouldn't get away with it."

"Get away with what?" I said in spite of myself. Was "he" really a "she" and was there any truth in what Oscar was telling me?

"It wasn't my idea. I hated it. But the whole place would be shut down. Don't you see?" he whimpered. "It's not my fault."

"Wait a minute. You talked with Jamie?"

"She had the papers. Rene told me he gave them to her to keep, but they weren't there, and she wouldn't tell me where they were."

"Oscar, is that what's in the envelope you gave me? Did you write down what Mrs. McBeel said to you. Because if you did—"

"You understand, don't you?" His voice rose right over me, not loud but insistent. "You're the only person who's been nice to me. I need you to understand." I didn't like

SUSAN C. SHEA

the fact that his teeth were slightly bared. Okay, now I was scared.

"Stay here," I said in a firm voice. "I'll get help." But he had reached out and grabbed my coat with both hands.

"Do you have them, Dani? Maybe you have them." He struggled to pull me closer. "I have to get them. Everything depends on them. There's still time..." His voice broke and he began to twist the fabric of my coat roughly. I was almost too frightened to make a mental note that it was a Dior coat and would not recover from this physical abuse easily.

"I don't have them," I said, "but if we go see my friend, we might find them together. How would that be?" I heard myself talking to him as if he were a toddler, but how else could I get my coat back?

"No police," he said again. "They're after me, you know? You didn't tell them where to find me, did you?" He pulled my coat harder. "You have to get me out of here," he said, talking faster. "They're following me again."

I pried the fabric out of his hands. "No one's following you now, Oscar, see?" I said, waving my hand toward the street, which, unfortunately, was full of double-parked dark cars with tinted windows, idling until the service was finished. In his eyes, they were probably all waiting for him to bolt. I pushed him toward the low concrete ledge behind us. How much of what he was babbling was real and how much was the result of his hysteria, I couldn't tell, but I had a feeling the best place for him might be an emergency ward rather than a police station. I hunkered down in front of him for a minute and put my hand over his restless ones. "I'll get my car," I said to him. "It'll be all right."

I figured if I said I'd get a cab, he might not want to get in. I'd improvise when we got to the curb. Maybe I'd actually

240

deliver him to the station, and maybe I'd wrangle him into the cab and run the other way.

Abruptly, he sat, folding his arms, dropping his head onto them, and rocking back and forth, making ugly, gasping noises. He didn't look like a murderer, sitting there sobbing. *They all say that*, my inner voice noted.

I ran around the corner and down the steps, waving frantically to the first cab I saw. He rolled down his window and I told him to wait a minute, that I'd be bringing someone over who was prostrate with grief. The cabbie looked skeptical, but turned his motor off. I ran back to Oscar who, thank heavens, hadn't moved. I tugged at him, but it was hard going. He wasn't paying much attention to me anymore. He kept mumbling as I dragged him a few steps toward the street.

"He promised no one would know. But I heard someone coming, and then you were calling for help, and I thought—"

"What's going on?"

For an instant, I stayed frozen in place. Oscar heard me come in to Jamie's office suite? He really did kill the most glamorous and powerful woman in San Francisco?

"What's happening here?"

I turned around to see Charlie Sugerman standing on the steps, a uniformed cop behind him.

Seeing the uniform, Oscar snapped upright. "You got the police. I told you not to!" he shouted. Suddenly, he grabbed me by the arm and yanked me up to the step he was standing on. Grabbing me in a bear hug from behind before I could recover my balance, he dragged me up the steps and back around the corner. I could hear Charlie yelling and got a glimpse of the uniformed cop jogging, but Oscar was pulling me from side to side as we stumbled backward and it was a blur.

"You bitch!" he screamed. "You said you wouldn't tell. You tricked me. You're a liar like everyone else. Now look what you've done."

This was a new and frightening Oscar, and I didn't like it one bit. I tried to twist away, but he was strong and determined. One of my shoes came off, which didn't help. Then, Charlie was tangled with us somehow and I began to feel like Gumby, being pulled in two directions at once. My hair had come loose and was catching on something. I thought Charlie might manage to pry me loose, but all of a sudden he stepped back, hands up in a placating way, at the same moment I felt a sharp point in my neck.

"Okay, okay," Charlie said. "Let her go, Oscar, so we can talk. You need to throw away the knife, okay?"

Knife? I tried to turn my head to look at the pressure point, but Oscar jerked me back to a position where I was directly facing Charlie. The knife was still pressing into my neck. He must have been running on pure adrenaline because both arms were still tight around my torso. I couldn't budge. I was breathing hard and looked to Charlie for a clue, but he was focused on Oscar, who was still cursing nonstop.

"You gave them the envelope, didn't you?" Oscar said, in that curious combination of anger and whininess he used. "I told you to give it to them only if I got killed, but you screwed up."

"She didn't give us anything, Oscar," Charlie said in a firm voice. "No envelope. I don't know what you mean. You need to drop the knife now so this doesn't get blown out of proportion. Then we can talk."

"I know how you guys work!" Oscar shouted. "You're all in it together. I'm not going to take the blame, do you hear me?" He dragged me backward toward a paved path that led to the adjacent building. I tried again to pull away, and the knife pricked me.

"Ouch," I said. "Don't hurt me, Oscar. Look, you heard Char —the policeman. I didn't get you in trouble, I promise."

Oscar's voice was harsh and keening. "No one keeps their promises. Not even Rene." His voice broke for a moment. "He said we'd be able to keep the lab running, and that I'd be the next director. But he didn't get me tenure, did he? And when the jar was stolen, Mr. McBeel got mad. He said he wouldn't give us any more money, that the lab would be shut down."

"Oscar, I can help you get the funds," I said. "Remember, I said talk to the university people? Well, I'll do that for you. Will that work, Oscar?" Without seeing him, it was like talking to the wind, but I had to try.

But he didn't seem to hear me. "Mrs. McB said she'd help me, but then she tried to run away."

"Oscar," Charlie said from his position close by but not close enough, "let the lady go. She's not involved in this and you know it. Come on now, drop the knife before things escalate."

"You're all the same!" Oscar shouted as someone opened a cathedral door and the combined boys' choirs sang out, sounding like an angelic chorus to his solo. Part of my mind registered this, the part that had decided not to get practical and help me out of this mess.

Charlie was advancing, step by step, as we retreated. *Like Astaire and Rogers*, my inner voice chose that moment to add. Astaire and Rogers, dipping and swaying as one organism in those old movies Dickie and I loved to watch. Tears sprung into my eyes. I had a powerful longing for those days suddenly. How had life gotten so lonely and scary? I felt sorry for myself, locked in this hostile embrace, in danger once again, with no one to rescue me. Maybe I should have been nicer to Dickie.

Astaire and Rogers. His arm around her waist, them bending gracefully, as one. I had an idea, but no way to alert Charlie to what I was going to do. If it didn't work, well, I wouldn't think about that. For the first time since we had begun this awkward dance, I became keenly aware of our surroundings. Behind Charlie, I could see lots of uniformed cops, alert, several of them talking into their handhelds. Farther away still, held back by the police, a few TV cameramen, probably here for the funeral, were training their steadicams on us.

Oscar was still at it. "Rene should have trusted me to take care of it. This is all his fault."

"It's always someone else's fault, isn't it, Oscar?" I swallowed the lump in my throat and said loud enough to break through his rant, "I don't even know what you're talking about. I never opened that envelope, know that? Never. And here I am, about to get stabbed for trying to help you."

The pressure of the knife didn't lessen but Oscar's voice wobbled. "You shouldn't have called the cops. I thought you were different. I trusted you." I could smell the sweat coming off his body and feel tremors in his arm.

We were still shuffling slowly backward and onto the path. I couldn't see behind me, but had to guess there were cops there, too. Maybe they had guns. Charlie was still walking with us, arms held out, probably so Oscar could see he had no weapon.

Without warning but with all the force and speed I could muster, I jerked my torso toward the ground, tipping my head away from the knife. We had never been moving smoothly and, while Oscar wasn't so off balance as to tumble, his upper body did follow me far enough forward so that his balance weakened and he lost his grip around my middle. I was too far into my plunge to move away from him, so I rolled onto my shoulder and kicked out at his legs. He roared, and would have kicked me back if Charlie hadn't rushed him from the front and a few other pairs of feet hadn't converged on us all at once.

It got chaotic then, yelling, bodies, hands pulling at me, a foot in running shoes connecting with my chest, and then someone holding my head down. I was conscious that my cheek stung. I grabbed the hands on my skull to pry them off, only to have Charlie holler, "It's okay, Dani. Stay down, stay down."

So I did. Took deep breaths and sank into the pavement, waiting for whatever was happening to stop. My shoulder hurt from slamming the pavement. My collarbone hurt, probably from the running shoe's kick, which must have been Oscar. The pinch on my neck tingled, and my cheek hurt more. I reached up and my hand came away with blood on it. A lot of blood, actually.

Right about then, the chaos ended. I looked up. Oscar, doubled over, hands behind his back, was weeping as four policeman manhandled him toward a waiting police car.

A woman cop bent over me. "How are you, ma'am?" she said. I assured her I was basically fine, but couldn't see how bad my cheek was. To me, I sounded like someone who had finished running a record race, panting and gasping for air.

"We've got the rescue squad on the way. Less than a minute," she said. "You did good, ma'am." She grinned at me for an instant before standing up and calling, "Over here."

A young guy in a windbreaker plopped down next to me on the path. He made me lie down flat, which I protested, but uselessly. He checked me out and said I was lucky. Oscar's knife had grazed my cheek when I dropped down, but no stitches were required. The prick in my neck was even milder.

"You're lucky," the woman cop said.

Lucky? How's that, I thought as the EMT helped me sit up, then stand. I pushed hair away from my face, tried to straighten my clothes to something like normal, and looked around.

Oscar was sitting motionless in the cop car, his chin on his chest. There must have been a dozen cops surrounding the car. Charlie was talking and gesturing to a couple of them, who nodded and fingered their belts. The media that had turned out for the funeral were clustered as close to the police car as possible like a pack of straining hunting dogs. I wondered if the people listening to the boys' choir inside the cathedral knew that such a drama was taking place so close by.

Closer to where I stood, another cop was standing over an ugly knife that lay on the walkway. What had Oscar said? The research lab would be shut down? His job gone? Just now, he had blurted out that everything was Rene's fault. Had Oscar turned on his mentor to prevent him from telling their billionaire supporter something that would jeopardize their funding? Maybe I had the right idea about ransom, but the wrong person. Oscar might have taken the jar as a crazy means of securing funds for the lab.

Charlie came over, worry lines furrowing his brow. "You scared me, Dani," he said, taking my arm and steering me toward a police car, its rotating red lights raking the cathedral walls. "It was an awful chance to take. How's your cheek?" He took my chin in one hand and gently lifted my face, no doubt examining the bulky bandage that covered that side of my face. Those amazing green eyes blazed at me.

"I'm fine, really," I said. "I wanted to signal what I was going to do, but couldn't figure out how." Now that it was all over, I wanted to cry, preferably in his arms. I restrained myself, turned partially away from him. Crowds, cameras, no place to be weak.

"You did fine, but it was a bad moment. He could have done a lot more damage with that hunting knife."

"Are you arresting Oscar for Jamie's murder?"

"We're arresting him for attempting to murder you," Charlie said, his voice turning hard. "As for the rest, I expect we'll be asking him a lot of questions and looking for evidence the rest of today and tonight. Dani," he said, stopping and pulling me gently around to face him, "we're going to need your help if you're up to it. Do you think you could be on hand at the station for a few hours?"

I felt crummy, but we were so close to unraveling this. I wanted to know who had the jar, damn it. Were Keile Obarri, Simon, or Tom involved in any way?

"I'll be okay if someone can bring me the orange juice the EMT told me to drink," I said.

"Good girl."

» » »

I was at the station half the night, parked in the same small conference room I'd visited before. Weiler questioned Oscar alone, then with Charlie, then alone again. Charlie kept coming in to ask me things I mostly didn't know, like names of people who worked in Kenobia's museum and who Jamie

McBeel spent time with. I wanted to go home and sleep but Charlie apologized.

"We need help here, Dani. The guy's still not making a lot of sense."

"Tell me," I said, sighing and wishing the fluorescent tubes overhead would stop clicking and flickering. "This is not my area of knowledge. I'm a simple fundraiser, trying to find out where my employer's precious object is. The rest of this is way over my head."

Someone brought me a Styrofoam cup of sour coffee and some powder that was supposed to make me think it was cream. I asked for water, and a half hour later, the same person strolled in with a plastic bottle of "clear mountain stream water," probably from a tap somewhere in South San Francisco.

At one point, there was a sudden flurry of activity and conversation in the hallway. Weiler opened the door and peeked in at me, as did a guy with a well-cut suit and a halo of silver hair. I recognized him from photos as the district attorney and the leading candidate for governor in the next election. I caught a glimpse of Wayne Lawson behind the politician, talking on a cell phone pressed close to his ear. Charlie leaned in, too, then pulled Weiler away as he spoke urgently into the older man's ear.

Forty minutes later, Weiler came all the way in and sat across from me, chewing on his upper lip. He slid down on his chair and ran his hands through already mussed hair before speaking.

"We got a problem here. What did this Oscar guy tell you? Go through it again."

I repeated as much as I could remember, admitting that I might have it wrong since Oscar wasn't all that clear in the telling of it.

"So he told you he killed Bouvier and Mrs. McBeel?"

"Well, sort of. I think he said Rene's death was an accident. And I wasn't sure if Oscar meant it literally when he said that he killed Jamie until he told me that he heard me come in to her office. He confronted her about the missing artifact and some papers," I said, not wanting to get into the ownership details right now.

"Did he say why Rene Bouvier was killed?"

"I'm so tired I can't think straight, Inspector. He did say something about Rene not protecting his job at Warefield. Tell me this, anyway," I said, feeling a sudden wave of anger, "has he said anything about where the King's Jar is?"

"I'll get someone to take you home," Weiler said, pushing himself up from the table. "I can't see that we need you here any longer tonight. Oh," he added with his hand on the doorknob, "thanks. You helped catch the bad guy, and that gets that society bigwig and the DA off my back."

And that was that. A serious young officer with a buzz cut and huge biceps ran me home in a marked car to an indignant cat and a bed that seemed especially empty. I'm not at my best when I'm sleep-deprived or scared, and I was both. In addition, my cheek was burning so much I gave in and took one of the pain pills someone had handed me. Fever picked up on my funk and curled up close to me after scarfing down his midnight dinner. I guess we slept.

chapter 19

THE PHONE RANG twice while I was showering in the hottest water my skin could handle, trying to ease my stiff muscles. Victoria's message said to call her back right away. So did Simon's.

I picked up the phone as the doorbell rang. And rang. I looked out to see a silver Porsche parked at an angle across the driveway, blocking any cars wanting in or out. Impossible. I don't know anyone other than my ex who drives a silver Porsche and has such a total disregard for parking conventions.

"How did you get here?" I said when I had recovered from the shock of seeing him at my door.

"Why isn't there a police guard right here right now, damn it?" he said as he stormed in.

"You haven't shaved, and it's way too cold for shorts."

"You're hurt." He would have touched the bandage on my cheek if I hadn't pulled back. It throbbed this morning, as did all of me.

"It's nothing," I said. "But what are you doing here, Dickie? You're supposed to be on the ocean somewhere."

"Lucky for me, there were seats on a flight out of Miami, once I got that far. Are you okay?"

"Really, I am. Just achy and tired. You didn't have to do this."

"If you could stay out of trouble, I wouldn't have to," my ex said. "You have coffee?" He headed into the kitchen. I wanted to be angry. Who was he to come slamming into my house and my life uninvited? But I remembered that moment of helplessness, locked in Oscar's embrace, feeling alone even with all those cops nearby.

"When did you get in?" I said, getting down mugs and dropping cinnamon bread into the toaster. "You're still in boat shoes. And those shorts make you look kind of silly, actually."

"Thanks. There wasn't time. I hitched a ride on a private jet to get to Miami. I heard on TV about that bastard taking you hostage. Geez, Dani, you scared me to death."

"The news? I can't believe it's out there already."

"Internet, sweetheart. It was probably online an hour after they pulled that leech off you."

"But it's not that important in the larger scheme of things. Why...oh, the McBeel connection." I sighed as I buttered the toast and pushed the plate across the table. "What was I thinking? Jamie's funeral. Of course it made the news."

"That's not the point," Dickie said. "I want to know if the danger's over. I want to know why there are no cops outside. Tell me everything."

I was too tired to give him a verbatim account of the last week, with all the nasty surprises and weird bits and pieces, so I did a fast summary.

"I don't know," he said. "Oscar seemed like such a passive guy. Something doesn't compute."

"Whatever. I'm sick to death of the drama," I said. I didn't want to talk to anybody, which reminded me I had to talk to Victoria and Simon. I made a deal with Dickie. If he went home and cleaned up, I'd stay at the apartment until he came back. He could escort me to the museum. Somehow, I felt that everything would be all right if I could sit in my office chair and pretend to work for a couple of hours.

Reluctantly, he agreed, but I had to promise not to budge for the next forty-five minutes.

I called Victoria first. She'd gotten a garbled message from Oscar yesterday before the funeral. "He said he had to know if Jamie had given me something to keep for her. He said I had to tell him, that it could mean life or death. I didn't want to call him back without talking with you first. I can't believe what's happened."

"You'll have to tell the police," I said. "What about the key?"

"Before I had to be at the cathedral, I went to the three bank branches Jamie used, but none of them identified it as theirs so I plan to give it to Charlie Sugerman this morning, like we agreed. Dani, are you okay?"

"Tired," I said.

"Simon called me. Should I tell him about the key?"

"Nothing, tell him nothing," I said. I hated to admit it to myself, but he had told me he didn't know Jamie, and until I knew he didn't have the jar, I couldn't completely trust him.

Victoria clearly didn't believe Simon was involved in anything criminal. "Dani, remember that he may have been the last person to talk to Mrs. McBeel before she died. He could have the information we want."

"Please, please, take it straight to the police, Victoria. We can't take the chance someone else is still looking for it."

She agreed. She was probably as spooked as I was about the accumulating violence around the missing treasure. "Now that the funeral's over, it'll be quiet. The next job may be closing everything up. I'm too depressed to go in, to tell you the truth."

Simon, when I reached him on his cell, was impatient to meet. "I've been frantic. Are you all right?" His voice sounded warm and sincere, which made me feel guilty for being even a little suspicious of him.

"I guess everyone knows about it, huh?" I said. "I think I'll hide out until the fuss dies down. Either that or think of something more original to say every time someone asks about my health."

"Get used to it, Dani. You're a celebrity right now."

"Ugh. Half an hour, that's all I have," I compromised, "and someplace where I can be anonymous." What if I could get Simon to admit he'd been having an affair with Jamie? Would he tell me what he and Jamie talked about in her office the evening before she died? I might be able to bring information to Charlie that would soothe my bad conscience. I might find out what *"Can Simon trust Tom?"* meant.

I was headed out of my apartment when I remembered my promise to Dickie. He wasn't picking up his cell phone, which made it easier to leave a message saying I had to get to the museum right away for a special meeting, but I'd call him as soon as I could. There's a small bistro not far from my apartment. Their espresso is perfect and they have the best croissants this side of the Left Bank in Paris. If I skipped the croissants for a year, I might lose ten pounds. But then, I'd have nothing to cut the strong coffee with.

Simon had seen the local TV news and fussed over my bandaged cheek. He was more relaxed than he had sounded on the phone because, he explained, Oscar was no longer a threat to me.

"Simon, Oscar wanted to tell me something and he asked for my help. But he went out of control."

Simon's shoulders twitched impatiently when I said Oscar never got around to telling me anything specific. He pushed me to go over everything Oscar said, but gave up when I explained it was all a blur, and reached for his coffee.

"I'm glad you called," I said, shaking my head at the waiter who wanted to know if I was up for another espresso. "Tell me more about Keile Obarri. I'm remembering his hostility toward Jamie at the gala, and his long history with the missing piece. Do you think he's involved with any of this?"

Simon barked a short laugh. "With the artifact, you bet. With murder, I don't see it. He's an operator and doesn't mind bending the rules, shall we say, when it's to his benefit. Maybe in the old days in Kenobia he might have been involved in violence. But today? Nah."

"I did some research on him, Simon, after I saw him with Jamie at the gala dinner. There were photos of Obarri, McBeel, and Rene in a Kenobian newspaper. You were in the group, too."

"It must have been an old paper," Simon said.

"Yes, about twenty years old. Right around the time Fritz purchased the jar, if I have it right."

"Those were the days," Simon said, his voice deepening as he morphed into the storyteller of television fame. He notched his expressive eyebrows up, drained his coffee cup, and turned his gaze to the ceiling. "The wild west, African style. It wasn't just Obarri, you know. Everyone was angling for an advantage—the archaeologists, the heads of the native crews, the entrepreneurs who hired out gangs of Kalashnikov-toting security guards. There was almost more bullshit than science being done, I can tell you. Crazy times."

"Sounds like you enjoyed it," I said, making it a question.

"Sure, why not? I had no real stake in the game, but I got to watch and take notes. My first book came out of that time, caused quite a stink, in fact."

"Because...?"

"I pretty much named names and told stories I'd heard, all of them true but not always flattering. Rene hated it, wrote to the *New York Times Book Review* editor, blasting him for giving it a front-page review."

"Why? Did you bad-mouth him?"

"No. In fact, I admired the guy, even when we didn't see eye to eye. One time, I had to point out that some of his data was off on a paper, and he did the right thing and pulled it, even though it must have hurt his pride."

"Oh, was our Tom Burns one of the authors?" I said. That would explain Tom's cryptic remark.

"Might have been. It was a long time ago. My point is Rene was a real scholar. But he had so much at stake—after all, his team needed to get their permits renewed every year—that he was always worried something would go wrong in Kenobia. He was pissed that I described the ministry the way it was, basically a gang of con men out for themselves, ready to do whatever any Westerner wanted for a fee."

"Such as?"

"Falsify permit approvals or denials, restrict access to material the postdocs had recovered, delaying their ability to publish, insist that the foreign teams use certain providers who charged three and four times the going rate for cars, cooks, and supplies. They encouraged bribes, then blackmailed people for it. Not that I blame them, in a way." Simon put his hands flat on the table and leaned forward.

"Kenobia was dirt poor, badly scarred by constant warfare, ravaged by drought and famine five out of every ten years, and most men didn't have jobs other than what Westerners provided. The atmosphere was like Bogart in *Casablanca*."

"Mary McBeel said you were an insider in Kenobia in those days."

"Mary was too. For one thing, there were so few Kenobians who were trained archaeologists in those days, not like today."

"Mary says the export sale of the artifact was, well, a little unorthodox."

"Yes, but it was for real. I told you I more or less brokered it. The decision-makers at the MACPCA in those days may not have known what was important to hang onto. Most of the archaeologists itching to bring home the loot weren't exactly open about the value of what they had, either."

"Which is where Obarri came in. I read he was the head of the ministry of something or other."

"MACPCA, yeah, but not always the head. You can get a lot done in the smallest office at the end of the hall if your relative is the president of the country."

"Would Obarri kill to get the King's Jar back now?" I said bluntly.

"No way. The government's doing a good job of creating stability and respect for processes. There's some foreign investment and a lot more kids in school than in the past. I'd lay odds that ten years from now, the Kenobian government will begin proceedings to repatriate the King's Jar and a lot of other stuff from various archaeological sites. By then, Obarri might be president and it would be a huge political win to bring back an icon of the country's rich history. He'd be a fool to jeopardize that with something as crude as murder at this point in his career."

"Okay then," I said, not sure if I accepted his theory but aware that I had to get up and leave in a couple of minutes, "would you?"

"Would I what?" Simon said, looking puzzled.

"I'm no detective, Simon, but I feel like I've been yanked around by a lot of people with secrets ever since poor Rene got hit over the head and the King's Jar went missing." My body was practically pulsing with pent-up anger. Probably fatigue, but something emboldened me to ask him point blank. "You were having an affair with Jamie. You were with her the night before she died. I know she gave you something, but Victoria and I can't find it. Was it the jar?"

He looked at me like I'm sure I looked at Oscar the day before. I could see his face turning red under the celebrity tan and his mouth was clamped shut.

"I hope I'm not hearing you right," he said. "I did not sleep with Jamie McBeel," he said in a low voice, "much less kill her, and I cannot imagine how you could consider such a grotesque scenario. I might sleep with a married woman," and here he shrugged, "but I'd never, ever kill someone."

He rose, and I scrambled to my feet, stammering that I was only talking about the missing artifact, not murder. His voice was stone cold as he stared at me. "I'm sorry you think I'm some kind of psycho." And the Most Eligible Bachelor proceeded to thread his way through the tables and vanish from the café and my life. Just like that.

My own face was red now. It didn't improve my mood when my cell phone rang and Charlie asked me, in brusque tones, to come over to the station immediately. I snapped back, but, twenty minutes later, feeling like a fool and a failure, I found the last parking space up on the roof next to the station.

It was hurry up and wait. I chose to stand rather than sit on a wobbly plastic chair wedged in a row along one wall. When my cell phone rang, I knew without looking who it was.

"Dickie, I can't talk now. I'm at the police station."

"Well, at least no one can attack you there. You were going to wait for me to escort you, remember?" He sounded angry. "I'm coming down."

"No, Dickie. Charlie—Inspector Sugerman—asked me here. Something's come up. I don't know what, but I expect he'll be taking me in to an interview room or something." I was becoming way too familiar with how the cops did things, it occurred to me.

"Even more reason. I'll call Dad's lawyer and we'll meet you there—"

"Why would I need a lawyer, for heaven's sake? I was the intended victim. I'm fine. Can we just leave it like that?" I looked around and there was Charlie, walking into the lobby slowly, his eyes red-rimmed and his tie half undone. "Gotta run, Dickie. Bye."

"Reporters?" he said with a grimace.

"No, my ex. He's worried about me. Wanted to bring me a lawyer." I hit the silent button and jammed the phone in my bag as Charlie took my arm and steered me toward the elevator.

"Had enough of our badgering?" he said. "I'm sorry you're in the middle of this one. I don't know how you do it, actually."

"Do what?" I said.

"Get tangled in stuff like this."

Before I could think of a defense, he changed the topic. "Your pal Victoria Peerless came by early this morning. She found something that may help us, help the Devor, too."

"Really? What was it?" I said in what I hoped was a tone of genuine surprise, mentally thanking Victoria for pulling it off.

"I'll let you know when we've had time to check it out. I have cops working on that now." Punching the elevator button, he said, "Right now, I need you to do something for us." He waited until we were alone in the elevator to continue. "Oscar's insisting on seeing you. He's in an interview room, not a cell. Of course, someone will be listening from outside the room, but I'll be in the room with you. The idea is to find out why he wants to see you, if there's something specific to the museum or your artifact that's behind his request for you. This won't be a long interview, Dani. We want to book him quickly."

I nodded, remembering my complete failure with Simon, and hoping I wouldn't repeat that fiasco. "So he did murder Jamie? Do I need to ask him certain questions?"

"Don't ask anything except why he wanted to see you. If I need clarification, I'll ask the questions. Ready?"

We had reached a gray metal door, and Charlie opened it. There, facing us across an equally gray metal table, was Oscar, his hair disheveled, eyes redder than Charlie's, shirt rumpled. He was leaning forward, resting on his elbows. He looked exhausted. The room smelled like sweat and old sneakers. Instinctively, I fingered my handbag, wishing I could take out my spray cologne and spritz myself and everything else in the space. Of course, even aiming the little bottle at anyone would probably have set off every alarm in the building.

Not knowing what else to do, I said hello as I sat down on the metal chair across from him. Oscar looked back and forth from me to Charlie.

"Does he have to be here?"

"Yes I do, Oscar," Charlie said in a friendly tone. "You wanted to see Dani and here she is. But we don't have much time, so why don't you tell her what's on your mind."

"I'm sorry I hurt you," Oscar said, his whole face puckering in what looked like sincere distress. "I didn't want to. Is your face all right?"

"It will be," I answered. At that moment, Oscar looked like such a wimp I was having a hard time believing any part of the last day was real.

"Did you find it?" Oscar said suddenly, leaning toward me. "Is it safe?"

"I have no idea where the jar is," I said, instantly annoyed. "Why would I?"

"Damn," Oscar said, frowning. His gaze fell to the table and he fell silent.

"Fritz McBeel seems to think I know, too."

"Rene said she had it—Mrs. McBeel had it. When I went to her office, she said that Mr. McBeel could have it back anytime if he gave her what she wanted. She said no one else knew where it was."

"But," Charlie said in a casual voice, "you thought Dani knew?"

"It seemed like the museum would be the safest place," Oscar said. "I was sure Dani or Tom Burns had it. I even wondered if Anderson gave it to her."

"Hardly," I said, snorting. "We've all been frantic. We thought whoever killed Rene stole it. Isn't that what the police think?" I said, looking over at Charlie.

"Oscar, tell Dani what you told us," Charlie said.

"Fritz—Mr. McBeel—told me if it wasn't returned, there wasn't any reason to keep funding us. He got angry. He was sure Simon Anderson smuggled it out of the country. Rene wouldn't have gone along with that, though," Oscar said, looking over at Charlie. "He always believed the jar should stay in the U.S. until Kenobia could care for it. I mean, it's the holy grail to a lot of people."

I opened my mouth, but Charlie held up a hand. "So, Oscar, is that why you wanted to see Dani?"

"Yeah, I thought she must know," Oscar said, shrugging his shoulders and staring at me. "I have no idea where it is, and that's the truth."

"Jamie never said anything to me about it after it went missing except what I told you already," I said to Charlie.

"I want a lawyer," Oscar said. "You called Mr. McBeel and he's sending his, right? He promised he would."

"A lawyer is waiting outside," Charlie said, still in his good-cop voice. My cell phone began to vibrate audibly, and Charlie used that interruption to get us out of the room.

"Dani," Oscar called out, urgency in his voice, as I went through the doorway, "I'm really sorry, okay? I really am."

Oddly, I believed him.

Something Oscar said was bugging me, but I couldn't grab the thought before it faded. The caller was Dickie. I thought about ignoring it, but knew he would not quit until he reached me.

"What is it, Dickie? You're driving me crazy. I told you, I'm in no place to talk."

"I know," he said. "But someone from Burton and Ballot is on the way over to make sure you aren't being harassed, and I'm on my way. If they won't let us see you, we'll raise holy hell."

"Stop," I said, "stop right now!" I was shouting and Charlie, who had been talking quietly to a uniformed cop a few feet away, turned and looked questioningly at me. Dickie was still babbling. "Listen to me, Richard Argetter. I am not in police custody. I am not in trouble. I am not in danger. I am perfectly fine and able to take care of myself. The only person who's harassing me is you." Charlie grinned at the other cop, which only made me madder for some reason.

I spun on my heel and walked as far away as I could before I spoke again. Dickie had shut up. I could imagine the hurt little-boy look on his face. I flashed back to the moment when Oscar held me at knife point and, thinking I might die at any moment, I had thought of Dickie and the happy days of our marriage. My voice was softer when I said, "Dickie, I'm sorry. I didn't mean that. You're really sweet to want to help and I give you my word I will accept your offer if I need it. But right now, everything is fine. They have Oscar and he can't touch me. Okay? Can you call off the lawyer for right now? I promise to fill you in. In fact, why don't you come to my office? That's where I'm headed now. We can get coffee or something."

My ex sounded a little wary as he agreed to meet me at the Devor. That may have been the first time in two years I actually suggested we meet. No wonder he might have thought it was a trick.

When the phone rang again instantly, my mood shifted. If that was Dickie, the offer of coffee was off forever. But I saw that the caller was Tom Burns. Charlie had just signaled that he'd be back for me in five minutes and walked down to the end of the hallway with the other cop.

"Dani, you're not going to believe this." Tom's voice was pinched with excitement. "We found it. We found the King's Jar."

"No way," I shouted. "Tell me." I waved my arm toward Charlie, but he rounded the corner. I began to trot after him.

"It was only by chance," Tom said, "which gives me goose bumps. Late yesterday, the intern came across something in a cabinet with no acquisition number." He sounded breathless with excitement. "She didn't pull it out of its wrapping, but included the information in her daily summary. This morning, we reviewed the handful of questions in the report and there it was. The jar, Dani, the goddamn Song Dynasty celadon jar, sitting right there on a shelf, in perfect shape right up to the little rhino figure, wrapped in brown paper." His voice broke.

No Charlie when I rounded the corner, so I stopped and focused on Tom's news. "Have you told Peter? Has anyone called the police?"

"I left an urgent message for Peter, but didn't want to get people talking, so I didn't tell Dorie. I don't know how it got there and hope we're not somehow blamed for this."

"And the police?"

"No, I wanted to talk to you or Peter for the same reason."

"Are you sure it's not a fake?"

"Absolutely. Remember, I've examined it many times. It's in my office. Believe me," he said, with a laugh that rang through the phone, "it will not be out of my eyesight for one minute until it's photographed, acknowledged, and in our vault. I'll sleep here if I have to."

"But how the hell did it get there?" I said, as much to myself as to Tom.

"Had to be someone with access to the archives. Dani, I know he's your friend, but my bet's on Simon," Tom said. "No one on the staff would do it. He's been in the archives a lot lately. But why? Don't ask me."

Of course. That had to be what Jamie gave Simon. The rat—he had known all this time and hadn't told anyone. "I'm at the police station right now and I'll tell them. Sit tight, Tom."

» » »

The next few hours were a blur. I got back to the Devor without killing anyone in my rush. Peter was marching around Tom's office, alternating big grins and ferocious looks, and Tom was pulling so hard on his hair, I worried he'd be bald by night. The intern who had made the find was clearly loving her role of taking a parade of people into the archives and repeating her story.

The cops wanted to take fingerprints from the ancient vessel, which Tom and Peter objected to on the grounds that the chemicals might damage the material. I vaguely understood they came to some compromise. The museum, being a small community, was buzzing within minutes of our arrival, and everyone wanted to do high fives and fist bumps. Teeni smiled and said simply, "The Devor should be proud. Tom was doing his stewardship right, and it paid off. I'll remember that when I'm a curator."

Teeni had brought Dickie up to my office, and he was pacing back and forth. She wouldn't tell him what had happened until someone gave her the okay, and, he told me later, he was afraid something new had happened to me, seeing everyone rushing around, whispering. When I came in the door, he grabbed me in a hug so tight I could hardly get my breath.

"God, Dani, you scared me to death," he said in a ragged voice that was buried in my hair. I hugged him back for a moment, admitting to myself that it was nice to have someone care so much. I had to tell him the news just to get him to calm down.

Charlie, Peter, Geoff Johnson, a silent but beaming Dickie, and I wound up in Peter's office, sprawled on the sofas. Geoff looked at my bandaged cheek and asked about my injury. "You're a brave girl," he said. I ignored the "girl" part. Geoff meant well and was too old to change.

He told us he had talked to the police chief, who was satisfied the case was wrapped up. Fritz McBeel's attorney told the police that Rene had called his billionaire client the day before the old man died to say the treasure was being held "privately" until McBeel agreed to revised terms that would allow repatriation to Kenobia in time. Rene had explained that Mrs. McBeel—the second Mrs. McBeel, that is—had been persuaded by Dr. Bouvier to help somehow, for the sake of the object's safety. McBeel refused to agree to the terms. He had intended to speak to his wife but, alas, the lawyer said, she died before he could do so. He said nothing about a divorce settlement, which didn't surprise me. But it had to be why Jamie had agreed to help hide the jar. It was the only rational reason she'd get involved.

Geoff said the police chief told him that Oscar Shelby had attempted to get the King's Jar back in a misguided effort to curry favor with Fritz.

"So Fritz told him about Rene's decision to put the Song jar into a hiding place?" Peter said. "He actually wanted Shelby to rough up the old man?"

"Good lord, no," Geoff said. "The chief says Oscar confessed to killing Rene accidentally, meaning only to scare him into saying where it was."

"I wonder how Oscar got from Rene to Jamie," I said. "It was hardly intuitive."

"Do you think Rene confided at least some of this to Oscar before he died?" Peter said.

"The chief's not saying much," Geoff said, "but he did tell me Oscar met with Fritz to discuss the situation at the lab after Rene's death. Oscar is a strange character. He may have decided the way to get on Fritz's good side was to keep looking for the artifact."

I pictured the scene in Jamie's office, the empty file folder on the floor next to her. If McBeel had mentioned that he thought his wife knew where the jar was, Oscar could have concluded McBeel wanted him to find out. He obviously hadn't found the documents, because Jamie had taken them out of the folder and locked them up somewhere. But if she had threatened to call the police when Oscar badgered her for information about the jar, he could have gone into his panic mode, which I had seen more than once, and killed her to keep her quiet. He had said, on the cathedral steps, that she tried to run, poor woman. Act first, think later seemed to be his style.

Geoff reminded us that the police chief and the district attorney were holding a press conference to announce solving the case. Peter and I agreed we needed to hold our own quickly, to tell the media that the King's Jar was safe and would be the centerpiece of the new exhibition as planned. Geoff, Dickie, and I left as Peter was calling Tom to come upstairs and consult. I seriously doubted that even the boss's directive would dislodge Tom from his vigil until the artifact was in the Devor's most secure vault.

I walked Geoff and Dickie down to the lobby.

"What people will do for money," Dickie murmured as we stood there.

"Oscar, you mean?" Geoff said.

"Yes. He wanted money for the lab, right? And Fritz held the keys to the bank, so to speak. So sad." He shook his head as he squeezed my hand. "I'll see you later, Dani."

Geoff and I lingered a little longer. I thanked him for his help and understanding. "Well, it's difficult times, isn't it?" he said, shaking his head. "So many people suffering, and for what? Oh, Louise sent something over for you. I left it with that crackerjack assistant of yours on the way up to see Peter."

My watch said it was almost closing time, and my body said it was way later than that as I got back to my office. At the top of the stack of papers in my in-box was a white envelope with "For Danielle's eyes only" scribbled on it. I flopped into my chair, slit the envelope open, and unfolded several sheets of paper densely covered with typewritten text. Paper-clipped to the top was a thick, creamy business card embossed with grey ink. "Mary McBeel" was printed on it and under that was handwritten, "Here it is, dear. You'll know what to do with it. Best, M."

The pages were copies of the sale papers from Kenobia's museum of antiquities, stamped export forms, and a memo of understanding. The sale was to Mary L. McBeel, precisely as she had said. The terms were "*to be sold back to the Government of Kenobia for the identical price in U.S. currency in twenty years, or at a date acceptable to both parties not, however, to exceed forty years.*"

There was one other sheet of paper, a copy like the other. The original had been typed on an old-fashioned typewriter that appeared to be in poor condition. "To Whom It May Concern." It was signed by someone whose name I didn't recognize, but whose title, printed below his signature, was Minister of State Police and Internal Security. The text was short but powerful, and shot me out of my chair. "*The State of Kenobia this day suspends the charges of bribery and intimidation of national officials by F. McBeel in return for his permanent banishment from the State of Kenobia and his agreement that he will never purchase or own any object excavated from Kenobian soil.*" Fritz's printed name and scrawled signature was underneath the minister's.

So that was it, a criminal act that made it impossible for Fritz McBeel to possess what Oscar had called the "holy grail" of sub-Saharan history. It explained the behavior Teeni and I observed between Obarri and McBeel at the Pilgrim Club.

I would bet Rene gave the file folder containing those documents to Jamie when he agreed with her that taking the jar out of circulation temporarily was the only way to keep Fritz from circumventing the deal by imposing a no-repatriation demand as part of the gift to the Devor. Jamie realized then that Fritz didn't actually own it, and she must have been torn. She could blackmail Fritz with the old document, but if she did, could hardly use the jar as ransom in return for half of his assets since the document proved her husband didn't actually own it.

Rene must have alerted Obarri, whom he knew twenty years ago in Africa, that the jar was going out of circulation for a while in order to make sure it would get returned to Kenobia. Jamie's guarded conversation with Obarri at the gala made sense if she, too, knew the jar was safe. Obarri's diplomatically expressed warning to her to make sure nothing happened to the treasure also fit if Rene had told him Jamie was helping.

Ironically, if Jamie had returned the King's Jar and Fritz had given it to the Devor, she would have been helping him break the terms of the first Mrs. McBeel's prenup agreement, and Mary could have come after half of Fritz's assets. In either case, he stood to lose a substantial share of a whole lot of money.

That also made Victoria's and Wayne's conflicting directions to us about taking ownership clear—Fritz wanted something that would bind us all to a different agreement. Jamie wanted to keep it in play long enough to use as leverage in her divorce.

My head was spinning with the twists and turns these people had taken in pursuit of their diametrically opposed goals. Money, power, and influence. Shame, deceit, and pride. I might struggle with my weight and my love life, but at the moment I was grateful to move in humbler circles than Fritz McBeel and his satellites.

I folded the expulsion letter into an envelope, addressed it, and left it in my outgoing mail box. I walked the rest of the copies Mary had sent me up to Peter's office. I told him I didn't know what to recommend he do with them, but that I was headed home with a sick headache. My cheek was throbbing and my shoulder ached.

As I crawled through the early evening traffic, something nagged at me. *"You called Mr. McBeel and he's sending his, right? He promised he would."* When and why, I wondered, did Fritz McBeel promise to provide a lawyer to defend Oscar? I recalled the archaeologist's awkward, earlier attempt to ask for my help getting Fritz to commit to the lab without Rene, and his increasing paranoia when we returned to San Francisco.

And, all of a sudden I remembered seeing the politically ambitious district attorney and Wayne Lawson, Fritz McBeel's go-to guy, hovering together outside the room I sat in during my long stay at the police station. Mary McBeel said Fritz made sure the people dependent on him knew what would please him. And, with the power that came from enormous wealth and prestige, he was used to getting what he wanted. He probably had since he was a little boy. When Peter told me about the time McBeel bought a newspaper in Los Angeles and gutted it, what had he said? In the end, Wayne arranged it so McBeel's role was invisible.

Money moves behind the scenes. Dickie had said that, hadn't he? He had been talking about big money, the kind of wealth Fritz McBeel controlled. Dickie had been commenting about people who used their money as leverage to intimidate and manipulate, and who managed to avoid consequences for what they set in motion. Suddenly, I was overcome with a wave of revulsion and fury so strong I felt dizzy. I pulled over to the side of the street.

Was it possible Oscar was set up specifically to commit this mayhem on McBeel's behalf because the billionaire didn't want to lose a contest of wills over a mere object? Or, more likely, was he afraid he might have to choose between losing a large portion of his billions or having the "To Whom It May Concern" letter become public in a nasty divorce case, where it would damage his reputation as a noble philanthropist and supporter of important research? Was all of this chaos and death the result of a cold calculation? Did McBeel actually find someone foolish and inexperienced enough to be pressured into doing his dirty work?

chapter 20

THE STREET WAS QUIET at this time of night. Subdued lights showed in the mansions on the McBeels' block, but there were no signs of big parties, no valets standing around, no rental trucks, or slightly drunk people standing on the lawns chattering. Perhaps they were silent out of respect for Jamie McBeel, strangled less than a week ago, or her bereaved husband.

"Poor man," someone was probably saying over cognac in one of the houses. "It goes to show that you can't buy happiness."

But you can buy some things, can't you? I said to Fritz McBeel in my head as I walked up to his front door. I thought of Jamie, lying on the floor, vulnerable in death as she never seemed when she was alive. I saw Rene, old and bitter but brilliant and principled. Who said he had to die, and for what? And I even felt a little bit sorry for Oscar, who might have known a lot about archaeology and Africa but nothing—worse than nothing—about how to get along in the world, much less how to control his lethal panic attacks.

My chest burned with anger at the injustice of it all, and shame that I'd been blinded by a billionaire's money. It was my anger that steered my car here and my anger that made me ring the door chimes—and it gave me enough courage to ring them again and again when there was no answer.

"Hello, Gerard," I said when he finally opened the door. "I need to see Mr. McBeel. It's urgent."

"I'm afraid Mr.—"

"It's urgent," I repeated and marched past him into the hallway. I heard my own voice and wondered when it had become so rough.

He must have heard something, too, because he only said, "Wait here," and walked quickly in the direction of Fritz McBeel's study. I didn't wait but walked so fast behind him that I almost banged into him when he stopped at the open door of the study.

Fritz looked up from a book on his desk, putting his finger on the place in the text he had been reading. On the desk next to him was a brandy snifter and, next to it, a silver tray with a decanter. The little armor-clad figure glowed in its shallow niche in the bookcase behind him.

"Thank you, Gerard," was all Fritz said until the butler left, closing the door quietly behind him. Fritz waved me to a seat, for which I was grateful because my legs were shaky and my heart was banging hard in my chest.

He said nothing while I fought to calm my breathing enough to speak.

"Oscar has told them everything," I said.

"Good." He looked at me without blinking. "The man's obviously insane. The courts will decide what to do with him."

"Everything, Mr. McBeel. About how you persuaded him to kill that old man and your wife, both of them."

"I did nothing of the sort, young woman, and I urge you to watch what you say."

"You promised Oscar that you'd keep the research team in funds if he found the King's Jar and made sure the Kenobians never got it back. And you even promised to hire your own lawyer to defend him should he do something bad—like murder—in the process. You—"

"That's enough, Miss O'Rourke," Fritz said sharply. "You don't know what you're talking about. I did no such thing, and I'll thank you to leave my house at once. You're overwrought. I shall chalk up your strange behavior to the traumas of the last week and let it go at that."

"Oscar told the police you promised to get him a lawyer. I'll bet that was before your wife was strangled. And is that lawyer likely to defend him or is this a clever way you and Wayne Lawson intend to make sure he takes the fall all by himself for what you told him to do?"

Fritz slammed his glass down and jumped up from his chair. He began to pace between his desk and the far window. "Now you listen to me, you little busybody. I've had enough. No one talks to me like this. In one minute I will call my good friend the chief of police and have you arrested for trespassing."

"Yes, he's your friend, all right," I said, too furious to be cautious. "The district attorney's your friend, too, isn't he? And because they are, and because no one will stand up to you or take the risk of offending you, Oscar will take the complete blame for all of this."

"As he should," Fritz said, raising his voice and turning toward me from across the room. "He hit Rene over the head, he killed my wife. Why shouldn't he?"

I got up and put my hands on the back of my chair. "You're right," I said in the most conversational tone I could manage, swallowing the lump that was forming in my throat. "Oscar killed Rene, by accident, but, yes, he killed his mentor when Rene wouldn't hand over the jar. And Oscar, thinking he was doing what you demanded in return for keeping the research project going, went to Jamie's office to frighten her and get her to tell him where it was, and that went wrong, too, and she died."

Fritz was making an effort to maintain a haughty expression while he glared at me. "He will pay, perhaps with his life," I said, practically choking on my anger. "But who set him up? Who frightened him into thinking he had no choice, no future unless he brought you the treasure?"

"It was mine, mine to give to the museum. Rene had no right to hide it."

"But it wasn't Rene who hid it. It was Jamie."

"She was conned by Bouvier," he said, shaking his head.

"No. She wanted a divorce, and you threatened to cut her off without a penny, so she took it hostage. She offered to tell you where it was, but only if you released her from the prenup, isn't that right?" I was breathless. "That's the real reason all this happened. You didn't want to part with your money." Saying it out loud made me nauseous.

"You can't prove it, but even if you could, it wouldn't change the fact that Oscar Shelby killed her and will pay with his life." McBeel's words were clipped, cold. He was standing in front of his bookcase wall, fingering the little warrior.

"You hope. Because otherwise, people may begin to listen to his story, and he will have a lifetime to tell it, won't he?"

"Jamie was foolish," McBeel said. "She would have changed her mind. But," he barked an odd laugh, "she misjudged me. She never could have kept me from finding it, and I never would have dropped our legal agreement."

"The truth is, you were in a bad place."

"You don't understand a thing," Fritz said. "My wife's decision to hide the jar made no difference ultimately. It was still mine to give."

I took a deep breath. "No, it wasn't. It was Mary's all along. Only Mary could decide who would have it."

The room was silent for a full minute. "Where did you hear that?" he said. His head snapped up and he said in a harsh voice, "You have the papers. Goddamn it, you have the papers." He came at me in a rush and grabbed my wrist. "Where are they? Tell me."

"No. I don't have them," I said, pulling my hand away. "But the right people do."

"Mary," he blurted out, glaring down at me from barely a foot away. "Mary told you."

"Mary didn't want more people killed because of your warped sense of divine right." I moved as far away from him as I could in the enclosed space.

"Mary wants more money so she can give it to that scheming bunch of incompetents in Kenobia."

"Mary wants them to become competent, and why not? But I don't think she's after your money," I said through clenched teeth. "Truth is, if you persuaded the Devor to accept the gift in perpetuity, Mary could come back at you and invalidate the prenup."

McBeel licked his lips and looked at me, warily, but said nothing.

"But she wanted the original deal to go through, which would keep your prenup in effect and repatriate the jar someday." I was figuring it out as I spoke. "I'm guessing you thought you could convince her to change her mind."

McBeel was eyeing me the way I've seen snakes look at rodents on nature programs, his head swaying slightly.

He would strike, but I had to continue trying to work this out.

"Even if you did, you'd probably have to give her a lot more of your money than when you divorced. And," I smiled a little at the thought, "she'd probably give it to that museum in Kenobia when you died, anyway."

He looked startled for an instant, then clenched his hands. "I will never," he said, coming closer to me again, "let that damned Obarri get his hands on my prize. I saved it from him. I would kill him first."

"But why?" I said.

"He plans to be president someday," he said, waving one arm high in the air. "He wants to be a hero. He wants to point fingers and lay blame and find a scapegoat to cover the fact that he took a massive bribe to let me buy such a precious object in the first place. He would accuse me of bribery but hide his own part. I swore he would never see it again if he made the first move."

"So you were using the King's Jar as a kind of blackmail all along? You would have hidden it yourself?"

"I would have destroyed it," he said flatly, looking straight at me. "But, I didn't have to. When the Devor accepted it, they accepted my stipulation that it never leave the museum."

"You used the Devor. When you want something, you manipulate other people to do the dirty work." My voice wobbled, but I was not going to cry in front of this man, this paragon of society, this greedy bastard. "But your first wife isn't dead. And she intends for the Kenobians to get it back someday. You can't have her killed, Mr. McBeel. You won't find anyone else to do your dirty work for you. It's too dangerous now. There's too much attention, isn't there? Even if the police can't touch you, they know about you now. And I promise you, the community's going to know about you."

"I don't know what you're talking about," he said, but I could hear the first bit of uncertainty in his voice.

"The paper you signed. The one that says you're banned from Kenobia for a crime you committed there. I have it."

He lunged for me and grabbed my arm again, this time much harder, and twisted it. His hand was like a claw. "Not only me," I said fast. "I sent it to the chairman of the board of the Devor. If anything else happens connected to this sorry business, he'll give it to the police, maybe even to the media. Did you know the Devor's holding a press conference tomorrow?"

McBeel twisted my arm harder and squeezed. My elbow screamed. "You can get it back."

"No, Mr. McBeel, I can't." I was gasping a little from resisting his effort to pull me closer. Why hadn't I insisted on leaving the library door open when I came in? "Nothing you can do will get you the King's Jar or the record of the sale to your ex-wife, or the paper that says you're not the upstanding person you claim to be. In fact, when Rene's set of documents turns up, I think everyone will learn about it. It will be big news, bigger than the best PR firm can spin."

"No one will care," he said, his voice rough.

"Oh, you'd better believe they will. You may be able to avoid being charged as an accessory to your wife's murder, but there will be gossip from now on. San Francisco's tight little social circle will make sure the news gets into every corner. Not just here, either. People will connect the dots and wonder what role you had in Rene's and Jamie's deaths. I think it will be enough to make people think twice about inviting you to be on their charitable boards or at their dinner tables."

McBeel let go of me, only to take a giant step over to the wall and grab the little armored figure off its shelf, holding it up as if he were going to throw it at me.

"I have to be at the police station soon, to give them background on the museum's stake in the King's Jar," I said in a low voice, the implication being they'd come looking for me if I didn't show up. A blatant lie since, my inner voice reminded me, I hadn't thought to let anyone know I was headed here.

He growled. I held my breath but didn't dare move for fear he'd throw the sharp little figure. We stayed frozen like that for what seemed like hours. Finally, he looked at the warrior and lowered his arm, replacing it carefully into its niche.

"Get out," he said in a dismissive voice.

"With pleasure," I said, feeling close to tears. Oscar's panicked face swam before me. So easily manipulated by this evil man who had figured out his weaknesses and used them ruthlessly.

Gerard, possibly sensing a change in the air, was nowhere in sight, so I found my own way out, nodding good-bye to the tapestry lady and her horse as I went.

chapter 21

OF COURSE, PETER made no mention of Fritz McBeel's role at the press conference. The police and the district attorney remained officially satisfied that the case was solved with Oscar's arrest and the artifact's return. Rene's copy of the twenty-year-old "To Whom It May Concern" letter from someone in Africa that they eventually found in Jamie's bank deposit box didn't mean much to them and didn't change the facts of the case.

The letter was interesting to Geoff and a few other prominent people in San Francisco and New York who somehow saw it, however. Ambassador Obarri sent me a message through Mary McBeel, hoping I was recovered and that I might visit Kenobia someday, perhaps when he returned to assume a higher office, to see the treasures in the new museum.

Oscar, never having had much finesse or self-control, fell apart, Charlie told me. He had nothing, not so much as a scrap of paper, to prove that Fritz McBeel had asked him to commit either murder, although he swore that was the truth. When Fritz's lawyer suggested he plead guilty by reasons of temporary insanity to avoid the death penalty, Oscar bought it and the district attorney went along with the deal. The researcher went to prison as confused as ever.

Fritz closed up the Pacific Heights mansion even before the case came to trial. At the prompting of a high-powered PR firm hired for the business, the social columns noted that he had retired to a secluded villa somewhere in Europe to live quietly after the tragedy of his wife's murder. Word is, he's become a recluse, rarely seen and a bit strange looking, and staffed only by a few people. Interestingly, Wayne Lawson isn't one of them. These days, he runs the McBeel Foundation like a lord, dispensing gifts and grants and reveling in his status. Someone told me Gerard works for him now. I see him at VIP events occasionally, but we rarely speak.

Victoria manages the social life of another San Francisco celebrity these days, an older woman with a sense of humor that's rubbed off on Vicky, as everyone calls her now. We've bonded over our secret and have lunch every couple of months.

The pale green Song Dynasty porcelain artifact with the crackle glaze and the mysterious little rhino on its lid, known popularly as the King's Jar, remains the star attraction of our new exhibition, in part because of its recent history, I'm sorry to say. We've all come to terms with the fact that someday the jar will be returned to its proper home in Africa. Tom Burns is a happy man, although I think he checks on the jar every day before he goes home, to make sure it hasn't moved. He put up a discreet wall plaque to note Rene Bouvier's unique contribution to understanding pre-colonial Africa's ties with the rest of the world.

A package came for me in the mail during the trial, a signed first edition of Simon's first book, with a note. "You did great! You understand I had to stay out of this publicly, but when Jamie asked me to babysit the jar, I knew where to leave it so it would be perfectly safe and the intern would find it quickly. Jamie wanted me to ask Tom Burns for help, but it would have ended his career to be dragged into this mess. Forgive me."

I also got a short note from Mary McBeel after the dust settled, saying how pleased she was that MACPCA had broken ground on a state-of-the-art museum. "Things work out eventually, don't they, my dear?" she wrote.

Not everything, I could have told her. I went on a diet for three months and managed to gain a pound. Dickie persuaded his mother to loosen her death grip on a first-rate Henry Moore statue and fund a small sculpture garden at the Devor, to be named for the dear departed Richard Argetter II. It's a wonderful idea except it means I'm seeing more of her and of Dickie as we plan the inaugural event. He's not so bad these days, though. We went to our friend's wedding separately, and he didn't insist on sitting at the table where I was hanging out with some of the groomsmen.

We had a quiet dinner after the excitement about the return of the King's Jar died down, and I told him what had raced through my mind when I'd had a knife at my throat. It had been an important reminder to me that he and I had good times, and that I wouldn't be quick to forget that in the future. But, I had added quickly as his hand reached for mine across the table, I had my work now, and a life I liked, independence and a stronger sense of myself. I couldn't give it up, I explained, although I hoped we could be friends.

He had looked at me for a long minute before nodding slowly. "Yes, you have changed. I like it on you, kiddo. We're both older and wiser, but you may be wiser than me. You know, I'm getting involved in a couple of philanthropic projects, getting outside myself? Having all this money doesn't do much good if it can't help people. Without strings, of course. That was what McBeel didn't get."

He put his arm around my shoulder as we left the restaurant, but only lightly, and dropped me off without more than a pat on my arm. It was a lovely evening, the best time I've had with my ex since the days when we hiked or curled up on the sofa with popcorn and old movies.

I feel Dickie's accepting that I won't get back together with him. I'm good with that. Really. After all, I've decided he's more like a brother to me, which is why I told him to beware of the motives of the ridiculously overdressed woman—girl really—he brought to the last donor cultivation dinner I arranged for Peter. It's not that the Armani wasn't gorgeous on her, but a satin smoking suit seemed a bit over the top for a business dinner. And then she talked nonstop about her prep school reunion and her grandparents' place in Malibu, which meant I couldn't discreetly ask the elderly couple trapped with me if they liked the idea of sponsoring the traveling exhibition of Hudson Valley painters I was trying to promote.

I had planned to bring Charlie to that dinner, seeing as how he has gotten to know the Devor so well. But at the last minute, he and Inspector Weiler got called to a murder scene on Telegraph Hill and he had to beg off. Teeni came instead, and I'm still waiting for her to tell me what she and Dickie were doing off in a corner of Peter's office whispering—and why they kept staring at me. I was stuck making small talk with Ms. Overdressed for the Ball, who so charmed an elderly trustee that he told me at the end of the evening she was "the cat's meow."

She's on the hunt, my inner self and I agreed, *even if Dickie can't see it yet.* Men can be so clueless.

acknowledgments

ALTHOUGH WRITING IS a solitary business, what surrounds the actual writing is anything but. Thanks to Terry, Ruth, Martha, John, and Carole for reading portions of the manuscript and for their astute comments. Enormous gratitude to Stephen M. Shea, expert in sub-Saharan African history, whose willingness to engage in "what if"s on the story's behalf must have chafed against his passion for facts at times. To the extent that the invented King's Jar and its history ring true, the credit is Steve's; any problems are entirely of my own making. Bows go to D.P. Lyle, crime author and physician who is also the go-to guy in our business for forensics help, and to the gorgeous Metropolitan Club in New York for providing the inspiration for my invented Pilgrim Club. Bisous to my gem of an agent, Kimberley Cameron, and very special thanks to Alex and Jen at Top Five for their insights, enthusiasm, and hard work. My heartfelt appreciation to Brian, Amy, Lonnie, Gwen, Alexander, and the friends who cheer me on. And a belated thank you to author and friend T.P. Jones, who first suggested I choose a fundraiser as a protagonist, reminding me to write what I know. That said, this book is a work of fiction, peopled by invented characters who move through some real places and some that exist only in my mind, doing things I have conjured out of whole cloth.

about the author

SUSAN C. SHEA spent more than two decades as a nonprofit executive before beginning her bestselling mystery series featuring a professional fundraiser for a fictional museum. Susan is on the board of the northern California chapter of Sisters in Crime and is a past board member of Norcal's chapter of Mystery Writers of America. She lives in Marin County, California.

www.susancshea.com

Author photograph by Charles Barry

a note on the type

The text of this book was set in Fairfield, a font designed by artist and book illustrator Rudolph Ruzicka for Linotype in 1940. Fairfield harks back to the modern typefaces of Bodoni and Didot, but has a distinctly twentieth-century look. The titles are set in Memoir, a font designed by Stephen Rapp in 2008 to mimic the handwriting of an earlier era.

Printed and bound by Edwards Brothers Inc. in Ann Arbor, Michigan